THE
DREAM
MERCHANT

ALSO BY FRED WAITZKIN

Searching for Bobby Fischer

Mortal Games

The Last Marlin

THE
DREAM
MERCHANT

FRED
WAITZKIN

THOMAS DUNNE BOOKS   ✦   ST. MARTIN'S PRESS, NEW YORK

THOMAS DUNNE BOOKS.
An imprint of St. Martin's Press.

THE DREAM MERCHANT. Copyright © 2013 by Fred Waitzkin. All rights reserved. Printed in the United States of America. For information, address St. Martin's Press, 175 Fifth Avenue, New York, N.Y. 10010.

www.thomasdunnebooks.com
www.stmartins.com

Design by Steven Seighman

Library of Congress Cataloging-in-Publication Data

Waitzkin, Fred.
    The Dream Merchant : a novel / by Fred Waitzkin.—First Edition.
        p. cm.
    ISBN 978-1-250-01136-7 (hardcover)
    ISBN 978-1-250-01137-4 (e-book)
    I. Title.
    PS3623.A35658D74 2013
    813'.6—dc23

                                                        2012042088

St. Martin's Press books may be purchased for educational, business, or promotional use. For information on bulk purchases, please contact Macmillan Corporate and Premium Sales Department at 1-800-221-7945 extension 5442 or write specialmarkets@macmillan.com.

First Edition: March 2013

10 9 8 7 6 5 4 3 2 1

For Bonnie, Katya, Josh, Desi, Jack, and Jeff

PART I

1.

I met Jim in July of 1983 on a tropical island rife with offshore breezes and nights lusty with renewal and reckless hope. I came here to fish in the Gulf Stream each summer, to get time off my back.

We were the only two customers in the tiny End of the World Saloon, but I barely noticed him when I sat down at the sandy weathered bar.

Hello, Ebb Tide, said Cornelius, a heavyset bartender who wore gaudy gold rings from a half-dozen years earlier when he'd worked for Colombians off-loading bales of marijuana. I had known him since I was a kid. He always called me Ebb Tide, the name of my fishing boat. Cornelius pulled a Heineken out of a beat-up cooler and set it on the bar in front of me.

The End of the World was an unpainted plywood shack set precariously on the windy south point of Bimini Island in the Bahamas. I loved drinking beer here at night so close to the channel you could hear the tide running and the sound of jacks crashing on schools of baitfish. A hundred nights I drummed on the rough wooden planks to the refrains of Bob Marley coming from

Cornelius's rusty boom box. Each time I come back to the island I expect to find the place has been blown into the channel by a hurricane or nor'easter. Someday it will be.

I brought you a nice one, I said, lifting a white plastic bucket off the sand floor of the shack. There was a six-pound Nassau grouper curled inside. Cornelius smiled, showing off his two gold front teeth. Grouper was his favorite. The one in the bucket was big enough to feed his wife and kids with enough left over to make a peppery soup the following night.

Where'd you catch it? asked the stranger who had pulled up a stool beside me. He stuck out his hand and we shook. He had a strong grip. He was wearing a tight T-shirt and looked battle tested like an aging fighter. On his muscular arm he had the fading tattoo of a full-figured mermaid.

A couple hundred yards off the concrete ship, I lied. Cornelius smiled a little and then walked to the far side of the bar, where he opened the lid of another cooler. He knew there weren't any groupers on the sandy bottom near the old wreck.

What kind of bait?

I shrugged.

What'd you catch it on?

Cornelius was back with my bucket, and scratching around inside there were three small crawfish. That was our deal, fish for crawfish.

Jim caught my eye. In the Bahamas crawfish were out of season and these three were shorts. He glanced back in the bucket.

What bait? he asked again with a naughty grin. What's the big secret?

Like many fishermen, I feel authorial pride about the wheres and gimmicks of what I do. Three, four times this stranger asked without giving me room to breathe. I didn't want to tell him, but he was in my face bullying and at the same time challenging me to keep my secret. He was a tough guy but also funny.

Why not? Why not? he pushed.

It felt like he was prying himself into my life. I couldn't shut him up.

I caught it with conch slop.

I didn't know they ate conch . . . will you show me?

Show you what?

We could go out together. I love fishing.

Jim's salesmanship felt familiar, but I didn't pin it down immediately. I wanted to say no, but turning him down on the spot felt like an opportunity lost. And he knew it.

Jim looked amused. What other fish do you catch off this island?

You can catch anything, almost anything, I said. That's the beauty of fishing here. The Gulf Stream comes right up to the shore.

What about tuna?

I found myself describing the big schools of black fin that come up at dusk off Picket Rock and Gun Cay. Before long I was telling him what lures I use and how far behind the boat I troll them. He wanted to hear every detail and I fell into a rhythm of giving up hard-won secrets, one after the next. I was saying so much that I felt ridiculous, but I kept talking until we started to laugh. Then he punched me hard on the shoulder. My shoulder throbbed, but I tried not to show it.

Jim was fast and powerful for a fifty-five-year-old, with big appetites, and handsome, with a worn-out toughness.

A sultry offshore wind was rushing through the open windows of the shack. Jim breathed it deeply. It must have been around ten o'clock by now and we were still the only two customers at the bar. We had been exchanging memories of our parents, wives, women we'd enjoyed. One story opened up the next. We were drinking beer and laughing at ourselves as if we had the truth collared.

————

This place is like my backyard, I said, pointing out the rotting window frame of the shack toward the bay with expanses of mangroves to the south and east.

You wouldn't believe the fish you can get right here in the harbor. Big snappers, tarpon, sharks.

Right here in front of this bar?

I pointed to a little jut of sand a hundred feet away.

One night when I was a kid, fourteen or fifteen, I came here with a bucket of bloody tuna scraps. Some local guy told me you could catch big sharks right over there at night. I had brought a hand line and a big hook, the size of my hand. I tossed my bait as far as I could and let it drift out with the tide. There was no End of the World Saloon twenty-five years ago. No one was around. The wind was blowing like tonight and it was the dark of the moon, pitch-black. The tide was racing out of the harbor.

Right over there? Jim asked, pointing at the nearby beach.

I nodded.

For a kid, battling a man-eater seemed like all of the adventure life had to offer, I continued. This was my coming-of-age moment. I was scared to death, also really excited. After a half hour, I hooked something very big that ran back and forth in the black water just beyond the small breakers while I hung on for my life, dug my heels into the sand. I was determined to hold on. After ten minutes I had this big thing tumbling in the surf and then I hauled it up on the beach. I pulled and pulled until the shark was about twenty feet from the water. It was heavy, maybe ten feet long, and sat there for a while stunned while I took it in. Suddenly the shark started jumping and thrashing around. Must have sensed it was no longer in the sea. Soon it was all covered in wet sand like a second skin, a disgusting sight. I was repelled by my shark, but I forced myself to touch it a few times. Then I didn't know what to do. The shark was too far from the water and half-burrowed in the sand. I didn't know how to push it back in. I wanted to show off this prize catch to my dad, but he was asleep in our hotel room up the road. I wanted to show it off, but no one was on the beach but me. I'd expected a big celebration from this victory, but now all I had was a sandy shark flopping on the beach. I didn't know what to do. I left it there dying.

Jim took that in. We didn't talk for a bit. I felt like we were buddies, that I could say anything to him. It happened very quickly.

Then, finally, into his sixth or eighth beer, he said, I've been going through a run of bad luck. Jim was drinking two to my one. I lost my wife, my business, my home, he said. I lost everything I had.

Everything I had.

He didn't spell it out, but it was my impression there was something illegal and shameful about the affair, some terrible disgrace.

I went to the Brazilian Amazon, he said. To make back everything I lost, and a lot more.

The Brazilian Amazon! He was in a different league. My victories and defeats were so much smaller than his. He'd lost his wife and business, his home. I had some melancholy moments to relate. I had local fishing knowledge. I lied that I was a novelist. In truth, I wrote freelance articles for magazines. I was trying to keep up with him. Before long I created a brief love affair, then blushed. I sensed that he could look right through me. If telling the dark truth had become a competition, Jim won easily.

At the time, I was renting a tiny cottage on the north end of the island. During calm summer afternoons, my wife and I trolled the Gulf Stream in an open twenty footer that I bought used in Fort Lauderdale for thirty-five hundred dollars. My father had first brought me here as a teenage boy. In our New York life he had usually been preoccupied with some business deal about to close or he was furious with Mom or with a customer who had crossed him, but on this windswept island he became mellow and yielding; "I feel like a new man," was how he put it. Our island visits imbued a longing that went beyond catching giant marlin or breathing the heavy night air suggesting pleasures I did not yet know. Every year of my life I return to Bimini hoping to alter my life's direction or, more modestly, to feel like a new man.

Jim had spent the past three months cruising the Exumas with his young wife, Phyllis, on a plush sixty-five-foot trawler yacht. That captured my interest. He had been healing, he said, since returning to the States after nearly three years in Brazil. Following this leisurely cruise he wanted to start a new business in Miami. He was going to shop for a house on a canal where he could keep his yacht tied up in the back.

I'm good at making money, he remarked matter-of-factly. I've made a lot of people wealthy.

What a crass thing to say, but I didn't care. I hung on Jim's words.

Why don't we team up for a week? I suggested, trying to hold his interest. I know fishing and you own a big trawler. I'll teach you to fish. I can take you to the best reefs for diving.

I'd never been more awkwardly out front in my life. I barely knew this man.

But Jim didn't seem surprised by my suggestion.

He and his wife had been planning to anchor for two nights off the north end of the island where there was a pristine and mostly deserted beach. He proposed that we should leave for our cruise in three days. We'd meet at the fuel dock of the Blue Water Marina Thursday at noon. We shook on it.

It was past midnight and I was sitting in the bar by myself finishing a bottle. Cornelius had left an hour earlier with the grouper. Jim was gone—maybe he'd stepped outside to take a piss. I'd had a lot of beer. I didn't remember him saying good night. I had this notion he'd put the idea of the cruise into my head. That he'd toyed with me.

I turned off the lights and closed the door behind me. When I walked onto the narrow Queens Highway Jim was nowhere to be seen. The wind had picked up and there was no one around. I walked down to the little jut of beach where I had once left the dying shark. I half-expected to find some trace of it, some lasting marker.

Three days later my wife and I were standing on the dock at the Blue Water Marina with our duffel bags and fishing rods, looking around. It was twelve o'clock, but there was no million-dollar trawler yacht tied up at the fuel dock. There were a few pelicans sitting on the pilings and it was very hot. I was sweating, embarrassed. Why the hell would some stranger I met in a bar agree to take me on his yacht for a week? You couldn't buy such a trip for five thousand dollars. Sorry, I said to my wife, feeling like a fool and getting ready for the hot walk back to the north end of the island. Right then I spotted the high bow of a trawler coming around the point of South Bimini. In another ten minutes the boat was approaching the concrete fuel dock and Jim and Phyllis were waving extravagantly from the bridge. Jim came in hard against a piling and then he didn't notice the stern drifting off with the tide. He was grinning, not paying attention. He wanted me to take the measure of his pretty boat.

Hey, guys, we need a stern line! I called.

They didn't seem to know anything about boat handling. A lot of wealthy people buy big boats with no idea how to run them or navigate. It is amazing that they survive at sea.

Phyllis came down from the bridge and walked pigeon-toed to the stern where there was a coiled line. She weakly tossed it my way and it fell into the bay. She had to gather it from the water and throw it twice more before I managed to catch the end. She was an awkward, voluptuous woman of about thirty with a daffy smile. It was hard to pull the heavy trawler against the tide, but we finally got her tied up.

Our first days on their yacht were a dream vacation fantasy. Phyllis's sumptuous four-course meals followed long days on the water spearfishing and trolling. He was all about gamesmanship, betting, proposing dares, playing in the sea, enjoying the best cigars, discovering life's possibilities each morning after his oatmeal. Jim was six foot, and powerfully built, particularly in the chest and shoulders, his sandy hair thinning, and with a light complexion that burned easily in the Bahamian sun. Phyllis served him hand and foot, literally. Every afternoon after diving she gave him massages. She walked along his back cracking his spine with her little feet. She smeared goop on his lips to protect him from the sun. Phyllis mixed his drinks and handed him Cuban cigars. She seemed good-hearted, affable, and dumb—that was my first impression. In the evening she showered on the deck and waved whenever I glanced her way. She was nice to look at. The girls cooked together in the galley, got along okay, although I didn't think much about them. I was focused on Jim.

On the third day out I guided him to an isolated atoll about seventy miles south of Bimini called Orange Cay. It was hardly more than a large rock. But the surrounding reefs were untouched by local fishermen who couldn't afford the fuel to travel halfway to Cuba. There were lobsters, snappers, and groupers carpeting the bottom, so much game here that it felt unsporting to drop a line or dive down and spear them. But I never said that to Jim. He was in heaven and I wanted to please him. He had that effect on all of us. Every afternoon he came out of the water with his pole spear like James Bond and presented a bucket of fish and crawfish for the girls to cook. Of course any idiot could catch fish in such a place, but still I felt like a big shot for having brought him here.

I suggested playing gin rummy. It felt like a manly contest and I was good at cards. The first night playing with Jim I won thirty or forty dollars. I knew that I would. In my circle of friends I nearly always won. The second night I gradually lost back nearly everything. With a swagger that was not my own, I suggested raising the stakes. Jim didn't seem to care. Whatever you want, buddy, he said. I held my own for a while and then I began to lose. I was down five hundred before we quit—much more than I ever lost at cards. But it didn't matter. Jim evoked the larger picture while he racked up the score against me. What was five hundred when we were having such a good time bantering about women, diving for lobster, eating caviar and the best seafood, drinking wine beneath a galaxy of stars? He knew how to live. He would take me to places that I could not begin to imagine. This was implicit in the largess of those unforgettable days on Jim's yacht.

On the fifth night out, we were sitting on the aft deck drinking beer and watching gulls from the tiny island wheeling behind the stern in the glow of our anchor light. I knew that he wanted to play cards and he was waiting for me to ask him. The girls were below in the galley. Jim reached for a cigar in his shirt pocket, but then he put it back. In that moment all the banter went out of his face.

Look there, he said.

What?

He was pointing off the stern at a pinpoint of light in the distance. Hardly anything at all.

What is it?

Wait here, he said curtly. He walked into the salon and I watched him disappear down the stairs.

Minutes passed and I began to feel uneasy on the aft deck by myself, peering off the stern at a light growing larger in the blackness.

The sting of Jim's voice had put me on edge. I could hear our wives inside the galley, laughing. I wished they'd be quiet. Possibly it was another fishing boat, but that would be unusual, so far off the beaten track. These days, the *Miami Herald* was filled with stories of cocaine trafficking in remote areas of the Bahamas. American cruisers anchored in the wrong place had been attacked by Colombian drug smugglers; tourists were shot to death and thrown over the side. I tried to steady my imagination. But then the lights went off in the salon and then the anchor light went out. Everything was very quiet, but I could hear my beating heart and also the rumbling of an inboard engine idling closer.

Jim returned holding two automatic rifles. He slammed a clip into one and put it into my hands. I didn't know anything about shooting guns and the weapon felt heavy and forbidding. The girls were still laughing, but now they seemed miles away. My stomach knotted up. I was thinking, Put the guns away, Jim, before something terrible happens. His expression was entirely focused, but also he seemed to be relishing the moment, which alarmed me more than the approaching boat.

What the hell are you doing, man? I said, and Jim cut me off with a hand slammed against my mouth.

What are you doing, man? I repeated to myself. I was beginning to shake.

Not a sound, he ordered.

He didn't want to hear from me, not when the speedboat was only a hundred yards off and edging closer in the dark calm water. Now I could make out its narrow sleek hull. It was sliding right up to our stern.

Then a voice called from the boat in a heavy Spanish accent, Do you know where we are? What a preposterous question to ask in the middle of nowhere. How were we supposed to answer? The sleek boat kept edging forward and Jim motioned for me to get down on the deck. Once again, Do you know where we are? The man's voice was cloying with sweet innocence. It was disgusting.

Jim seemed to see something. He raised the gun fast, hesitated a beat, and he squeezed off three rounds.

Holy shit.

In a second, two thousand horsepower was roaring and the speedboat wheeled on its haunches, throwing white water on us, and for a moment I saw the alarmed face of the man at the wheel staring back as the boat shot off into the darkness.

Did you see the other guy pointing a rifle from the companionway? Jim asked, lowering his own gun. I hadn't seen a second man. I had never seen anything like this before in my life. I was trying to pull my heart back into my chest.

Were they gonna kill us?

What do you think?

Are they coming back? What's gonna happen?

He shrugged. I still didn't get it. Was this for real or a paranoid fantasy that Jim was filling up with life? I had no idea if he'd hit the men or shot to scare them. I hadn't seen any rifles except our own.

We'll have to stand guard through the night, Jim said as though situations like these were normal in life. I tried to imagine how we'd hold them off. Where I fit in. I was a writer from New York, not the right guy to go into a gunfight. The rifle felt clammy and too heavy for me to hold up. Honestly, I wanted to hide down below.

He led me up the companionway and positioned us on opposite ends of a Boston Whaler on the top deck. He took my rifle and clicked off the safety so that I was ready to shoot.

Don't pull the trigger by accident, he said. I've seen that before.

I nodded, pulling my right hand away from the stock. Looking across the taut canvas cover, I could see two lights in the distance moving back and forth. No, three lights. What the hell was going on out there? I couldn't tell if they were coming closer or moving off. How could we defend ourselves against an armada of drug smugglers? But why were they coming for us?

Jim had stopped answering my questions. The waiting was too much. After a half hour like this, clutching the gun against my knee, I was simply going crazy. To break the tension, I asked, What'd you do in Brazil?

I didn't expect an answer, but Jim coughed two or three times and put his rifle down on the deck.

I spent three years in the jungle mining for gold.

Tell me, I said, still trying to breathe normally.

It takes over your life, he said while keeping his eyes focused on the boats that now seemed to be moving a little farther away. Everything changed for me the first day I walked into that camp. The smell of pig shit was everywhere. Jim shook his head slowly, remembering.

I had a friend in Canada who had signed a lease with the Brazilian government—they call it an *alvará*—to work twenty thousand acres in the deep jungle south of Manaus. He made a proposal for the two of us to go into business together. Why not? I was fifty-two years old and my life was in ruins. I found out that my partner didn't know anything about surviving in the jungle. His first visit to the camp the guy got scared, and he never came back in. I ended up doing it myself.

Jim took the cigar out of his pocket and put it in his mouth, but he didn't light up.

Now just imagine a few Brazilian Indians sifting dirt and gravel at the edge of a riverbank in the middle of the Amazon, he continued. On this first trip, I brought along four men from the city. I didn't know them at all, but they were supposed to have experience finding gold.

I was exhausted and hungry. I trekked through the jungle with the men for four days to get there. One of them spoke ten English words, but mostly I was guessing about things I'd never seen before. My partner had said there would be some basic house where we would live. I figured bunks and even a shower. There wasn't any house. There was an old pigpen made from tree trunks rotten with termites. It was all that was left from a mining operation ten years earlier. The jungle had grown over everything. The hovel was filled with shit. I guessed some wild pigs still used it. I couldn't imagine sleeping a night there. For lunch we ate a large anteater that one of the natives shot beside the river; it was a big animal with claws the size of a man's hands. My guys considered anteater great eating, but the animal had a terrible smell from ants. They cooked the meat with a sweet guava paste to kill the smell, but it was just awful. They cut up the rest of the anteater and tossed it in an old rusty barrel for later.

It was hot, a hundred degrees or more, with humidity worse than anything I had ever felt. I needed to get cool, but I was frightened to swim in the river because of snakes and who knew what was in there. I was thirsty and bitten raw by mosquitoes and ants. Worst of all, after walking sixty miles in the heat I was dead tired; maybe I was sick. I needed to sleep for a week in a cool room. There aren't any cool rooms in the jungle. But these little men I hired, they had such energy and patience. Hour after hour they sifted the dirt with large sieves called *batillas*. I was sweating and thinking, What the hell am I doing here? Maybe I was sick with malaria. I had no idea. I looked into one of those sieves and I saw a few clumps of hard, shiny metal. It was gold.

Jim paused a minute and lit his fat Cuban cigar, which seemed preposterous given our circumstances, but it calmed me a little. He wasn't thinking any more about the boats. He was remembering and barely nodding his head to some interior music.

Just seeing it, my God, what runs through your mind. The lust. What I could do with this! I mean, there was so much more money in this dirt than I had ever made in business. More than I had ever dreamed of. To hell with everything else. It starts exploding in you, that I could do anything, I could have anything on earth. I could be a billionaire like De Beers. This goes through your mind. Why the hell not? It's all around me on this property, tons and tons of gold; just look at the clumps rolling around in the *batilla*. I'm calculating the money, all the things I'm going to buy, when all of a sudden I'm looking around to make sure that no one sees what we've got here, this fortune that's just a half a foot beneath the ground. We've got to protect this property, because someone could take it. Maybe someone is watching right now from the trees across the river. How can we protect it? We'll need guns. People would kill us to get this gold. And it was mine. All mine.

Jim looked at me squarely. Are you getting this? Do you understand?

Looking at the shiny chunks of metal in the *batilla* brought on some wild ideas, he went on. I could build a resort, a casino in the Amazon. Anything at all. I would have my own Learjet, like before I went broke. All I could think about was this gold. I'm going to become rich. I'm going to show everybody in the world that I made it again after what happened to me. I made it back on top, but much bigger.

One of the Indians was trying to gesture to me, no, no, Jim—he was shaking his head at my excitement—the clumps of metal aren't real gold. They haven't found it yet. This is false gold. He is pointing up the river. We have to search other parts of the property until we find the real thing and begin our mining operation.

It's not real gold, but I can't turn off the faucet.

I don't give a shit about anything. I'll eat anteater, heated-over anteater with maggots stirred in—that's what we ate for the next three days from the barrel. Only someone completely mad could eat such vomit. I would sleep on the ground with bugs crawling up my legs. I'm going to make it, whatever it takes. We'll cut an airfield into the jungle with machetes and our bare hands. We're going to bring in heavy equipment. Whatever happens, I'm going to find the gold, because other guys in the jungle are finding it. In Manaus, all I would hear about was gold, gold; men were putting together expeditions with every dollar they could muster.

It was something more than just getting excited. A force was running through me. On that first day the rules changed.

After a few days on the property we started to find the real thing, small amounts, but it was gold for sure. And I knew nothing was going to get in my way. All the things that I went through in my life prepared me for this. I had no fear. Nobody's going to take anything away from me. If you get in my way, I'm going to trample you. You could put a gun to my head. That happened to me, and I didn't give a shit. I was one son of a bitch. I had to deal with my people and some of them were brutal. I did bad things. People died. So what?

Jim looked at me a beat and then back toward the moving lights. So what! I thought.

I loved it, he said. I loved it. One time I was speeding along a rutted street outside Manaus and this euphoria built up in me and I just started screaming into the night like I was on something. Because I was.

People can see it in you. You could see it in me. They called me *gringo maluco,* the crazy American. I was another person. As if you had a dream about wanting to be a certain type of guy—a real tough guy, you see them in the movies. And these guys can do things you could barely imagine. Well, these guys are for real, a lot of them, because they have something inside. A lot of CIA agents, or people who are killers—well, they have this drive. It's a fever. Some people who kill a lot of people—these multiple killers— what do you think they have inside of them? Something's driving them. Nothing's stopping them. Nothing was stopping me.

Now Jim was quiet for a time, looking out at the dark ocean.

Are they coming any closer? I asked for the third or fourth time, unable to get my mind off the gunmen in the boats.

Hard to say, he answered.

Jim was returning from the jungle and didn't seem concerned about the boats. I imagined that he was thinking where this experience had left him—whether a man can come all the way back and be normal, live again with his wife in a neat little house in the suburbs as if he never left.

The plan was for us to keep our vigil, behind the Boston Whaler where the Colombians couldn't see us if they came back. That way, surprise would be on our side. Jim told me that he was a good shot, and I didn't doubt it. We would have a fighting chance, if we stayed up the night and remained alert. That was the key. He'd learned about such things in Brazil. He had a plan and I believed him.

In the morning, when I woke up, I was still clutching the rifle. It was a calm, picture-postcard day in the Bahamas with no Colombian speedboats anywhere that I could see. Jim was sleeping beside me on the deck, snoring like a bull.

2.

Jim raises his bare thigh a little and Mara, in shorts and T-shirt, settles on him, her body moving smoothly against his dry white skin. The petite, shapely twenty-six-year-old spreads her legs a little and raises herself, rubs her sex back and forth against my friend's thigh. I am sitting to the side of them in his old La-Z-Boy recliner, moved hastily, two weeks earlier, from his apartment with Phyllis. Jim is grinning, his left eye tearing as it has for the past eight or nine years.

I've just met this girl who now turns back toward me, strikes a pose, and smiles as though to ask, Do you like this? I feel aroused watching them and confused about why she is performing like this on my first visit to their tiny dark house. This pose, this angle, staring at her small raised behind, legs spread, is about the same view as the snapshot Jim had showed me five weeks earlier on my last trip to Florida, before Mara arrived from Israel, where they'd met. In the picture, her head is turned to the side on a pillow after they had had sex. She is spent, entirely pleased. Jim had made a show of snatching the photo from my hand, but first he'd wanted me to relish her youthful ass and bushy dark hair with their wetness spilling onto her inner thigh. And now he is grinning at me. Do you like her? They are both selling me even while they sell each other.

Jim is now rounding the bend to eighty. He and I have been best friends for twenty years, although it feels like a puff of time since the night vigil alongside Jim's Boston Whaler. And yet there have been so many lavish dinners with Phyllis in their condominium, fishing trips to the Bahamas, fervent promises and plans for the future, money schemes, so much history flashing past, it is hard for me to take her in, this brand-new leading lady. Or maybe it's that I can't quite see where I fit in.

Jim and Mara are flat broke, but he doesn't seem worried. Jim has been a moneymaking machine his whole life, but now his boundless energy and ambition have narrowed to this twenty-six-year-old who has been a shock to his family, friends, to a virtual army of customers and salesmen, to everyone who knows him. How could he leave Phyllis, his faithful devoted wife, his home, his business (though it wasn't doing very well)?

Here they are in a worn-out bungalow with aged matching appliances. Two children are sleeping in a closet-sized bedroom, her kids. Empty pizza boxes are strewn in a corner—not a trace of gracious living anywhere to be seen. For most of his adult life Jim has lived in gorgeous, spacious homes. This? This would have been a tragic place for my friend, banishment.

Mara brought a few thousand from Israel, just enough for them to scrape by for eight or ten weeks. Then what? He cannot move back to Canada, where he is still a fugitive. Returning to Phyllis would be humiliating and bewildering, though she would take him back.

I could never have concocted this late chapter. I know him so well. I can often anticipate his words, practically read his mind as I could my own father's, particularly in the last years of his life when he was very sick and no longer on top in his business life. When he needed me I traveled to his shabby rooms in Cambridge, Massachusetts (rank smelling, and fashioned in nearly the same torn-and-crumbling endgame style as Jim and Mara's). I became my father's source of energy and hope. He no longer had vocal cords, so I became his voice. A few times I drove his Buick to the office of an electrical distributor he knew in Boston, held Dad's arm as we walked inside. I made his audacious pitch while my father grinned and tapped on the desk with a pencil. I was going to do the same service for Jim, help him make his way as an old man. His wife, Phyllis, never minded our scheming and intimacy—in fact, she found us amusing. I looked forward to our afternoons together on his spacious, breezy terrace over the Intracoastal, replaying our greatest fishing days or listening to him tell stories of his life in the jungle.

But this? This?

Mara is beautiful in the half-light of the small living room, a kid with smooth milky skin, without a wrinkle or a bulge. She could be his granddaughter. For an old man, what a miracle she is. She is wearing shorts and a white T-shirt, no bra. She wants me to look at her. No, she dares me to look.

She begins to kiss Jim on the mouth, hungry kisses; her tongue is working like a puppy—perhaps for my benefit—while she moves steadily against his leg. He's getting aroused and beginning to giggle. She won't stop. Mara's quite a salesman herself, plays us both smoothly. She has decided that to make this sale she needs to seduce both of us. She's amused by his stiff cock, turns back toward me. She is entirely comfortable speaking this language. Speaking English is more of a strain. Although her English isn't bad.

Don't you trust me? she asks. This is our new life together, she seems to say with her smile.

Their new life together. She waits for my answer. I nod my head, as if to affirm, Of course I trust you, even while I am not sure.

She is soft with me, and seductive, but underneath, a fierce woman. What does she want from Jim? Love? I don't get it.

Jim watches us, amused. He is so proud of her selling. She has become his everything.

Mara wears too much rouge on her cheeks, which makes her look trashy. I wonder, with time, if she will wear less. Except, how is it possible that for these two time can move ahead in unhurried, evolving years? He is an old man.

Jim and I could spend our life in bed. But our bed is too soft, she continues. We need a good bed.

He could die there, I say.

Not a bad way to die.

I can't shock or even jostle her. She is very sure-footed.

We'll buy a good one tomorrow, baby, he coos.

What will they use for money? He has no more credit cards.

She attaches herself to his neck, burrows into him, making a mark. She won't let go. She is digging into his life. Jim has promised to marry her. Soon they will market the Wow Card together. They will be business partners, fifty-fifty. Phyllis is out. Jim and Mara will have a new home by the water and a yacht in the backyard. There won't be any regrets. She wants a little white BMW convertible. Jim will be a millionaire once again. His whole life he has made it and lost it. Who is winning, making the sale? I fear she is winning. Jim is hooked very deep.

I am resolved to confront him about this precipitous course change, but the words that pop into my head are too miserable: Jim, what about all of the adventures, the promises you made? What we were going to do? I would pester him with questions about Brazil—a hundred times we had vowed to go back there together.

Instead, I ask him, Jim, what will you do when there's no more money?

In six weeks we'll be ready to put the Wow Card in stores, he answers smartly. There is nothing in the world like the Wow Card. Did I explain the marketing plan? We'll sell millions of cards; actually, we'll give them away. That's the beauty of it. Hold one in your hand and it looks like any other debit card, but it throws off a hefty residual income for the rest of your life. Let me show you some numbers—he still has ardor for the hunt despite a run of failed deals and the specter of oblivion, which he greets as a new and beguiling acquaintance. Jim has never been reluctant to experience new tastes, to walk new paths, even now while he walks the plank. This seems like the final chapter for my friend, but who knows? Jim has crashed before.

Even now, living with the girl, who feels like my enemy, he pulls me back in. I am enticed by his scheme, maybe "connected" is more accurate, preposterous and gaudy though it is. This has nothing to do with logic. Jim's ideas are the dreams of my own father.

Jim lays out the terrain: stacks of Wow Cards piled high in stores across America. He'll put them in topless bars, gas stations, and eventually they'll go into supermarkets. The Wow Card is a debit card that works in ATM machines, but its primary purpose is to allow a buyer to rent pornography anonymously at steeply discounted prices. Jim talks a little about the value of pornography while the girl smiles as if he's preparing to open a flower shop. My friend can turn a deal on its side and make it seem adventurous or cozy or sexy or the very answer to a life of pain and wanting. I've seen him do it many times. For me his pitch is a child's song.

We'll soon buy a big fishing boat together, he says to me, a sixty footer. We'll cruise the islands in style.

She listens to each word and seems to adore him.

He's laughing. The gap from his missing front tooth looks ridiculous. There's no money for a cap, but having nothing, starting again, unhampered, is so much sweeter than standing pat and being mediocre. The greatest thrill for a gambler, he'd told me years before, is losing a fortune and bottoming out. And now he's flat broke, never been this low since he was a child growing up on the outskirts of Edmonton. And he feels content watching her clean their little place and listening to the yammer of her Israeli children, or turning on Frank Sinatra.

She smiles. She loves him. I don't know. Maybe she loves him.

3.

When the girl frets or feels idle or homesick, he uses the past like roses and chocolates. Jim has described to her the houses: the last condo he and Phyllis lived in had seven bathrooms, the girl was amused about the bathrooms, never having had more than one herself, and the river of money, for years everything he touched turned to money. She squirms when he talks about high times, his two new Rolls-Royces parked in front of the cavernous modern house Jim had built on a peninsula for his second wife, Ava. There were two smaller houses on the property for the servants. Some called it the finest estate in Canada. In the morning, Jim chose between the white convertible and the silver sedan depending on his mood or whom he was meeting for lunch. He told Mara about the night Tony Bennett crooned from speakers in Jim's Learjet "Fly Me to the Moon" while Jim and Ava screwed face-to-face in his buttery leather recliner, screwed and laughed, and then he pointed to a glowing full moon blasting through the oval window as the plane descended from thirty thousand feet into Vegas. That was when Jim was at the very top. I heard Jim describe the moment at parties in the big condo on Brickell Avenue above the Intracoastal where he often entertained with Phyllis—it was the perfect address for Jim's marketing business.

There was always a subtext to his tales, usually narrated to several eager men standing off from the main group (most nights of the week you would find Jim holding forth at some party or business gathering); more or less, the stories all led to the same happy conclusion: If I can have yachts and planes, gorgeous women, all the thousands I need to play at Caesars, so can you. It's easy. First you have to understand your hot button. What is your hot button? Take a look at yourself. Be honest. What is it that really turns you on? Do you love beautiful young women? Do you love big-game fishing? Fast cars? Cars? Have you seen my new BMW 740? Come on, let's walk outside a moment.

For sure, Jim was gauche with his Cuban cigars and ornamental women, his flashy Liberace suits festooned with a pocket handkerchief folded into a pouf (his suits were inspired by his father and Jim owned a hundred in his heyday, had a hanging closet the size of a nice bedroom, lined with fine shoes on custom teak racks, a hundred poufs, three hundred silk ties, on and on), but so what if he might have been more understated? Jim was always fun to be with, charming, a good storyteller, and best of all, he tantalized with the impossible, opened hearts with the lure of opportunity. Jim promised very big things. He intrigued lawyers and doctors who resented working for an hourly wage, grand though it might be, and failed entrepreneurs who could feel the deep dream of wealth, the very essence of their life's meaning slipping away, the aching sadness of it; but in his later years he devoted more of his energy to the vast dispirited army of the unemployed and the nearly unemployed, maids, janitors, repairmen, and the like, who had never tasted the sweet life, didn't have a clue. He'd educate them. Are you ready to make a move? he'd ask when the moment was right. Jim dallied in the late afternoon with cranky, aging housewives, had them buying and sometimes offering withering favors. His favorites, no question, were the ones barely hearing, bent and shaking with years; Jim called to them with his music, a sinuous stirring refrain to awaken forgetting seniors stacked in rank, forgotten rooms around North Miami. Are you ready to make a move? He just got a warm feeling selling the ancient and near to dying, tapping into the greater good. Look at my BMW, he said. (Or, That's my yacht, or, Have you seen my apartment with its own gym, seven bathrooms? or, Did I tell you about the years I lived in the Amazon? Yeah, the Brazilian Amazon. Or, Do you like a good cigar?) Feel the softness of the black leather, go ahead, sit down, sink in. Let me turn the sound system on; feel how it surrounds you, makes you feel like a new man. Go ahead, grab the wheel. Look at the glint in your eye. The years are falling off you, man. You're a free spirit. Would you like to own one of these? The company gives me this for free. You could have one.

Why not, if Jim could do it with his high school education? Actually, he was a dropout, and look at the way he lived, where he'd been, what he owned, the big boat docked in the backyard, his joie de vivre, no despair, no despair on the horizon, you could have all of this, but custom-tailored to your own desires. First, understand your hot button. He laid it out step-by-step—how to get there, layered in the joys of life, the myriad sensual pleasures he knew so well.

The products changed over the years I knew him—it is inevitable in network marketing—but Jim was a constant, selling hope, new chances and possibilities, the big time. How could anyone turn down a resplendent, prosperous, sensuous, healthy, never-ending future? Many didn't. Jim brought tens of thousands of men and women into his organizations, no exaggeration, tens of thousands. . . . His present state, his poverty and occasional listlessness ("docility," as Phyllis described it to me—perhaps defensively—one afternoon when I was visiting her) as we see him now, at this late hour in the story (except when Mara touches him and Jim begins to awaken in her hand, his sweet smile then like a country boy coming of age in western Canada), is assuaged by the restless army of dream workers waiting behind him; he will tap them again, when he is ready. Jim is getting ready.

4.

It's been nearly forty-eight hours since my first visit to Jim's new life. I would have returned the following afternoon to their place in Homestead, except before I drove off Jim had leaned into the open window of my compact rented car and said, Buddy, do me a favor, skip a day or two before you come out again. You know, enjoy the beach.

Reasonable, I suppose. A new couple needs their space. But I felt angry and talked to myself the whole forty-five-minute drive back to Miami. What the hell did Jim think I was doing in a cheap motel near the Miami airport?

Every year I come down from New York to visit him four or five times—twenty years of visits. He picks me up in the airport in a shiny new Mercedes, Jaguar, or BMW—bad times or good he drives a luxury sedan.

These trips—usually three days or five days, occasionally a week if we're going fishing—have burrowed themselves into my psyche. Usually from the airport we drive to a fancy waterfront restaurant on South Beach, called the Blue Moon, and pick up the thread of a dozen conversations about women or pro football or making money or how life is soon going to take a fantastic turn. Most of my Florida time we are in Jim's condo. While he makes his calls I sit on their terrace and smell the ocean. I read a novel or work on the draft of an article or interview. My ideas feel fresher, more enduring, within the familiar glow of Jim's wholesale optimism and glamour—okay, tarnished glamour.

Instead of coming over I spent the last two days sitting in my motel room stewing in my juices. I tried to read but couldn't concentrate.

Now I am driving back to their place along an unfamiliar road. I feel disheartened and lost. I've just called his cell. I think he said, Take a right, then a left, right at the church. I don't see any church, but maybe I've missed it in the bleak landscape of run-down homogenous strip malls, one after the next. Jim was speaking so quickly on the cell. She was talking in the background and he was distracted, not thinking about what he was saying. Jim is getting old, forgetful. I've already called him twice for directions, but I have to call again. I know that he'll make an annoying joke that I've never been good navigating on the land.

Soon he and I are standing on their back patio that is irretrievably grimy, as though sixty years of tenants have never once bothered to hose down the rough crumbling concrete. There are some worn plastic kid toys piled in a corner. Jim tries to push the sliding glass door closed so we can talk in privacy, but the tracks are bent and the door catches in place, remaining partially open.

My old friend leans in close, striking an intimacy that leeches away my anger. He wants me to understand.

I had to do this to save myself, he explains quietly. For the last year with Phyllis I was broken into pieces that didn't fit. I no longer knew who I was. Jim pauses for me to take this in. I began thinking about suicide. Did you know that?

I shook my head, no.

Well, I became obsessed with the idea, he said in a quavery

voice. Every day I sat by the bay window in front of the canal and imagined putting a gun to my head.

He gestures toward the door, where we can see Mara puttering in the kitchen and from time to time looking our way, trying to catch his eye.

She makes me feel young again. When we make love I could be twenty years old. Jim glances her way, and his expression turns daffy.

All of our conversations soon loop back to Mara. In fact, everything that we talk about is a prelude to expressing his love and gratitude or some detail about his girl that charms him to distraction. He is like an adolescent boy.

Jim is now drawn into the kitchen, where they kiss a few times. I watch through the dirty glass feeling stiff as a board.

After twenty minutes he rushes out the front door to buy beer and pizza. It is awkward for me to be alone with her. I really don't know what to say, but apparently Mara has been waiting for this opportunity to speak privately and goes right to the point.

I want to know about him, she says in her fetching Israeli accent. Everything. Tell me about his girlfriends. How many lovers Jim has had? Please.

I shake my head, no idea.

Tell me. I'm so curious.

Sixty, I answer. Who knows how many? Mara, come on. This is ridiculous.

But she persists, flirts, how many lovers?

Mara wrests open my delight while I should be alerting my friend, Caution, Jim, storm warnings ahead.

How many in the last year before he met me? I know that you know this. He tells you everything. He whispers to you.

Then she pauses a beat: Why is this wrong? I love him. (She lingers on the word "love." How could he ever resist her?) What's wrong? She repeats looking into my mind, my mistrust.

Jim doesn't tell me everything, I offer weakly. But in truth, Jim eludes me, especially now. I don't understand how he moves on without regret. How much has he told her? I wonder if he described the girl in Brazil, eighteen years old with a voluptuous body; she forgave his sins and he desired her endlessly. (Jim is circumspect about certain events, and for good reason. He speaks with careful pauses or he coughs for time.) One night after dusk the two of them were in a hammock in the jungle clearing, wrapped in mosquito netting, drenched and dozing or making love while an armed guard stood a few feet away like a stone figure. Jim held the girl in his arms and decided that he loved her, he would marry her and bring her back to the States. He can still hear the rustling, screaming sounds of nights in the rain forest with terror and ecstasy all around, the smell of her in his hair and fingernails. But he can't remember her name. Maybe tomorrow he'll remember.

Jim has a history of shedding past lives, molting. Bankruptcy is absolution from debts and love and remorse, particularly remorse. He can no longer recall half the deals or whose fault it was. He confuses the names of his ex-wives. Does he feel remorse for Phyllis? I can't tell. Even when his face approaches real grief or guilt, Jim listens for the phone, jumps to grab it lest he'll miss an opportunity.

After pizza he and Mara are back lying on the ratty sofa making out. The girl doesn't mind the missing tooth. She explores the dark hollow with her tongue and then takes a breath. I love you, Jim. I love you too, baby. Jim's discolored toes are curled every which way like stubby claws; some nails are missing. One ankle is swollen and stained black-and-blue. She has perfect toes with pink nail polish, shows me her feet for approval. She keeps looking at me until I nod and say they are beautiful. Mara tests me even while I test her. She smiles finally, but it enrages her that I will pass judgment, tell Jim what I think, yes or no, like passing on a heifer.

He puts a trembling hand—his hand always trembles now—on her girlish ass without sag or even a trace of cellulite. Her toes curl into his. I love Jim's feet, she says, and then begins to kiss him again, ardently. I wonder if she is going to suck his dead toes. I'm afraid she will. She doesn't, but I can feel the weirdness of their turn-on, shivering explorations and discoveries, their laughs and little nips, her small rosy nipples; he savors them between his stiff fingers. His chest is powerful but sagging despite curls, push-ups, and crunches every morning. She soothes his tearing, hooded eyes with her cool mouth. Her hand finds his gray pubic hair, while I watch. No secrets, she says to me earnestly.

This Israeli woman keeps Jim coming time after time as though he were a boy, three times, one night five times. She milks him with her soft hand, entices him back. In the morning Jim wakes up hard. She mounts him, laughing, rides Jim while he tenderly holds her adolescent breasts, careful not to hurt his little girl.

Whenever we are alone he describes their sex, every detail. It is painful to listen, but he needs for me to know as though I am his Boswell, chronicling for all time the great miracle in his life.

I am back watching them from the La-Z-Boy. In the huge condo this was my favorite television chair for pro football. He and I used to bet one hundred dollars on every game we watched together. He would let me choose either team. It didn't matter to him. What mattered was the action.

They are curled around each other, fondling, kissing. Jim puts a shaking hand to his chest, a habit whenever he feels stress. His heart is fluttering. He calls it a warning. He notices that I notice and raises a finger. He doesn't want the girl to know.

5.

Jim has been telling me stories from his life since the first days of our friendship. From time to time he's even suggested that I write a book about him. Journalists hear this a lot from people. But Jim is a very smart man with a sense for time passing and for the uniqueness of his story. Also, he's very persistent. For years he has wanted this from me and my reticence has annoyed him. Some years ago he said to me there is another writer he knows and if I won't write the book he'll begin talking to the other guy, give him the scuffed-up tan briefcase that still smells of jungle rot and is crammed with memorabilia and yellowing photographs of Brazil. Ridiculous. It was the kind of blackmail I grew up with in my father's home. Except my dad had a feather trigger and it was very dangerous to cross him—he would take away his love for years. Anyhow, Jim's book became a tease and a tension between us. I would tell him I was thinking about it. From the scenes he recounted to me over the years, it was a story with incredible runs of glory and degradation. He hinted at violence, lots of it, but held back telling me these parts. During the span of our friendship I was writing pieces for a half-dozen national magazines, hustling ideas to editors, pressing to meet deadlines. So for me, Jim's "book" wasn't a real option. In any case, I was more interested in our fun together, listening to the shoptalk of salesmen, sometimes going fishing and diving with him. Writing his book would almost surely change things, maybe ruin us.

But Jim's final rebirth turned me around. I have long harbored a fantasy about leaving my home for distant lands, saying good-bye to my family, my worn, comfortable chair beside the front window, starting a new life and, more important, a different way of seeing the world. I've wondered if I could shed my fears and basic format, even outrun the shadow of my age, or if I would quickly fall back into myself. As I've gotten older this fantasy has seemed both more far-fetched and also more poignant and impossible to neglect. With Mara onstage, Jim's "book" began to percolate inside me.

Now when I visited him in their shabby place, I began to ask questions about his past as if he were the subject of a piece I was researching. I took notes and a few times I brought along my little tape recorder. Jim was delighted by this display of his importance. Even then, they fooled around on the sofa, acted like they couldn't wait for me to leave so they could retire to their cubbyhole bedroom. I wanted to hear about the businesses in Canada, his partner, Marvin. Yes, Marvin. From the little I already knew, Marvin was physically disgusting and a world-class schemer, a true Svengali mastermind. And Jim's wives. I knew Phyllis of course, but about the alluring Ava I knew next to nothing except he had never fully gotten over her. Of course I wanted every detail about my friend's life in the jungle. But their sex was always in the air and that's what Jim really cared about, or that's how it seemed at the time. I still hadn't fully committed to writing the book. Jim was still enticing me, pulling away the bait. He was such a con artist.

Meanwhile, the girl was angry with me for acting like the judgmental rabbi. She showed herself off shamelessly. I could have you, I could break you, she seemed to say. I tried to turn her my way by talking up the book. I told her that a book about Jim's life would bring him fame and would be good for his business. She took this in.

Jim had me begging to write the book. I was afraid he would die in her arms before I had the story.

The first night I was able to get him talking, Jim skipped around, while she and I had to struggle to keep up, tried to imagine details and connections. They sat on the sofa and I pulled the La-Z-Boy closer. He jumped decades in a sentence. Jim wanted to move fast and hit the glamour spots for her, hunting jungle animals, the close calls, his considerable physical courage. Jim watched her face and when he thrilled her he smiled back with his love-goofy expression.

She got into the swing of it. Jim, say the beginning, she prodded. Say when you were a little boy.

Then Jim smiled at me to say, Look how smart she is.

She was smart but also very literal and dogged. She kept nudging him to fill in the blanks. How did we get from there to here? Finally, she dragged him back to the beginning, his grandfather's farm in western Canada where the story begins.

Jim coughed for a time to gather himself.

What first came to him was the smell. He hadn't thought about it for a while, maybe since she'd come to live with him, but now he remembered the sweet sickly odor and fear spreading out from his neck and shoulders like the dark pool on the narrow concrete floor, some of it reaching the edges, where the floor came against a buckling wooden wall. Jim could see the puddle through a crack in the workshop door, viscous and blackening on the concrete slab. After sixty-five years he recalled it vividly. The afternoon was hot and he swatted flies and sweat from his face. Jim was afraid to push hard on the door, which was blocked by an unyielding weight. He was nauseated and shaking all over. In the kitchen sink there had been clumps of black hair. He didn't want to open this door, not then and not now when they had no money, he and Mara and the kids eating chicken legs every night, not even enough to take her out to lunch. They drove to the Winn-Dixie in a twenty-year-old Volvo with bad brakes he'd picked up for six hundred dollars. A better car was out of the question. His stomach was in a knot at their poverty, or maybe it was the lingering stench of blood. He paused before starting to speak about the early years of hunger and heartbreak. He coughed, to steal another few seconds.

Jim's dad, Nathan, in a fancy suit with wide lapels and a perfectly folded handkerchief in his pocket, striding off past the pigpen of his father's farm, kicking at a few chickens while he crossed the dirt yard. Through the kitchen window Jim could see the old Chevy moving away from the farm on a narrow winding road. He ran outside to watch the taillights flicker and disappear. Where's Dad going? Sally shrugged.

A little boy on a farm in western Canada is wealthy with things to see and wonder about. Jim awoke to the dry rush of prairie wind through his half-open window. Outside, the trees were bending. Something wild was happening. Get up and race to the swing on the big maple tree. Feel the wind on his face. Smell the fresh-cut hay and the manure of horses, smell it way up his nose into his cheeks. Good. Smell the turned-over earth, even better than eggs, made him feel all opened up to living. Get up and search for worms and bugs. Dig some potatoes for Sally and smell your hands. Get up. Smell the fried eggs sizzling in the summer kitchen, a big cool pitcher of milk set on a great slab of ice below the floor. Dad sets his beer gently on the ice that doesn't melt all summer. Dad's face is filled with wanting something. Get up. Through his little window Jim looks at the rolling hills, and a picture of cows grazing down near the river. Lovely, peaceful cows that don't move until Jim comes very close.

From his window Jim could also see a little shack, a workshop where his dad sometimes did carpentry for his own father. Nathan held rough pieces of wood in his vice that smelled of oil, and after a few days he carried a finished chair or little table from the shed. Jim wanted to learn how to do this trick. He wanted to stand beside his dad, who always smelled good. Jim shuddered at the pleasure of Nathan.

Jim petted the cows and wiped away flies from their ears and noses. They had big dopey faces. He played with their ears, touched the drool on their soft mouths. In the corral they were bored, swishing and stomping in mud and cow dung. He liked them better in the field. Most afternoons he walked toward the river and learned how to track them in the grass and dirt. He called to them in his biggest voice and shook the chop bucket. The lumbering beasts followed him through the gate when it was time for milking. Jim was master of the cows.

Nathan pursed his lips, looked very serious tying his tie in the mirror. He was the boss. Jim watched his father shine his shoes to a deep luster. Jim wanted to be the boss. Nathan said to Sally he wanted to ride in a Cadillac. She sighed. I'll never be able to own one, but at least I could see how it feels on the road, he said, while Sally washed the dinner dishes and tried to push down her disquiet.

Nathan walked out the door with a slam. His work was dressing up and going out. What's a Cadillac? Jim asked. What a nice name, Cadillac. Sounded rich and bold like his dad. Jim wanted to go out and find Nathan. He wanted to smell perfume on his face and body. Mostly he wanted to dress like Nathan. He practiced with a ribbon tying his tie. Practiced pursing his lips like Nathan when he tied his tie. Sally shook her head. Jim practiced folding a napkin and putting it in the pocket of his filthy flannel shirt. He sat in bed folding it over and over, a hundred times.

A Cadillac is a big fancy car, Mommy, must be good to ride in. I want a Cadillac. Where is he, Mommy? She wouldn't say. She washed their clothes, worked even when she might have rested an hour. There was always work to be done on a poor farm like this one. Toil was respite from worry and questioning. Grandpa took care of the big family as best he could. Whenever he gave Sally a few cents, she saved it in a rag. Actually, there was a box of knotted rags. The secret stash had been growing for some time; maybe something important would come of it, though she couldn't imagine what. Nathan had all the big plans.

Sometimes Nathan didn't come home for a couple of nights. Sally accepted his infidelities without a word. There was nothing to do. From the kitchen window she would watch her husband leaning against the old car, staring at the hills.

Again and again Jim's dad dressed up and threw himself into the night, rode hope into town, and took what he could, except he was turned away for not having a buck, couldn't go to good restaurants or buy things that might have appeased him. Nathan resented the successes of other men, the tailored cut of their suits, their pretty, made-up ladies. Much of the time he was drugged and blackened by lusting and resenting and could not focus on his sturdy wife and pauper children. Doing the work of the farm, which he understood would someday pass on to the eldest of his twelve brothers, was futility and malaise. Nathan chased his urges and stole small favors, whenever he had the chance.

One fall afternoon, before Jim turned seven, Nathan announced that they would have to leave the farm, Grandpa couldn't afford to keep them around anymore; he couldn't feed everyone in the big house and keep it warm. It was something called hard times. Jim wondered why his uncles could stay for hard times and they couldn't. He worried about leaving the cows but then decided he'd be returning soon. He couldn't imagine not coming back to where he'd lived his whole life.

The family took a bus to a tiny village outside of Edmonton, about seven hundred miles to the west. Nathan had heard there was work there. They found a small house in the country and rented it for eight dollars a month. The front room had a dirt floor. In the kitchen there was a little wood stove. There were three other rooms, but only the kitchen was heated as long as they had wood to put in the stove. There was a toilet but no bath and not a stick of furniture in any room. They would have to sleep on the floor. It was a cold, forlorn place.

Sally spread some blankets and then, sitting beside a flickering candle, she showed Nathan her money saved over the span of five years, a little more than two hundred dollars. She counted it out slowly, with a hesitation, wanting to please him, but also feeling the urge to pull it back and knot it away again—her secret life dissolving with this pile of dollars and loose change on the blanket. But maybe he would love her again now that he was away from the farm. That was her hope. Nathan was astonished at such a sum, and sobered to discover that his wife had kept this big secret. She saved her pennies milking cows, mopping, digging, planting, cooking, cleaning, sixteen hours a day without ever taking a holiday. She kept it from him and now they had it. He called her a good girl and hugged her on the cold floor. There was enough money for Nathan to go and buy furniture and a new stove for the kitchen, to put food in the pantry and to buy cotton for Sally to sew new shirts for the kids to wear on their first day in school, so they wouldn't be embarrassed, and make curtains for the front room and the kitchen. She wanted to make it a cheerful place. Then when he had a job they would put in a wood floor in the front room. That would help. They would manage until he found work.

Nathan brought home meager provisions for the kitchen—a few cans, some cereal, milk, enough for a few days—but next to nothing sitting on a shelf made a desolate picture. While she waited for the furniture to arrive, Sally did what she could around the house and ran after the kids.

For weeks, Nathan looked in Edmonton for work, but he

couldn't find a thing, not one day's labor. Thousands of men were looking.

Nathan told Sally he was going to ride the trains and look for work farther west. During depression times many men were riding the freights. Sally was impatient. Where were the furniture and her new stove? They would be delivered to the house in a few more days, he said. She didn't want to wait for Nathan to find employment and start sending her money—he wasn't a good bet. Sally had already talked to a few neighbors who agreed to buy her fresh-baked bread, and occasionally she would sell them some cookies and a cake. Sally was a resourceful and energetic worker—she wanted to get started and needed the stove. In her mind her little business was already taking shape. But now they had next to nothing in the house. They needed to make some money fast. The kids had big holes in their shoes. She tied rags around their shoes and sent them off down the road to school with a couple of pieces of bread and jam.

The night Nathan left on the train she confronted him about the furniture, stood in front of him, hands on her broad hips while he weaved around. Where's the furniture, Nathan? Where's my money? Or else he would have walked out the door without a word about it. And he wouldn't have cared, on the wondrous first night of his odyssey, lying on his back, looking up at the stars from a speeding train. He told her he had taken the money and gambled it on pork options, lost every last penny. He explained this while he gathered his things, folded his suit, put on his new shoes, searched for a clean handkerchief without sense for the outrage of his vanity, let alone the import of his crime.

We might have made a fortune, but it didn't work out, Sally. I tried, he said with heaped-on repentance. She shook her head and didn't say a word.

What did it matter if he spent her money on pork options or poker or more likely on some women who thought he was a business

owner having a sporting weekend on the town—what did it matter? Or maybe he was leaving them with a hundred in his pocket
and a dream about where he would go and whom he would meet.
She could feel his festive stirrings—she knew him. But what did it
matter how he lost it? They were a desperate family. In a few more
days they would owe eight dollars for the month's rent. She didn't
have two dollars. What would she do when the lady came for her
money? Nathan left them this way, rushing out the door for the
whistle of a train.

It was deep into the fall and the prairie wind was frigid even
before dark. Wind seeped through the thin wood walls, rushed
through loose window frames and beneath the front door. Even
with the stove hot, the house was cold and the children wore most
of their clothes to bed at night. They smelled from never bathing.

Sally begged in the church and when she had nothing, she
pleaded with strangers on the street. She heated a little soup before bed and gave the boys bread in the morning. One man took
pity and gave her three dollars—it gave her just enough to pay the
rent a week late. But what about next month? If they were put out,
where would they go? How would Nathan find them?

One morning Jim woke to go to the bathroom and the toilet
was frozen solid. Go out back, said Sally. They were living in a
frozen house. The four of them began sleeping in the kitchen hud-
dled together around the fire. There was no tub to bathe in. In the
morning, they went to the bathroom in the yard beside a broken
shed. The earth was too hard to dig a hole. She sent them off to
school, walking across snowy fields with holes in their shoes. At
least it was warm in the school. Sally spent her day walking the
streets looking for work, and then it was a five-mile hike back from
town. She came into the freezing place bone tired and hungry, lit
the fire before the kids arrived from school. But then, gripped with
fear that her children would starve, she rushed back out to the
church, two miles down the road, and mopped floors until night to

earn a quarter or two. She was driven by terror, and often took the two little ones into a store and begged for an onion or a carrot. If she was lucky she would cook a few vegetables in her little pot with some butter. The four of them dipped bread into the pan.

Months passed and the family starved. Not a word from Nathan. But Jim was certain his father was doing something splendid. Starting a business was what usually came into Jim's mind, although he wasn't altogether sure what that meant. He had many fantasies about Nathan. Some days he worked in a wood-paneled office dressed in his fine suit with a folded handkerchief and shining shoes. Other days Nathan was out west searching for gold in the mountains. That was the story Jim liked most. His dad was striking it rich in the mountains, maybe in Alaska. On some days Jim allowed himself to join Nathan and they found gold together.

One evening Sally came home with her face flushed and a bad smell on her breath. Her speech was rambling and her message unusually candid.

We need to start making money or we won't survive, Jim. We'll all be dead, she continued, grabbing her son's hand. This is your father's fault. The way he left us with nothing at all. How can we pay the rent? What are we to do?

Sally careened into Nathan's history of idleness and lavish spending and told the boy how his father had stolen her money. She spoke to Jim with candor and detail, as though he were her confidant and last chance rather than a kid. She wept. She beseeched him, What are we to do?

Jim narrated this early history in a dilapidated cottage with filthy sheetrock walls, soiled rugs, and broken furniture, a house wreck presided over by a flagrantly sexual and opportunistic girl. Who says you can't go home again? I couldn't help thinking that Jim's father would have died for a Mara. He left his family in a freezing house without a few dollars to pay the rent or buy a morsel of food. The family would have starved to death except that Jim was clever and charming even then.

There was a dairy farm a few miles down the road. Jim decided he would go there and speak to Mr. Hayes. Jim wasn't really sure how much he knew or didn't know about cows. More than a half year had passed since they had left Grandpa's farm, a long time for a boy. But he had moxie and seemed to understand he'd have to introduce himself in a way to catch the farmer's attention. Jim planned to tell Farmer Hayes that he knew how to talk to cows.

Jim knocked on the door and waited until a big man in overalls opened it up. The hulking farmer did not exactly embrace young Jim. These days Hayes was bothered too often by poor people looking for a nickel or something to eat. When he said, I can't use you, go on home, kid, Jim didn't budge. This familiar place warmed him inside, the barn and the machines, the smell of the tilled earth. But Jim felt something besides nostalgia. The farmer's vast green meadow spread out before Jim like a calling. Jim wanted to make this first big step into the world. He camped on the porch and the farmer shook his head and went back inside. He didn't need a boy who talked to cows, but he couldn't help chuckling.

A little later, Hayes came back out with a piece of apple pie and an offer: You go out and find my herd and bring them back to the barn for milking. If you can do it, I'll give you work to do around here. It's like a test, he said, while Jim savored his last bite of pie. Mr. Hayes was only getting rid of a little beggar in a tattered coat. He was a good man, but he didn't want the boy's misery around his farm. He was sure Jim would get tired or bored in short order and head back from where he came.

The cows are out there. The farmer gestured with his hand and shut the door firmly. Out there, beyond the meadow and distant tree line—somewhere, it might have been the end of the earth he was pointing to.

Jim set off to find the cows. If he had been a few years older he might have experienced this as an agony—a test to save his starving family—but for an eight-year-old it was just a game. Starvation was a mother's concern and Jim was still licking apple pie off his lips. He felt at home in the big meadow, picked a few daisies and smelled the spring. He headed off for the trees, about a mile and a half away, swinging an empty bucket he picked up in the yard. It was a game he'd played before. Find the cows. In the meadow there was no dirt for tracks, so he searched for bent underbrush. He was an Indian crisscrossing the meadow until he found a route of trampled grass pointing toward the trees.

In the shade of a narrow stretch of tall pines Jim found some hoofprints in the dirt. This would help. He walked along the trees for a half hour and wondered how the cows would look and how many he would find. There was no question of finding them. In fact, he wanted to draw the game out; more hours in the country meant time away from their house that was cold even in the spring, their rooms permanently imprinted with chill and a mother's sorrow. He came to another stretch of meadow and lost the tracks in a confusion of trampled grass and brush. He found tracks again approaching the river and walked along the bank for a mile.

Sure enough, the small herd was drinking at the river's edge. Jim approached casually, as if he didn't have a care, and then he started talking softly to himself, and when the cows looked up he turned away as if he weren't really interested. Talking to cows was just a trick. Jim kept up his prattle to some trees rustling on the bank, to the swollen river, soothing words to go with a spring afternoon. He yawned. By the time he began calling the cows he'd become a part of their place. They swished their tails and looked up at him, licked water off their faces. They didn't come to him. Not yet. He knew they wouldn't. They didn't know him. But they weren't afraid. He kept speaking to them while he walked to the riverbank and scooped a couple of handfuls of gravel into his bucket. Then

Jim called to them again, this time in a louder voice, and he shook the bucket as if it were filled with grain. The cows began to walk to him as they had many times before when he carried the chop bucket on Grandpa's farm. Jim knew they would come.

It was easy to fool cows, although the farmer could hardly have been more surprised when Jim came back leading a procession of twenty Herefords ready for milking. He gave Jim two quarters and was true to his word about the job. Each afternoon after school Jim found the cows and then did some chores for the farmer. Most evenings Jim gave the quarters to his mom. It was enough to pay the rent and put a little food on the table.

Young Jim was tireless and seemed endowed with a precocious sense of responsibility and limitless goodwill. By the hour he listened to the woes of his abandoned mother. He soothed her. He rubbed her blistered feet. At first light he was delivering newspapers in the snow before school, and afterwards he worked for the farmer. When there was an hour Jim gathered wildflowers in the field for his mom to sell in the church. If there was a job to be done Jim never had to be asked twice. Before the age of nine Jim was the breadwinner and patriarch of his home, adored and fully relied upon by his faithful mom. But this hardworking, better-than-good boy had a secret passion that burned stronger with the years. He lusted for his father.

6.

In his daydreams Jim reaches for Mara while he drives their creaky Volvo for the morning paper or takes her children to school. He burns for her. When they walk together on the street she puts her hand inside the pocket of his tight jeans and smiles tenderly. She touches him a little. He feels empowered by their rebellion, this fevered, improbable chapter even in a long life of fresh starts. Imagine a seventy-five-year-old man turned on while walking across the intersection headed to the supermarket. He is with a woman young enough to be his granddaughter. Her two young kids trail behind calling him Daddy. He hasn't worn such tight-fitting pants for twenty years or more—she chooses his clothes. Mara kisses him deeply, defiantly, in front of the Wynn-Dixie. She will show everyone their love. Old ladies turn and shake their heads. She is wearing sexy white shorts on a hot fall afternoon, presses her shapely tanned leg against him, kisses his ear. She is amused, but it is more. She is incited by the spectacle of her and Jim. It is their desire that presages everything good down the road, belittles the stares of ladies in front of the Wynn-Dixie and the bitchy arguments against their chances from Jim's friends like me, and Phyllis, his abandoned wife.

The girl smiles. They don't have our happiness, baby, she says.

When they are alone in their shabby rooms, Mara seems oblivious to his age. She talks exuberantly about their lives in twenty years, in thirty years: their homes, cars, long-term mortgages. The best colleges for her kids, who will soon be their kids. She is a careful planner. In the mornings they sip coffee and use the sunny palaver of young couples just starting out. She usually calls him baby.

One afternoon I ask Mara, What will you do when he is sick, when he can no longer go places with you? She seems completely confounded by this question. What about when he is too old to fool around? I ask.

He is not old, she says simply. But her face has turned crimson from surprise or perhaps the cruelty of my question. I'm not sure what to make of it. I wonder whom she sees when they are making love. Or when his bunions are hurting and he can barely make it from the car into the pizzeria. Is it that she is imbued with a child's transforming optimism that I can barely recall?

Jim keeps placing me in front of them so that I will record all of this for "the book." He envisions his magical effect upon her as a part of his legacy. Although there are moments when a shadow passes and Jim asks me, What do you think?

The question cuts too many ways.

Before Jim met Mara he had been marketing a line of appliances—mattresses, blankets, pillows, back and ankle braces—purported to alleviate pain and foster healing utilizing magnetic therapy. After a half-dozen years of considerable success and high living the business had fallen into decline. Prior to his leaving for Israel, things had become so bad financially that Jim and Phyllis had been forced to leave their spacious condominium for a one-bedroom apartment that was also on the Intracoastal. Jim was humiliated about this move. He traveled to Tel Aviv, where network marketing was still in its infancy, hoping to revitalize his business by signing on new recruits (down lines), but more fundamentally trying to revitalize himself.

During his three-month stay in Israel we spoke on the phone every couple of weeks. Jim described his new life in considerable detail and especially his courting of an attractive young woman whom he met at one of his introductory recruiting meetings. He spoke about their unlikely romance and his own sexual rebirth at considerable length, and he described their sex with details and candor that embarrassed me and frankly put me on edge.

I tried to reel him back. Hey, Jim, it's time to come home, I said. You realize, it's the football season. Come on. Enough.

If I could just get him on the plane back to Florida the old life would take hold. I'd come down to Miami and we'd be back talking in the Blue Moon, betting the games and plotting the next moves. The girl would soon become another old story, some laughs in a bar.

Not yet, buddy, he answered firmly.

When I got off the line with Jim I felt unnerved.

The evening Jim met Mara, he had been standing at a lectern in the meeting room of a small hotel in Tel Aviv, looking a little tired, but natty as always in one of his custom-tailored Florida suits and sleek Italian leather shoes. He was looking at his notes and trying to summon the old pep for his bread-and-butter talk about the ease of building a residual income for life. It was one thing to give this talk when you are flying high in a palace on Brickell Avenue above the Intracoastal and another when you are depressed and alone in a foreign country, worried about the next month's rent.

Jim was looking around the audience—mostly middle-aged men, dressed badly, fidgeting and sweating as if they'd soon be asked to perform up front like Jim—when he noticed a young woman, lovely auburn hair to the shoulders, lipstick, a slight girlish figure. Their eyes met. She was staring at him, which was disconcerting but also pleasurable. His energy for the presentation came from her.

She came up to him after the talk, wanted to know more about the business. They went out for a cup of coffee. She and her husband had fallen into a financial rut. They weren't getting anywhere. The husband, Shimon, had no motivation to do anything. When he came home from his job, he plopped in front of the television, barely acknowledged the children. She touched Jim's hand to make her point. She was interested in magnetic therapy; could he tell her something more about it? And what is this thing you call network? Her accent was intoxicating and alive. No, network *marketing,* he corrected with a smile. She listened earnestly. But he wasn't up to this. The business trip had been going poorly. Hardly any sales of his products, and few recruits were signing up. Apparently it hadn't been such a good idea to sell his magnetic healing aids to a population preoccupied with war. When he wandered the streets of the city, young men and women rushed past him, fearful or quickened by the violence; older folk were just weary. Jim wasn't noticed, Jim who had always been the center of the party, but this girl hung on every word. She asked if he would meet with her husband, talk to him about the business. Shimon was sleepwalking through his life. Maybe Jim could wake him up. You are so convincing, she insisted. It was very hot in the room. She had dark hair under her arms, thick lipstick. She wore a short skirt, and when she slowly crossed her legs Jim shivered like an old horse. What if she noticed? She was so young and fresh. He tried to shake off this far-fetched desire. But he knew that he must get free of his loser mentality. Jim began to explain what the business could do for them, the many riches it had given to him and Phyllis. He talked past the ache in his gut, the sadness of recent failures, and described the palatial condo where he had once lived with Phyllis in Miami, the great parties they had held overlooking the Intracoastal Waterway, the smell of the sea air in the evening when storms blew in from the east. He didn't mention that his business had nearly gone broke and they had been forced to move into a modest apartment.

Jim and Mara walked back to his small rented room so he could give her material to study. When she took his hand he began to tremble as if the temperature had plummeted. Jim couldn't stop shaking. He didn't know if he could still make love. He felt so diminished, pared right down to old age. It was humiliating to be shaking on the street. The girl wasn't nervous at all. She wanted to stop for a moment and then she kissed him deeply. He almost said, Thank you, as though she'd given an old man a gift to remember, but her face was flushed with desire. Once they arrived at Jim's small room she took the lead. Mara nursed him back to life with passion served up with innocent eyes and much laughter. She could not get enough of her older lover, kissed his aging chest and legs with irrepressible relish. For Jim this was flattery that felt like redemption.

Jim didn't want to leave Israel, but he wasn't making a dollar. He called me in New York and asked to loan him the money for the flight home. It was jarring to think of my high-roller friend without the funds to buy a ticket. But I think he would have stayed in Israel and lived on nothing except the girl agreed to join him in Florida.

When Jim returned to Phyllis, he spent his days sitting in a chair looking out the bay window facing the canal, waiting for Mara to call. For the first two days he didn't tell Phyllis about the girl and she tried to regale him with the latest gossip about their aging friends along with a big dose of the optimism she had learned from him, except she had never been able to pull off his pep talks.

Jim couldn't pay attention to his wife for more than a minute or two. The enormity of what he had done, what he was going to do, paralyzed him. He couldn't think of how to explain the end of their long marriage.

But mostly, he didn't think about Phyllis at all, though she rarely left the room. She watched him sitting by the window and figured out the general drift before he said a word about the girl. He was afraid Mara would change her mind, wouldn't travel here to begin their new life. He shook his head like a victim. Jim was trying to keep their dialogue alive inside. Sitting in his chair, he tried to summon her smell, her taste. He didn't want to be interrupted. He couldn't bear the violation of Phyllis's voice or her long stretches of crying once she fully understood his intention.

Jim had no energy for his marketing business. Of course he needed money, but he was obsessed with Mara (it would take her nearly two months to settle her affairs and join him in Florida), and he couldn't bear the grind of travel and attending meetings, listening to endless sad-sack stories that were at the heart of signing new recruits. Suddenly these group sessions seemed to mirror an inner deadness. Their inflated promises and coarseness were inconsistent with the new feelings that stirred his being.

His former best buddies, the top guys in his organization, were bewildered by Jim's reticence to soldier on. They offered him a new product line with a guaranteed income and still Jim didn't return their calls. Top executives, distributors, casual friends, his grown daughter, his wife, the lot of them had been swept aside by improbable love.

When Jim and Mara are window-shopping the glamour stores in downtown Miami and happen to run into one of his salesmen or good buddies from the old days, and there have been many, he usually greets the man as "bub." It is hard to imagine the surfeit of dreams and shared aspirations that have suddenly and tragically drained into this tiny dismissive noun. Whenever I hear him use it I feel embarrassed for the friend, though at the same time I feel pleased to retain a place in Jim's much-diminished circle. It has become a circle of three, but only because I cling to him like a pilot fish. I feel like calling back to the spurned stranger, Wait, just wait! I still believe (or want to believe) Jim's infatuation will pass and he'll return to the old days with Phyllis.

She would take him back, even now.

7.

Why does he want to be with her? Phyllis asked me. She's a terrorist.

One night I was with Jim and Mara, and the next I visited Phyllis in the dimly lit one bedroom where she had waited for Jim when he was in Israel.

She has him hypnotized, hypnotized. Phyllis repeated this word slowly while looking at my face to see if she'd gotten it right. Phyllis has often annoyed me with her choice of words, not exactly wrong but not right either. I was tempted to say to her, Captivated, enthralled, fascinated. But I didn't. I was barely listening.

While Jim was in Israel for months loving Mara, it never once occurred to Phyllis that he wouldn't stand by her. They had been married nearly three decades and Jim was her lion. Like many of us, Phyllis resisted the image in the mirror. She didn't notice her dappled, bulging thighs, her spreading hips and pudgy face; she still lovingly patted on her morning makeup, slipped into a short skirt, and showed a plunging neckline. It was the way he had coached her to dress. Then she walked to the supermarket in the dreamy style of Jim's young lover, in Toronto, twenty years his junior, when she still had a tiny waist, thrilling hips, and a rolling Marilyn Monroe walk through paradise.

They met one night in a club in Toronto. She had been sitting at a table with a few friends and he sent over a bottle of champagne. Jim introduced himself and they chatted a little. He was a charming guy, but she had a boyfriend. Before the end of the night he'd coaxed her phone number. Jim called three or four times before Phyllis agreed to meet him for lunch. He stopped by for her in his new Mercedes convertible. Their second date was a two-hour ride that ended at a gated estate on Lake Ontario with tennis courts, two speedboats, servants' quarters, a gorgeous water view. She couldn't believe her eyes. It was his place.

That night he asked her to move in with him. She laughed at his audacity, but he wouldn't let it go. He asked her again and again, triangulated all of her incredulity and doubts with enthusiasm and a stream of promises. Jim promised to take her on his private jet to Vegas. He would show her things she couldn't imagine. It was very hard to say no to him.

I was resolved to be honorable to both Jim and Phyllis, but it wasn't easy. I left Jim's place the night before feeling lusty and troubled, as though my youth was seeping away. Mara's aura was all over me, her heat and a vague invitation I couldn't pin down. Was I losing out? Surely I was losing out. I was growing old with my wife. Mara gestured with her hand, pulled me into another room to tell a secret. For an instant, her beautiful leg brushed against mine. Jim wanted me to feel what she brings. He encouraged it. He was selling her to me, selling wildly.

Now I was seated in Phyllis's apartment of grief. She and Jim had been forced to move here after Jim could no longer come up with the mortgage payments on their condominium. Phyllis had quickly found this modest place, not far from the water. Jim would be able to take walks in the afternoon, looking at passing boats. They didn't have money for the security deposit, but she had convinced the doddering manager of the old apartment complex to let them move in with their boxes, the big projection TV, and their stainless refrigerator. The bedroom had termites, and Jim needed to rip the framing off the door and kill the bugs or at least slow them down. He tore off the wooden frames with an old man's fury. We will be out of here in a few months, she said to calm him down. Jim sat by the bay window, looking out, hardly speaking. The view of the canal reminded him of the boat he had been forced to give up. Seventy-five years old and he had lost nearly everything.

Phyllis had preserved Jim's dark mood of a half year earlier, before he met the girl, or even deepened it. She wanted to tell me secrets about Jim's girlfriend, terrible things. What could Phyllis tell me that would be convincing? I was reeling from Mara's seductiveness, her undertow; we can't swim against it. In this dark place, his lover's leap made perfect sense. Mara is youth that we can only barely remember. Young girls live every night. Every night is the night. Jim's wife was speaking, but I could barely hear her.

I was angry with Phyllis. She had always been so fast to defend him, said whatever it took to get him off the hook. It wasn't Jim's fault. Never Jim's fault, no matter how many promises he broke, how many thousands were lost, how many innocents lost their savings in one of his marketing schemes or phony investments. It was the accountant's fault. Jim was misled.

Cardboard boxes littered this apartment, which she would have made picture-perfect if he were here, if he would only come home. Everything had stopped in place. He had taken the big TV two months before so he could watch sports—she had wanted him to take it for the games—and there was a gaping hole between two cabinets where it had sat against the wall, an unseemly tangle of antennae and speaker wires left where they had fallen. On the glass dining room table, where she had carefully laid out splendid table settings for dinner parties in the big condo, there were piles of discount coupons ripped from magazines, hundreds of coupons. She used them during the final months in the condominium, so he could entertain, to buy cheap cheese and crackers. She no longer bothered with them, but throwing them away felt reckless.

Their jewelry and most of the paintings were gone, sold for a fraction of their value. Nearly everything of real value was gone. Her remaining share of the lengthy marriage was in the cardboard boxes. Her share of Canada, her portion of Florida waterfront homes and start-up companies with skyrocketing futures, were all in those boxes. In several of them I could see ribbons and wrapping that she used each December for her Christmas presents. Every year she would slowly accumulate gifts to send out from her and Jim.

She had a keen feel for what his grandchildren would appreciate and on the floor were their books and art supplies wrapped in favored pastel colors with lovely ribbons. She knew much more about these two kids than he did. She knew more about his daughter as well. Phyllis and Jim had been living in separate homes now for two months, but remarkably, Jim's fifty-year-old daughter still hadn't been told about their separation. She loved Phyllis and he couldn't bear to break the news. In a couple of weeks, after the New Year, she and Jim planned to travel together to the coast and talk in person to the woman. Jim would sit on the sofa looking contrite and weary, as though the world had pushed him into this unseemly affair—Jim's daughter would be horrified by her father's runaway lust—while Phyllis would put an upbeat spin on their separation: It was all for the good. She and Jim remained the very best of friends, Phyllis would say, easing the way for him.

For so many years Phyllis had selected Christmas gifts for his most important clients, his up lines. It was one of her responsibilities. This year's presents were also on the floor. She prided herself on knowing what people really liked, and selected each gift with care and conviction—many years ago she and Jim had agreed that sending the presents to his up lines was money in the bank. She had written all of this year's cards, each of them with a personal touch from Jim and Phyllis, no mention of the breakup. She couldn't bear to tell anyone, not yet, although all of their distributors were discussing it on the Internet. Phyllis wanted to send the Christmas gifts but didn't have money for postage. It would come to several hundred dollars. She'd have to speak with Jim about money for the postage. The stacks of unsent presents made her desperate. What was he thinking? Without his contacts, he would be ruined. She would be ruined. They were still dancing together in Las Vegas. She couldn't stop dancing. Phyllis was up nights fretting about Jim's contacts. It was painful to listen.

She was sitting on her knees, beside me on the chesterfield, wearing red Dr. Denton pajamas, a big woman in a child's outfit, enormous melon breasts hanging free, wide fleshy hips, her puzzled face heavily made up in the Vegas style that Jim favored. He'd taught her a lot. He'd taught her how to be the younger woman, to excite the room with novelty and risk like Ava had before her. That had been Phyllis's job. She was still poised to do it. . . . She'd lost weight, to please Jim, still needed to lose another thirty pounds. But not so large as before. Maybe Jim could accept her now. She seemed to be showing herself to me with this question in mind. Phyllis was titillated by his new sex life. I could feel it. She was coming alive herself after years of repose, readying herself for him, stimulated by their sex. She was starving herself. She wanted to be a small woman, for him. Most days she went jogging on sweltering Miami streets, her face flushed from effort, dripping sweat, hoping he'd drive by and see her in sweats and the stylish ankle weights he had given to her as a Christmas present some years back. She yearned to please him. This remained her primary drive. She couldn't turn it off.

She blew her nose. When he came back from Israel he spent his days looking out, she said, pointing to the curved bay window. We still might have worked it out. This woman wouldn't allow it. She was calling every hour from Israel. She was afraid Jim would forget her, his little sex trifle, so she called him every hour. She wouldn't give him a moment with me, didn't want to risk it. She wouldn't give me a chance. He raced for the phone. Otherwise he was glued there, by the window. Despite not being in contact those first few days of separation, she called fourteen, fifteen times in a day. Jim and I would begin to talk, he would tell me how he was feeling or that I was his very best friend; I cried when he said that; he remembered a moment with his son in Canada. I gave him a hug and the phone rang. As if she had a camera in the room. This terrorist. And he would cradle the phone in a corner so I wouldn't hear, but I heard everything. He called her baby. His baby. He was calling her these love pet words in the corner. Sometimes I couldn't help myself and I raced into the bedroom and picked up the phone. I needed to hear it all, to wash myself in their stupid endearments. Oh, Jim, I'm so depressed, she would say with her little hot voice. Jerking him off. Oh, Jim, I can't sleep. I miss you so much. I'm so afraid. I'm laying on the floor, Jim. What will I do? I have a stomachache, Jim. I miss you so bad, baby. These phone calls came at all hours in the night, so I couldn't get my balance. I couldn't sleep. She never thought about me, not for a minute.

Sometimes after he got off with her he was very dark. He wouldn't say a word until she rang again or he'd say terrible things. Phyllis, I can't make love to a woman with big breasts. I always had big breasts and he loved them. I even made them bigger for him. She took a deep breath. He told me that he loves her feet. He always loved my feet for being so small, but now he loves her feet. She has feet like a man. Every night I rubbed his back, I walked across his back and he called me his darling. But after this woman, he said to me, Who could love you, Phyllis? Who could love you, Phyllis? He said that. Look at yourself. You're a fat woman.

She started to weep. Now, I was crying as well. I embraced her. We were both sobbing, our faces wet and gummy from her makeup. We laughed. Maybe I loved her for the first time that night. We were just people getting older.

I held Jim in that chair, she continued, after he said to me he felt like blowing his brains out. He was so depressed, he didn't know what to do. I love you, Phyllis. He said that. And then she called, at that instant. She was pulling him away from me. I love you, baby. I love you, baby. Phone sex. She had him. She had him. And he would speak to her in the corner, over there, clutching the phone for his life. They did baby talk. An old man speaking baby talk. If he went out for a few minutes, I picked up the phone and when she heard my voice she hung up. It would have been so human if she had said, Phyllis, it is Mara, could I please speak to Jim? But she heard my voice and hung up. She terrorized me. I was trying to get Jim together. He was so down and confused. What kind of person does such a thing?

Once I knew she was coming, there was no changing it; I found the house for him myself. I knew he couldn't manage. He was just sitting over there by the window. Each day was passing and he was sitting there. She was coming in four weeks. She was coming in seventeen days. He was paralyzed. I was afraid for him. I always did things for Jim. I drove him around until I found a little house that would work. It wasn't much, not his style, but it was in a safe neighborhood with a good school system. That was important to her. Once the husband, Shimon, decided she could bring the kids to the States, she became fierce about her children. She wanted the best for them. The boy needed gymnastic classes, whatever they cost. He must have gymnastic classes. Believe me, there was never any question about whether she would bring her children. That was just talk for Jim, part of her act.

I picked out their furniture, the silverware, the matching glasses, the children's swings for the backyard. There wasn't much money, but I tried to imagine what she would like. I can't explain why I did it except he wanted me to. I wanted him to be happy.

Did he tell you about her sister? Probably not. Mara's sister came here four years ago and married an older man and then she dumped him. The sister is living in Miami. She has a young boyfriend with a flashy sports car and a house on Key Biscayne. So what do you think is going to happen to Jim after he marries her and she gets the green card? Haven't you noticed the change in him? He's worn out by her. He's become an acquiescive person.

Phyllis caught my eye, and I nodded to her; "acquiescive" was the right word for Jim. His top guys from the company sometimes talk to me, she continued. Jim doesn't make business calls anymore. He doesn't return their calls. He sits and waits for her. He dreams. What does she want with an old man who dreams about the past? Just the green card. Then she'll walk out or she'll kill him with all her love. What could anyone say about it?

8.

After a month in New York doing rewrites for an article, I was back in Florida visiting again. On the first night the girl made us barbecued chicken and a delicious Israeli salad, a welcome departure from pizza, which almost always gives me heartburn. She laughed and served us red wine. She was definitely settling in, no longer a visitor. During the gap of time since my last visit, little secrets had taken hold like seedlings, modest changes in their home (a new red-and-white-checkered tablecloth with a Walmart tag still fixed to a corner), suggesting plans and movements that I didn't know about.

My God, didn't she ever notice that Jim was old? This question had begun to obsess me.

Jim was dressed in sporty Bermudas and a tight T-shirt to show off his strong tattooed arms, but he looked tired and gray. Too much Mara. Too much sex, and no more lounging on his outdoor patio selling optimism. He had taken on the pallor of their drab walls and filthy venetian blinds like a sea creature blending with the bottom. Also, the creases in my friend's face had deepened, and I flashed on my own dad's face during his last months, thinner than Jim's, but Dad's creases were so deep that they could have been knife wounds—they frightened me. Meanwhile, the girl had stopped wearing so much makeup, which made her look even younger, more adorable and fresh.

The following day I was driving from my motel back out to Jim's, musing about stories he'd been telling us, trying to connect the boy to the old man. As a kid Jim had called the shots in his house. There was no parent instilling the meaning of "no." When he was ten, Jim went to the best department store in Edmonton and bought a flashy expensive suit to imitate his dad. The family was still very poor, without a lot of basics, but Jim's mother didn't say a word. He told us that when he was twelve he fell in love with a friend of his mother's who had been renting a bedroom in their little house while her husband was away in the army. Jim thought about her incessantly and began bringing the woman wildflowers and then little presents from town. He couldn't get her out of his mind. Some days Sally would ask her son to take out the dirty clothes and wash them. Jim would hunt for the woman's underwear, put it to his face and inhale her. At the time Jim had still been sleeping on the floor with his two brothers. It was Sally who asked her friend if Jim could sleep on one side of her big bed—he was working so hard to support the family. The thirty-year-old had been amused and perhaps also intrigued to share her bed with the child master of their house. One night she allowed the boy to touch her ample body, more than allowed. Jim's mother had been complicit. She was so grateful to her hardworking son whom she depended on for everything. But if the thoughtful clever boy never learns the meaning of "no," what happens later on when doors begin to close in his face?

It occurred to me that Jim's sexual exploits with younger women, much younger as he's grown older, was perhaps born in the tabooed indulgence of the child with a shapely woman nearly three times his age, this sublime incongruity. Over the years, Jim's young lovers have given him confidence and vitality but most essentially the license to shed his skin and move on from static and occasionally dangerous circumstances—to stay alive as he saw it. Moving on for Jim, starting over, was staying alive.

I was thinking about Jim's younger women and had lost count of the lights and turns to his place. Fuck! I was completely lost. Again. It was humiliating. Each visit I have to call him on the cell and Jim gives me detailed directions: past the Catholic church, past a large empty lot, take a left, then the next right.

But it wasn't just my distracted driving. There was a desolate sameness to this neighborhood that played havoc with my sense of direction. The baking asphalt streets were interchangeable; each numbing house had exactly the same penumbra of sadness.

Eventually Jim hustled out onto Nowhere Street waving his arms so that I would stop circling. He was grinning as if I'd pulled into the number-one spot for happiness in the state of Florida. He never seemed to notice the rusty barbecues, jalopies, and broken bikes, the heat rising from driveways, or one of his neighbors carrying out the garbage with an alarming torpor.

For my dear friend, life's tawdry surface had been transformed by this young woman's allure and artful coaxing, by the public theater of their foreplay (her thick maroon lipstick and brazen invitations astonish me while they incite him), by the daily routine they had worked out: when the kids were at school she guided him to the bedroom for a quickie; and after their abundant evening meal with wine, when he was indolent with food and alcohol, his lips a little greasy from chicken thighs or liver, she led him into the bedroom. She was always moist and hungry for him. But if Jim happened to be reluctant, which was rare, she turned her back to him and lifted herself a little. She reached around and slowly opened herself with her fingers. The sight of her young wet pussy hit him with a reckless surge, her needy smell and little sounds. He stiffened and threw himself against her back and ass while she laughed and he reached for her little breasts. Baby, she said, pushing him inside, taking hold of his old hanging balls and caressing them like dice. Jim fucked for nearly an hour, thrusting into her with his still powerful thighs. My friend reported all of this while giggling and shaking his head to say, Can you believe this kid?

I'm getting younger, he said to me, sucking in his belly and looking at himself in the narrow mirror on his closet door.

But if Jim happened to wake in the middle of night wracked with dread (lost somewhere between lives; or, much worse, when he heard the call of his waiting wife, Phyllis)—and this had been happening two or three times a week—the girl put her hand on his shoulder. It's all right, baby, she murmured in her beguiling accent, pardoned his sins with a hand on his shoulder. He adored her voice and the smell of her after sex, her legs spread like a wild animal cooling down. Just a word or two and she flipped him from guilt back to rapture.

The August heat was blistering on the driveway outside their bungalow. Jim had walked inside ahead of me while I opened the trunk to get a six-pack. When I came through the front door I could hear them talking in the kitchen. I heard my name and something defiant from her. I couldn't make it out, but it made me sweat. There was rebuke lingering in the air and I felt betrayed.

After two or three minutes he came back into the front room. He looked distracted and I couldn't contain myself. Jim, aren't we buddies, man? I actually asked him this pitiful question. Then I remembered many years earlier I'd asked this very question to my dad when he was sick and I was afraid I would soon lose him.

Jim smiled at me. Sure we're buddies. You are my best friend, he said slowly and meaningfully. He took my hand.

At times I felt as though Jim were living anew and dying in the same moment. He would run off the names of his top salesmen to Mara and me, so we would know who he was or maybe just to jog his own memory—decades of salesmen strung out like a banner, men Jim had made wealthy. I wondered how many of them were now dead. Jim wouldn't know. He'd keep thinking they were all still making deals and living rich. Two or three times he told me about going to a fancy dealership in the late seventies with several of the guys to help pick out a Rolls-Royce for Todd Kelso, his top man. Just two years before, Todd had answered a newspaper ad, he was a young man sitting around without a clue, bowling on Friday nights, and Jim made him a millionaire. That's something.

I noticed the girl smirk. She all but blurted out, Baby, why do we need to hear so much about old salesmen? Mara was young and without much patience for nostalgia and intimations of demise. She wanted to move on with her life, with her suburban aspirations.

Jim smiled at her sadly. He was slumped back against the frayed pillows of the sofa. He was worn out, his ankles swollen from too much pizza and canned soup.

I also dreamed of aging salesmen, of my father and his buddies who sat ringside at the fights in Philadelphia showing off their tricked-out young women while Julio Mederos pounded the shit out of Harold Johnson, Jr. The portly balding men grinned whenever smatterings of gladiator blood or sweat fell onto their girls' white scarves or gloves or their enchanting faces. Some of my dad's friends bought country homes they couldn't afford and played at being barons in New Jersey for years, until that battering winter when favorite receptionists inexplicably turned them away and telephone calls weren't returned. None of the guys understood that the newest generation of handsome young selling lions had crowded them out; it was the way of life.

The girl decided that I was a saboteur, always dragging Jim

back to old times. She complained to him that I stepped all over their newly planted garden. It's true, I never accepted their shared illusion about his eternal youth. Their pretense seemed ugly and made me wonder if they were gaming each other. I was moved by my friend's old age, which was a real thing. But the girl was unsettling. She made me doubt myself. Maybe she was right—I was stepping on their garden.

Then after dinner, it was time for more stories. But first, Mara slid closer on the sofa, touched the creases on his face until he smiled, smoothed his shirt, made him a little more presentable for the narrative.

I don't know why their intimacies pulled the air out of the room, made it hard for me to breathe.

Jim was twelve years old when his father finally returned home. Nathan was nothing like the fantasy Jim had entertained of a hero dad arriving with riches and tales of success. There was no new Cadillac with a shiny bicycle in the trunk for Jim. His dad had come home poor as he'd left and was now suffering from tuberculosis and depression. Sally had taken him back with tenderness and concern— she always took him back regardless of his sins. Nathan was a broken man. Jim tried to buoy his wasting father with plans for hunting trips and far-fetched business ideas that would make the family rich. Now and then the boy was able to elicit a small smile. Jim still had his dreams.

Until the afternoon he came home from school and the pitiable house was filled with dread and clues that he did not understand or did not want to. There was cold soup sitting on the stove, as if Nathan had put it there and then changed his mind. He hadn't turned on the range. Jim would have heated it for himself, but he decided to make his dad come and eat with him. Nathan had to eat to build back his strength. Jim sometimes felt impatient with Nathan.

Jim went out back to the workshop. More and more he had to tell his dad what not to do, when to do what, as if Jim were the father. But really, Jim felt flattered his dad listened to his suggestions.

Dad, Jim called. He had ideas for their afternoon projects. The workshop door was closed. Jim turned the handle and pushed against the door. It didn't give. He pushed harder, managed to open it a few inches and smelled something sweet and familiar. Dad, will you listen to me. Jim pushed a little harder, and now he could see the dark pool on the concrete floor, some of it reaching the wall where it had thickened. He began to gag. Jim was afraid to push any more. His eyes went to the workbench, and he saw the stock of his .22 clamped into the old vise. It was a hot afternoon, and Jim swatted at flies that were buzzing around his face.

Then a high-pitched wailing was pouring out of him. The voice scared him, but it was hard to stop.

Jim had first told me about this many years earlier. Now I wanted to ask how the suicide affected him after waiting years for his dad's return and the great life to begin? Did it change him? It must have.

Jim didn't want to say much more about the suicide in front of Mara, as if he feared she would make some historical surmise and walk. But Ava? Jim was eager to tell us about Ava and Marvin Gesler. On reflection, it was Marvin Gesler who provided answers to the questions I'd pondered.

PART II

9.

Ava's walk was languorous and promising and she had a little smile that cut through Jim's purpose, whatever he happened to be selling—that's how he liked to remember her.

He met Ava on a warm spring morning with birds singing and a clatter of children and fresh chances all around her sunny neighborhood. They were standing on her small front porch. Jim, thirty, was selling waterless cookware. He was the picture of success in a three-button khaki suit with wide lapels, holding a suede Stetson.

I want to talk to you about this product I represent, he said. It could change your life. She looked him over, confident and unhurried. She had a wondering smile, auburn hair with a slight curl, a hint of a Southern accent. She was wearing hoop earrings and a low-cut blouse showing off her full breasts. Jim shivered. She was the most beautiful woman he had ever seen.

Are you from around here? he asked. Where'd you get that Southern accent? She widened her big brown eyes as he fed her his opening lines. I'll bet you have a boyfriend. A fiancé? I'll bet within a year or so you'll begin a family, a fine-looking family. How many children would you like? You'd want them to be healthy?

Anyone would. She was amused listening to his pitch tumbling out from too many angles and way too fast.

This is a terrific neighborhood for children, Jim continued, looking around from the porch, which cued her to do the same; and she noticed behind him, parked beside the curb, a brand-new Cadillac convertible with the top down, a red leather interior and yards of glistening chrome. It looked fast and rich. That car said it for Jim, where he'd come from and the way he was headed.

She said she didn't need cookware and he challenged her. Everyone needs it. Don't you want the best for yourself and the ones you love? This will be the greatest gift you could ever give to your family. Let me describe to you the benefits of cooking without water. What's the harm on such a great day? He invoked the beautiful sunny morning with his hands. Sizing people up was Jim's life. Was this one smart or just a gorgeous dumb brunette? He was spurred by her looks, no question, but also there was some reserve of savvy or maybe regret. What was her story? He'd have to know to sell her. Jim could find out things. People opened up to him. Let me describe to you the power of nutrients. Do you know what nutrients are and what they can do for our bodies? He felt her pulling away. What do you really like, Ava? What excites you? Jim's waterless cookware wasn't it. Wait. She shook her head and walked inside, closed the screen door softly behind her. For a moment or two he could see her as a hazy image receding behind the screen. He tapped the door frame twice. Too bad.

Jim sometimes went for two or three days without a rejection. He held a record with the company—seventeen closes in a row, stone-cold sales without leads, just knocking on front doors with his pitch and then worming his way into a heart or a heartbreak. He had grown into a handsome six footer with an enthusiastic, caring manner, almost the same good boy who trudged up hills delivering newspapers in the snow. But by now, selling had become a singular passion in Jim's life and he couldn't turn it off, though the products kept changing. At the moment it was waterless cookware and he sold it to friends at parties or on hunting trips or fishing on a pitching boat for cod off the coast. Selling was his music. Going door-to-door was his forte—anyone could sell with leads. But knocking on doors, fielding the boredom or scorn of strangers, that was something. He knew when to cajole or act coy or push, how hard to push or when to use the Cadillac or a little silver spoon he sometimes gave away. Jim's props and scripts were often hokey. It didn't matter. People were moved to buy from him. Jim was tempting and delicious and a little dangerous. But most important—and this was Jim's rare gift as a salesman—he could be the rare friend who challenged and stirred you deeply; it was clear from that first conversation that he really cared about you. Customers wanted to buy from Jim because it forged a bond. He instilled this need. You wanted to know Jim beyond this day, this transaction, and shaking on the deal sealed this possibility.

When he visited her again four days later, Ava yawned at his selling and proposed a walk into the spring evening of deep shadows and lush smells to pique a young man's desire. They held hands and traded pieces of their lives. She told him about her husband, also a "Jim," a second-string quarterback for the Winnipeg Blue Bombers, who rarely got into games. They were no longer together.

Ava said, Wow, for no apparent reason and Jim loved that and wanted her to say it again. Such a beautiful woman changes the essence of language and meaning. How could you ever judge if Ava was thoughtful or deep? Deep was the utter delight of her voice and the turn of her neck, the way she clicked along in French heels. Maybe you'll get back with him, Jim offered. "Maybe" hung in the evening light, became a lump in his throat. He yearned to touch her, to pull her close and smell her hair. When Jim looked at Ava all the sense went out of him and he had to turn away. They stopped at a store and bought a large bottle of red wine.

You're a married man, aren't you? Ava guessed correctly, with the suggestion that he was being a bad boy. Tell me about your wife.

Jim hemmed and hawed. He couldn't recall why he'd married her. It was embarrassing, like forgetting the name of someone standing in front of you. He pictured his wife in bed wearing rollers or standing in the kitchen in her drab bathrobe talking on the phone with a friend. Jim made a little distasteful expression as though he were ashamed of himself. Why had he married her? Because at twenty-three Jim had been rushing ahead, focused mainly on the road. That was all. Between his selling trips all over the western part of the country, they had made a daughter. For the first two years of the marriage, he returned home every two or three weeks. Now he hadn't been back for nearly six months, although he sent her a check each month. For long stretches Jim forgot that he had a family, and then one night in a cheap motel he would remember his abandoned little girl with a helpless shrug.

Jim talked about his life on the road with Marvin Gesler. He'd met Marvin a year earlier when both men were hustling picture-book Bibles. Ava smiled at their preposterous work. How could you ever make money selling Bibles?

Jim nodded. You wouldn't think so. But he had been making better than six hundred a week selling Bibles door-to-door, a fortune back then for a young man. Bigger deals, bigger opportunities, were just down the winding road: a new product line, a hotter blaze of hope.

Whenever he told us about the early years of selling I became giddy with adolescent emotion. I could summon the smell of my father while I sat on his bed and he smoked a cigarette and told me about his newest big deal. I could see the lot of them, Jim, my dad and his buddies, my uncles who were also salesmen, careening their big shiny sedans along the road to glory, all of them meeting up in Vegas to watch Sammy Davis Jr. bring down the house. Over Jim's desk, rescued from the last condo and now jammed in beside his bed in the bungalow, he still prized the photograph of Sammy Davis giving him a hug at the Sands. They were buddies. My dad had also had a close friendship with Sammy Davis Jr.

It was Marvin Gesler who came up with the idea of forging a partnership with Jim and training their own salesmen. They boarded them in motels, three to a sweaty room, coaching coarse men to read the body language of housewives and deliver their scripts, Marvin and Jim refining scripts by night and sending men out each morning with Wonder Bread Spam sandwiches and Bibles, and taking a share of their commissions.

As he told Ava about Marvin she tossed back her head and laughed. Marvin is a decent salesman, and smart, but he's physically gross, said Jim. That's what holds him back. Ava was alarmingly beautiful. Every man turned to look at her and they kept staring as she moved along, slow and hippy like the other Ava— she was that arresting.

Marvin is a Jewish guy about seventy pounds overweight, Jim told her, prematurely balding, and he wears a wig that doesn't fit right. He's often adjusting it, but sometimes he forgets and it falls onto his face. Marvin doesn't have manners or even a sense for what manners are. He finishes his meal in a gulp like a human suction and then he's ready to leave before you've started. She threw her head back and laughed, prodded Jim ahead. And he has this gross habit.

Tell me. Tell me.

He hacks up spit into his mouth, takes it on his fingers like this—Jim acted it out—looks at it, and then slides it back in his mouth.

Ewwee.

And sometimes Marvin, he doesn't realize; it's terrible even for Marvin.

Go ahead, she ordered sternly.

Sometimes he reaches into his pants like this and feels himself.

You're kidding.

And he smells his hand. He does it anywhere. In a restaurant, during a sales meeting. He likes the smell. Then he forgets where he's been, he'll throw his hand out, you know, he wants to shake hands, and you've been watching him hold himself. And you're standing there not wanting to touch his hand, which makes him confused. He doesn't understand because he wants to shake hands.

Ava was shaking her head, taking Marvin in.

But Marvin knows a lot, said Jim. He knows finance, politics, sports, you name it. He's a whiz with numbers. He can do any calculation in his head. He knows more about things than most people. And not just to know facts like a teacher. He has ideas you can't imagine, unusual ideas that make money, a lot of money. Marvin's a genius. Jim was getting excited talking about Marvin. Even in the moment, walking with this stunning woman, Jim felt the need for Marvin like an essential nutrient of his life.

He couldn't give all of Marvin to Ava—he couldn't and still be the guy for her tonight. At least that's what he thought. Marvin was an easy mark for Jim's ridicule, but when they were together talking in a restaurant or late at night in their motel the two men seemed to merge into a singular being. They radiated a kind of wall or sanctity and the other salesmen knew to steer clear, as if they'd be singed. In their sessions, Marvin did most of the talking. It was disturbing to look at them because Marvin's arms would swing around or he'd spew cheap Danish onto his shiny pants—he had no sense of style—and Jim, a really great-looking young man, fun loving, athletic body, a classy dresser, he sat there nodding with their heads only a foot or two apart, as if he were being defiled or his physical beauty were being absorbed.

Ideas just tumbled out of Marvin Gesler. He was a machine. He would become emotional and sweaty describing scams to Jim. Marvin had many more ideas than he could ever implement and this tortured him. He tapped his foot impatiently. Sometimes he made pleading expressions or he'd look petulant, like a spoiled child. His neediness was appalling.

Jim came to understand that Marvin couldn't pause long enough to get anything accomplished. He was prey to his own impatience and churning mind. Marvin revolted people, simple as that. Despite his scripts, it was a miracle he ever sold anything. But Jim also recognized that the two men were necessary for each other. Marvin gave Jim the opportunity to sell on a scale he could barely have imagined. Okay. Marvin would be the beast in the basement, planning, devising. It was Jim who catalyzed this torrent of ideas, but also he could slow Marvin down a little, guide him around, place him in front of a problem. Jim could make it happen in the world with his charm and way with people. Jim could sell anything. Marvin needed Jim. Marvin would listen to Jim. They'd make a lot of money. That was the important thing. They sat up all night and talked. Marvin told Jim what they would do with their millions. How millions would make more millions. Marvin talked about offshore bank accounts. What the hell was that? Where we'll bury the money. Soon enough they'd never have to work a day. Cookware had a bigger upside than Bibles, so that's the direction they went. Marvin wanted to get off cookware the second day, but Jim quieted him, got Marvin to focus on the scripts that were simple but brilliant. All the men were making sales. Soon enough there would be time for the next idea.

Marvin knows he's smarter than other people, Jim said to Ava, struggling to push his partner aside and retrieve the moment with this gorgeous lady. Marvin expects doors to open for him, but it doesn't work that way. People have to like you and trust you. They have to believe that you are acting in their interest, and that you are a good person. Marvin tramples on people's feelings. He doesn't care. It's his nature. He's disgusting and people want to step on him like a bug. Anything to make him go away, disappear.

She was interested in all this. The key to Ava was telling everything or nearly everything. No pretty stories. No sugarcoating. Put it out there. Let her pick through the garbage. That's her story. Ava was lurking behind that discreet southern belle accent and her high-class clothing and manicured nails. She liked high times and speed, ugliness, big gambles, putting it on the line and winning big or losing everything. That is how Jim read her. But Ava liked it darker than Jim could understand.

There was a small formal park in the center of town, a lovely white church across the street and a statue of some military figure in the middle of the park that was bordered by a sleepy sidewalk on all sides. Jim and Ava sat on a bench beneath the statue. It was dusk and the smell of cut grass was intoxicating. They were drinking wine. Ava drank with a real hunger. He liked that. They giggled about the Bibles and Marvin and soon enough Jim was feeling good. What a woman, so beautiful and willing to come here and drink with him like this. He wanted to squeeze her and she didn't mind. They began to kiss. Jim was dizzy with Ava and the redolent spring night. She smelled so good. She tasted of pastry and wine. He began to laugh when she kissed his ear and then Ava began to touch him. She was hungry and funny. She unzipped his fly and made him hard. He laughed and pushed her hand away. She teased him. I'm sorry, I thought you wanted me to.

I do, but look where we are. They were right out in the open. People were passing. Shouldn't we go back to your place? There were couples walking around the park, a lady in a wheelchair pushed by a young man, her son probably. This was a real church town, conservative, pious, and neat as a pin. Ava guided his hand beneath her plaid skirt. He laughed and so did she. She had a real proper voice, like a schoolteacher. She was wet and tight, slick, with a hard belly, astonishing body, lean but achy soft in all the places. He was sick with wanting to fuck her. She climbed into his lap and turned to kiss him deeply, urgently. They kissed for a while, and soon he couldn't help himself, had it out of his pants, and she raised herself and let him, right on the bench. Ava held him in place and moved slow. If you glanced over from the sidewalk, there was a girl on her boyfriend's lap beneath the statue. It was a handsome Norman Rockwell moment. Barely moving, but she was squeezing Jim inside and letting go and sometimes laughing in her discreet way.

10.

Three years later. Jim and Ava were on a raised stage beneath a colorful billowing tent on the outskirts of Montreal. There was a crowd of about three hundred, mostly men. It could have been a revivalist meeting or the start of a sideshow in a rural circus. Jim was holding a microphone, smiling, while rock and roll blared from big speakers. A storm was gathering outside and gusts of wind whipped the canvas. There was excitement you could taste, hunger. Ava was shimmying to the rock and roll that was raunchy and wild. Jim began describing the opportunity at hand. But it was hard to make out his words, such was the enthusiasm and welling of expectations. Ava stoked them, clapping to the beat, teased the guys to drown out Jim's words and make him suffer. Jim shrugged. I give up—the noise, the wind, and Ava were too much for him.

All of this was written into Marvin's script. She wore red heels, a dark skirt, and a low-cut blouse. She did a vampy version of the twist that sizzled. This new kind of dancing was like sex. Do you want to get rich? announced Jim above the singing of Chuck Berry. Do you want to have fun? Ava was clapping and shaking her head, no, no, no, deep into something while Jim, practically shouting, explained the deal in shorthand. Spend fifty dollars tonight on an electric iron and make twelve hundred sixty dollars during the next month or six weeks. When will you ever have such a chance to buy something useful and make money at the same time? Enough cash to buy a car or to put an extension on your house, to take the vacation trip you and the wife have dreamed about for the last twenty years. Where could you ever find such an opportunity? Buy tonight, get started, and bring friends to our next meeting in two weeks.

The script was about opportunity, taking hold of a dream, like Ava, who was rocking to her own music, bemused by something. Marvin gawked at Ava, with her perfect angel face and devil body, spittle gathering at the corner of his mouth. He watched her from his canvas office at the back of the tent where he counted the money. Most days in the week Jim, Ava, and Marvin were rubbing elbows, planning for the next big meeting, going over the script. With a glance Ava made Marvin weak and fevered. More than once his arms had jerked out toward her. She smirked and stepped aside.

If you don't buy right now, you could lose the chance, said Jim, selling with fervor. The moment is here and then it's gone. Our days are numbered. Our days are haunted by losses and missed opportunity.

Loss, loss, Marvin had hammered this reminder to Jim during their coaching sessions. Fear of loss closes the sale.

How many of you can tell a story about a house you might have bought and now it's worth five times as much? Jim asked the quickened audience of mostly workingmen, farmers, construction workers, a sprinkling of wives. It was a warm summer evening and the men were sweating.

You should have bought the neighbor's farm and today you

would be a wealthy man, Jim continued. And now you're old. Makes you sick, right? We get old so fast. Makes me sick, the chances I had. My daddy had chances, but he died a poor man. Poor and bitter. Spent too much time dreaming about gold. It didn't need to be that way. Believe me, it's only a question of deciding and making a move. Don't sit on your hands. You're not too old. Not yet. But it's coming, sure as I'm standing here; opportunity passes. Jim was saying what he knew to be true, what he learned growing up. Of course he understood that their Ponzi scheme was against the law, but he also believed that the business was more than a fair deal for his customers. What was the harm if he was giving back nearly as much money as he was keeping? Everyone was a winner in their money tent.

Years before Mara, when Jim had first described this scam to me, he showed me an old photograph of himself standing on a crude stage pointing at the crowd with one hand while holding a microphone in the other. He was dressed in a tuxedo, white shirt, and bow tie. His blond hair was long and wavy, and he had a fervent expression staring into the middle distance. What a great-looking guy he was at thirty. There really was a passing resemblance to Burt Lancaster's Elmer Gantry.

Marvin Gesler's conception was simple but astonishing. He first came to it three years earlier when he had gone to the supermarket to buy white bread and Spam to make sandwiches for his crew of Bible salesmen. He'd spend ten or fifteen dollars on groceries and the girl passed him coupons to paste in a little book. So many coupons could be redeemed for more groceries. That was the idea, basically, to buy what you want, what you need, and collect a bonus. The best ideas were simple.

But here was Marvin's wrinkle. What if the bonus was huge and demonstrable, not a few groceries but something to change your life, or get it rolling? Put up fifty dollars at a meeting to get a quality product, maybe an electric iron, and a few minutes later collect ten dollars, five apiece, from two others who put up their fifty bucks. Ten dollars doesn't sound like a life change, but a half hour later you'd collect five apiece from four others who put up their fifty dollars for irons. Before the end of the night, you were back up on a stage again getting forty dollars for your fifty-dollar payout. And the tent was filled with other guys tramping up to get money. You'd surely drive home eager to tell friends about this opportunity to buy something useful for your home while earning money from this business or whatever it was. The following week—or if the meeting was large enough all this could happen during the first night—you'd get eighty dollars, because sixteen others had bought irons. You've actually made a nice profit for your purchase. Now you are at the apex of a small pyramid of customers, people yearning to have more. Each week you are boosted higher on the pyramid, more people supporting your future, your prosperity. And the beauty of it is that people below you, creating this cash flow siphoning upward, are at the same time atop their own little pyramids with the hope, no, the probability of enriching themselves from others who come on below them. All that each of them has to do is buy an electric iron for fifty bucks to keep the money coming. Ava and Jim would make sure that this happened.

All your friends would surely come to buy; they'd make money and you'd make money until you got to the ultimate, the $1,260 payout, and then you'd have to put up another fifty dollars and get another iron and start all over again. And you would, right? Why stop now? Who wouldn't be game for these meetings with rock and roll and this beautiful woman, very sexy though a little preoccupied, passing out money, tens of thousands? She's just giving it away. Who wouldn't want to come to such a meeting?

This was Marvin's idea. Basically, he was selling an illusion.

Who's counting how much we're giving away? How much we're keeping? he asked Jim and Ava. They're gonna want the money in their hands, he said, licking his lips and glancing at Ava.

The music rose for a time, drowning out Jim's entreaties, and Ava clapped to the beat, shook her chest boldly. For the moment she had stolen the scene while the music swelled the tent with hope and anticipation. Then it was his turn, talking about hardship, growing up dirt poor, not bathing, not eating, freezing in the winter because Daddy made bad choices or no choices at all. Daddy was paralyzed and dreaming about the future, and Ava moved toward the money tree, all eyes on her slow walk; they switched back and forth, sex and privation.

Don't give it away too soon, Marvin coached. Frustrate them. Pull away the bait.

Jim and Ava were so smooth. They had been doing this routine for two years. The operation was getting a reputation around Montreal. It had started out with just a handful of reluctant people meeting in a small basement room, with no music, no real pulse. Back then Marvin hadn't worked out the intricacies, but he knew that he could make out selling electric irons for fifty bucks and giving away money—he smelled profit. Now he had complicated charts. He knew that he must cut the play off after twelve levels. He calculated that they would keep 56 percent of the dollars that came through the door. Now there were big crowds showing up for their tent giveaways. People were driving a hundred miles for irons and money. The three of them gave away more and more money each time and drove off in one of Jim's cars—he now owned three Cadillacs!—a suitcase of dollars in the trunk, sometimes a hundred thousand or more.

Onstage, Ava moved slowly to a large tree, a Christmas tree with money clipped onto its branches. She enjoyed being watched.

She liked to make men squirm. It made her feel alive. She'd even flirt a little with Marvin, although she'd quickly turn away, he was such a pig. There was fifty thousand in cash clipped onto the fifteen-foot tree, five-dollar bills, fifties and hundreds. There were poor people in the audience and the money tree worked like chum scenting the water. Poor people wanted that money for food and fun they couldn't afford; the dangling money made them feel unsettled. Marvin's scene might have been obvious and a little shabby, but Ava had a shine that spilled all over the room. She moved within a circle of light. The music poured over Ava's lush, swaying body as if she'd parted ways from her fundamental and fetching shyness. It must have been the sultry night air and money that made her wild and hot. Ava gave them license. Everyone wanted the money tree and this girl—even ladies could feel her pull; she incited an urge. MONEY. Jim's voice, The more we sell, the quicker you get to your goal, the $1,260 payout. Quick. There were two men laboring in the aisles with heavy carts filled with irons.

The music fell away and the spotlight found Jim in his tailored tuxedo. He seemed to be searching for the words. Ava stood to the side, the air gone out of her like a puppet on the shelf. They were a great team. Jim relished this long hesitation—what would happen— this building unease, and Marvin was nodding from behind the flap of canvas. Jim seemed to be listening for an inner voice.

Finally he said, I want you to meet someone. Jim paused and gained traction. I want you to meet someone. Chester, Chester . . . Chester!!! Where are you, man? Jim walked back and forth on the stage searching in vain for a man in the audience. Chester . . . Chester? Jim squinted a little and then he signaled with his hand. Come on up here, Chester. Chester was a butcher, a short powerfully built guy with coarse black hair on his thick forearms. Jim signaled for him to come up onstage. He had never been onstage before. Months earlier, he bought an iron, and this was his moment, what he'd been promised. And more. Chester, this is your life, said Jim, invoking the name and spirit of the TV program watched by millions. It was the moment a butcher became a star. This unfurling of fame was an essential part of Marvin's scheme. Every two weeks they made a little man a celebrity to be adulated for a time among his friends, at the bar, in his community. How much is fame worth? It was an ancient question with a new wrinkle. How much is it worth in terms of hawking electric irons? Chester had been a faithful customer. He had come to a dozen meetings, collected his payments, he brought friends and family to buy irons, and tonight was his night.

Ava was clapping for Chester to come onstage. But he was beet red and remained glued to his folding seat. How could he come to this woman? Her walk was an event, teetering on the stairs in her heels; guys reached out to help, but really they wanted to touch her butt or feel her bare arm. She slithered down the aisle and right up to him, put out a hand, her charming Southern accent: I've come to take you up there, Chester. Her hand touched the hair on his forearm. Up there, into the circle of light onstage. He was a short guy, five feet, three inches, and he'd never been near a woman like Ava. He closed his eyes and breathed her in, slow and delicious. He wasn't thinking about the money tree or what he might do with the $1,260. Chester was staring at Ava's chest heaving from her brave exertions. He wanted to plunge into Ava's creamy bosom, to swim all over her with his hairy body. Jim made a joke about where Chester was staring, but Chester didn't notice. Ava was the greatest thing he'd ever seen.

Look up, Chester, Jim said. Look up, man! Everyone roared with laughter, which roused him. Chester shot both hands up in the air and shouted, I like this! I like this!

Then, while she led him up the stairs, Jim reflected a little on Chester's hardworking life. He's the salt of the earth, Jim said with real emotion as Ava counted money out from the tree and put it into Chester's hand. But Chester didn't notice. He had fallen in love. He didn't want to leave her. Chester's nose was practically nestled into the deep cleft of her chest. Jim played on this until finally Ava led him back to his seat, leaned over, offering one last glimpse, and then she kissed his flushed cheek.

Now Jim and Ava were into the heavy work of the night, giving away cash. The air in the tent had grown thick and rancid from sweating men. But no one cared. Jim and Ava called men onstage, one after another, handing out fives and tens—they began by paying off new customers, but soon enough there were repeat winners, more and more of them. They came strutting off the stage grinning, waving dollars, as though they were moving ahead in life, as Jim had promised, while workers in the aisles passed out irons and stuffed dollars into shoe boxes.

Selling irons was sweaty pedestrian work. Jim took his pleasure from the earlier part of the evening and tried to play it over in his mind. He loved ambling into his stories and becoming caught up in poignant hard times. He took his customers years away from irons and cash giveaways, nearly freezing to death in the little house outside Edmonton until he had saved his starving family when opportunity presented itself. Jim touched his customers with his heroism and fineness. In his business life he might take shortcuts and deviations as long as he knew who he was; he needed to revisit this core of himself. He described waking up before dawn while his mom and brothers slept deeply; delivering newspapers in the snow. While other boys played after school, Jim took care of the farmer's cows.

Selling without strain or apparent intention was the highest art. And Jim was laying the groundwork for a stampede, until there was a moment, he would let out a wistful breath or raise a finger or look at Ava, some small gesture, often tinged with reluctance or regret (it was so sweet), and men would bolt from their grimy folding seats waving cash, fighting to spend fifty bucks on ten-dollar irons as if they were priceless—electric irons that offered an escape from lives fated to boredom, mediocrity, and slippage—and the supply was greatly limited; buy now, buy right now, before we fade into the ether. Look at her. He gestured to Ava, who was so depleted from her long efforts, but still lovely and offering. Buy them for her. He used her like bait. Ava was struggling mightily to make her mark, wanting to be something more than a sexy prop, and she trusted him. Everyone trusted Jim; again and again in these meetings Jim released a torrent with a word or glance. . . . Marvin had clever ideas, sure, but he couldn't dance. It was Jim who made Marvin plausible, as if a cartoon had suddenly gained flesh and force. Jim knew that Marvin must be coddled and cherished and that he could make Jim rich, hugely rich.

When they were all together, Ava did not exist for Jim, which was necessary but devastating to her. Over time she learned to stay out of their invisible cage where Marvin might touch her leg or ask for massages like a goon. He was impervious to her disdain. And when Jim didn't seem to notice Marvin's crudeness, she felt pitiable. Jim was entirely there for Marvin, listening keenly and picking through Marvin's manic opulence, although at other moments Jim would kick back and just smile at the marvel of his partner. Jim sometimes felt bad for Ava—that she had to endure this threesome—but Marvin was necessary and Jim would make it up to her. He loved Ava, and that gave him license to proceed.

In the dank canvas office with rain coming in at his feet, Marvin Gesler was counting the evening's take while Jim and Ava shook hands with a few lingering customers in front of the stage. The rain fell steadily against the tent, making a pleasant isolating sound, as if he were alone in a lair. They had brought in nearly one hundred thousand dollars—a good night, with some customers buying as many as ten irons. Multiple sales were happening more often at meetings. This had Marvin thinking. An iron was like a coupon. This business could operate on a much larger scale. Marvin was considering the efficacy of stores and warehouses. He wanted to tell Jim about his thinking. He wanted to design huge stores that had a racy, modern feel. They would make millions. He was impatient to tell Jim.

11.

Ava found the three-hundred-acre farm outside of Toronto and Jim paid cash for it, a little more than two hundred thousand dollars, most of what he'd stashed away working with Marvin for two years on their pyramid deal. Who knows how much Marvin had buried, but surely a great deal more than Jim. There was often tens of thousands lying in shoe boxes and suitcases in their motel rooms, and Jim made a show of not keeping track as if to say he was something more than Marvin. Perhaps Jim acted this way because of Ava.

She had been begging Jim to take time away from Marvin. She felt dirty from his incessant money talk and grossness. At first their work had seemed funny and rebellious. Now Ava wanted something else, although when Jim pressed her for specifics she couldn't find the words. Finally he packed Marvin up and sent him off on a bus to Virginia, where he had a cousin. Marvin was baffled by Jim's vacation idea. He climbed onto the bus muttering. Jim was amused, but at the same time he felt like he was turning his back on himself. He shipped his partner off for Ava. He worried that he was losing her.

The house was situated on an acre of green lawn and gardens that flattened out from a sloping mountain like a verdant mesa. Looking from the shaded front porch, you saw an expanse of valley, much of it their property, sections of burly green forest, some acres of planted corn, and down below a vast meadow of green grazing land dotted with a few cows.

Jim was immediately drawn in by this place that evoked early memories. He told Ava how great their lives would be here, and she listened earnestly, believed everything he said. She'd learn to cook gourmet meals for him. They'd make babies. They jumped in one of the Cadillacs and drove to a little drive-through hamburger joint, sat in the car eating and kissing. He loved to kiss her mouth full of munching food and she laughed at his ardor and mussed his hair.

Ava's first meal for Jim was an ambitious Sunday morning breakfast. The table was perfectly adorned with new place settings, polished silver, breakfast pastry in a basket, and flowers from the garden. Ava looked fresh and lovely with hardly any makeup. Jim smiled at his great fortune and went back to the paper. He sat at the table reading the sports section and glancing out the window, where he could see the old barn. He was ready to jump into the day's projects.

Ava couldn't quite get the flame of the gas stove where she wanted it and she fussed with the knob. The eggs were cooking too fast, but instead of taking the heavy skillet off the fire she kept adjusting the flame. She wanted this meal to be perfect. Ava took a deep breath to quiet her nerves.

For the past two years living with Jim and Marvin in motels and occasionally a rented room, there was never a kitchen. Meals were mainly sandwiches or something fast in a diner. She had cooked for her first husband, the football player, trying to please him, although he would often ridicule her meals and haphazard cleaning. Then he would put on a false smile and show her off to his football buddies or to his dad, who couldn't take his eyes off her breasts. Ava had sustained herself with a belief that she was drawn to mystical or artistic endeavors, acting or painting, even though in reality she didn't know anything about these things.

Now the heavy pan was smoking with hot grease, and even with the flame turned down, the eggs were burning at the edges and when she flipped them one of the yolks ran. Terrible.

Her husband had wanted the whole package, Hollywood starlet looks to go along with a homemaker's perfect touch, like Ava's mother, Beth, who kept an impeccable house. While Ava was growing up and competing in beauty pageants, her mom had won prizes for her pies and cakes in country fairs all over Tennessee, although mother and daughter rarely competed at the same fairs, because Ava's dad liked to prime and primp his little champion without the distraction of Beth's hobby. And Ava loved going off alone with her daddy. Beth went along with the arrangement.

Ava was a natural and she quickly developed a reputation throughout the state for her willowy good looks and perky manner. She knew just how to intrigue and charm the judges, particularly the men, with a broad grin or a shy giggle. She and Daddy came home all heady with victory, and the rooms were filled with the smells of roasts and glazes and baking bread and cakes. For nearly eight years they traveled on weekends to beauty pageants. The pageants were the central event in their family life. When Ava took the prize, the goodness of life seemed rolled into Mom's popovers, hams, and puddings and Daddy loved her so much. It was pure bliss when he brandished the check for a couple of hundred dollars, called it their fun money.

Of course, it occasionally happened that the first-place trophy and check went to another little beauty. At the judge's announcement Daddy turned red in the face. He became sullen and remote; he couldn't look at Ava during the interminable car ride home. He would say, acidly, her hair had been mussed or her shoes were scuffed or she needed to lose weight, and she nodded. Yes, yes, you're right, Daddy, yes. She had ruined their good times. It was worse if he didn't say a word and she imagined how hugely he hated her. He couldn't eat dinner, and Mom never said a word during those awful nights. Ava had let them all down.

Ava felt an urge to throw the eggs in the trash. She'd forgotten how her mind became trapped in a loop. The urge was unbearable, but she hesitated, worried Jim would notice. He didn't know about this side of her. The eggs were more than cooked, but she hadn't put the toast on. The bacon was getting cold on a plate. She couldn't serve Jim these burnt eggs. She needed to start again and get it right.

Ava tossed the four cooked eggs into the trash and nodded to herself. It was the only thing that helped. There was real pleasure in throwing them away and beginning again. It was a chance. She gathered the bacon strips into a paper towel and threw it away. She took a deep breath and began cracking open eggs. She wasn't very handy and bits of shell fell into the pan. She tried to take the shells out with her fingernail and then impatiently shook the eggs into the trash. That felt good. Jim didn't notice. And she didn't have to muster any stupid excuse.

By the time she was sixteen the family had moved from Tennessee to a small town in western Canada where her grandparents lived. Ava was in a new school. She was smart, a good student. But it was her looks that people responded to, a perfect angelic face, a cute ponytail that played against a ripening body that sent signals she didn't understand. By then, Ava and her dad were no longer going to competitions. For a time she brought purpose and prestige into his life. The trophies, cash prizes, and articles in the local paper had been his clever work, as though the little girl were a part of himself—the winning was his art.

Eventually she had grown sick of being adorable and that spelled the end of her winning. In their Canada life her father was unshaven and badly dressed, shrunken to a middle-aged car mechanic who went drinking with his buddies on weekends. He barely noticed her, or his wife for that matter. When Ava had been winning, their home had been cheerful and optimistic. Now she blamed herself for the family's decline. There was no one to share this with and Ava felt hemmed in and moody. Still, her mom cooked savory roasts and biscuits and cleaned with a dumbfounding smile. Ava was bursting at the seams.

On a fall afternoon she traveled to an away football game. After most of the kids she knew had left for home she talked to a shy boy she'd never seen before. She never asked his name. The boy was confused and she said it was okay and held his hand. She led him beneath the bleachers and began kissing his face and mouth and then she unzipped his pants and began to touch him. He quickly came in her hand.

Ava did other things. She began stealing from department stores. She put things under her coat and walked out. It was like filling up. She was never caught. These adventures appeased some craving she didn't understand. She could go on being the prom queen for a time, chaste and waving from the float.

One evening Ava drove the family car to a small, uneventful town about twenty miles away. She looked older than seventeen, particularly when she let her hair down, wore red lipstick, and dressed in heels and a tight-fitting blouse and skirt. She had been practicing her slow walk. She parked the car and walked into a bar. There were about eight or nine guys drinking and they all looked her over. She ordered a beer and soon a man wearing a felt hat came over and they began to talk. He was a grain salesman, a smooth talker. He described the business and Ava smiled at him and said she was a secretary. They finished their beer and she followed him to the back of the bar where there was a dim hallway. She'd thought this through, more or less, but hadn't anticipated the leaping of her heart. She didn't even know the guy's name. They began to kiss in the amber light. He was real hungry and she followed his lead. He pushed up against her and she touched him with her raised thigh. It thrilled her to feel his hardness. He reached inside her blouse and then he crudely pulled up her bra and began to suck on her breasts and squeeze them. His loving was desperate, as if a good deal would get away. Ava moaned the way she thought she should, although she imagined herself being milked and had to force down a giggle. She helped him slip his overcoat onto the back of a chair and that's when she felt a bulge in his pocket. Her mind was racing. She groaned and licked his ear. Ava rubbed her thigh against him and then pulled the guy's zipper open. She discovered his balls, handled them. The salesman pulled up her skirt and reached for her crotch. Not yet, she whispered hoarsely. Ava rubbed his wet cock with her palm, rubbed harder. She realized now that it was her show. She covered his face with urgent kisses, and while he was feverish and groping her breasts she slipped the wallet out of his coat pocket and tucked it into her purse. She hadn't thought about this part. She just did it.

While the salesman considered his lucky day and cleaned himself with his handkerchief she was back inside the bar and out the front door. The episode thrilled her, and she thought about it a lot. It kept her anger down. She was able to sit at the dinner table with her father without feeling riled and jilted. She had this reservoir to draw from.

Throwing the eggs in the trash was the good part. Ava felt free of the tension. Maybe she'd get it right this time. But soon she was muttering about the new batch of eggs that she'd flipped over without incident. They looked fine, but she still felt the urge to throw them away and begin again. She craved it. She wished Jim were sitting in another room so she could toss them. Each time would seem like a chance to get it right. Maybe it would be the last time. But that didn't matter so much. The urge mattered. Eggs were piling up in the trash. Her first husband had come into the kitchen and laughed at her. You're a crazy woman; look at you throwing away food. He'd smacked her. This made her feel like throwing away the food. It was all she could think about. She was trapped. She would have thrown the eggs away a third time except that Jim might decide she was crazy. But she could not serve him eggs that were less than perfect. She blurted out finally, I'm going to start again—which felt like throwing them away. She smiled a little.

He looked up from his paper. What? Come on, I'm hungry. Let's eat those eggs.

They are not right, she said obliquely. I wanted them to be perfect for you. A few minutes before, everything in her life had seemed to hinge on her ability to cook him a great breakfast. Now she just wanted to throw it all away. She slipped them into the trash and smiled sickly. She wanted him to know.

Jim had never seen her this way, but he seemed to get it. It's okay, baby. He took her in his arms.

But I wanted to do it for you, she said, resisting his embrace. I planned this meal and I've made a mess. I'm not sure I can do this, she said, meaning their perfect country life.

Sure you can, he said, holding her with his strong left arm like a dance partner. We'll cook it together. He began cracking open eggs with his right hand. Jim was a whiz in the kitchen, flipped them over in the air. He had learned all about cooking from his mother. Ava was baffled by his facility and it made her even more downcast, except he coaxed her to add a little pepper and butter the toast while he held her close. She'd counted on this meal being her coming out. It's okay, he assured her. They'd go fishing after breakfast and he'd teach her to track the cows. I'll teach you how to find them wherever they go. Soon the eggs and bacon were done and Jim and Ava were sitting at the heavy oak table with late morning sun streaming through the gingham curtains. He swept her up in his energy for the meal and the farm life, and his good humor and optimism were all over their breakfast. They would live in this beautiful place with farm animals and make a fat baby. They would take care of the farm, fish and hunt, and make more babies. It was a terrific spread. Jim said, Look what we've done, and he had drawn her back.

But also Jim was attracted to the quirky, brooding, and dissolute side of his wife. When she eventually described to him her obsessions and early sexual explorations, he relished them like her faint smile filled with whimsy. Ava showed Jim possibilities he could never have imagined. She was a powerful influence on young Jim, nearly Marvin's equal.

12.

Jim found the plush mattress marked down to $150 at Sid's Best Buy in North Miami. After six rapturous nights one side caved in as if the springs were made of asparagus. Now Jim had to reach uphill to find Mara, although that wasn't the worst thing in the world. But he should have known better. For all of his wheeling and dealing, Jim remained a sucker for a deal.

He procrastinated a week before returning the mattress, although there wasn't any reason to expect a problem. To the contrary, on his first visit to the store he and Sid had really clicked, and Jim had looked forward to seeing him again, maybe showing off his beautiful girl. He had it in mind to tell Sid about the Wow Cards and to make him a distributor when the cards were ready. But on this August afternoon, with the ruined mattress sagging on the roof of Jim's car, Sid wouldn't give him the time of day. Jim was embarrassed, getting brushed off by this sweating, fat shyster. He was going to have to drive the mattress back home. Then what? Sid was staring at Mara's thighs while talking about the fine features of a cheap dresser to an elderly black woman.

One thing led to another and Jim leaned over the counter and when Sid raised his voice Jim pushed his finger into Sid's flabby chest. Then Sid came around and there was a scuffle and Jim lost his balance and fell hard onto his back and hip. Jim was surprised this fat shit could push him over; he must have lost something. This came into his mind because Jim could really handle himself. He bruised both his elbows and came up hobbling. He and Mara left with her helping him along, while Sid dialed the cops and shouted, You come in here and threaten me! You fuck, I know your address, I know where you live. Did you see what he did? Sid turned to the black lady, who nodded solemnly. Jim felt disgusted with himself.

I was in Florida that week and stopped by their place in the evening. Jim was hurting. His left elbow had filled with liquid that wobbled when he moved his arm. He asked me to touch it two or three times. The elbow felt strange, like a water balloon connected to his bone. He couldn't believe it was there. Also, there was a hard knob on his hip. I was more concerned about his hip. But he could walk. At my age, it's bad when you break a bone, he said when she was out of earshot, as if she shouldn't know he was an old man. Come on. But he was more concerned about his elbow than the hip. He said he wouldn't be able to lean on his elbows. What will I do? he asked helplessly. For a moment, I didn't catch his meaning. They were planning to drive to Orlando to visit friends the following morning, had the babysitting worked out. It would be a whole weekend together without interruptions from the kids, and she was looking forward to it. He was concerned about leaning on his elbows with this flopping water bag.

Mara was out of character, edgy. She was afraid Sid had called the cops. What if they looked into her immigration status? She could be sent back.

Do you think the cops will come? Jim asked me, glancing her way. In a moment, their future had come unglued.

I think it'll be okay, I said to calm him. I don't think the police will care about this—they're trying to solve murders. A few minutes later he asked again and I said I'd call a lawyer friend and ask his opinion. It bothered me Jim was so off balance. The situation was trivial. I kept expecting he would snap out of this lovesick old guy and become the Jim I know.

Maybe we should take him to the emergency room, Mara said. She wanted me to look at Jim's bruises. She took him by the hand and led him limping into their tiny bedroom. I followed, a really weird moment. He took off his shirt and then lost his balance trying to pull down his pants. She worked them off for him while he leaned on her shoulder. Then she peeled off his underpants. Jim stood beside the sagging bed, completely naked. His chest and arms were still powerful, but he needed to lose about twenty-five pounds. His belly hung toward his drooping balls. His discolored ankles were swollen from gout or some circulation problem. Without clothes my friend looked like an old man. But Mara admired him as if he were a stallion. She touched his sagging flesh and seemed to feel the thrill of his virility. Her face took on a glow. He began to swell from her longing.

Maybe she was using him, like Phyllis once said to me, to get her papers, but also she craved him; anyone could see it. She felt his bruised hip with her hand and the pain left his face. Sure, they could go to Orlando tomorrow, he insisted. Look how I'm walking, he said, half-hard while he gimped around the small cramped room. He just needs massage, she said to both of us, and Jim nodded. Tonight I will give him a long massage. Won't I, baby? She cast him one of her looks—lips pursed and moist while she leaned toward him. She yearned to touch him. His being injured and hurting seemed to heighten their anticipation. It was clear where they were headed as soon as I left them alone. Mara looked at me squarely, until I blushed.

———

Mara could turn on a dime, one moment sexually provocative or even inviting and the next wary as one of Jim's gunmen in the Amazon. Her alarm bells went off whenever he and I walked into another room or outside on the lawn to chat. After five minutes she came to join us with her face flushed. Then she stuck with us like glue. One afternoon we'd been talking and I offered to drive him to the deli to get a six-pack. Mara said no. That was it. No, her face set in fierce determination. She was probably thinking I would drive him back to Phyllis, where he belonged. Jim accepted Mara's iron rule, which I found disturbing.

I wondered what she truly saw when she looked at him—a stallion or a dying old horse? Mara had closely held secrets; that much was clear to me, although Jim seemed oblivious. Maybe she was his equal as a scam artist? I began to settle on this idea.

Before Jim left for Israel, he was the best recruiter in Southeast Florida. Everyone in the business knew it. Three hundred times a year, more or less, he wore his custom-tailored suits, stood at the head of a chilly conference room with antiseptic linoleum floors, a green board with his scribbled circles and squares, Danish and bagels wheeled in on trays. Jim's recruits were seated on folding chairs, looking uneasy or beaten, despair and the smell of floor cleaner welling up in the fluorescent light of morning. Just glancing around the room he could usually identify the best prospects. Jim was tuned into neediness. Soon his mellifluous voice began invoking a business that would give them a sense of empowerment and independence. It is called a mailbox business, which means that while you go to dinner with your friends or go to a show, or watch the game, men and women across the country are earning money that will go into your mailbox; even while you dream at night, checks are on the way. Later, after making phone calls and taking a quick nap, Jim and Phyllis hosted recruiting parties on their balcony overlooking his fine yacht, enthusiastic mixers of old and new friends with music and Phyllis's hors d'oeuvres and Jim holding court with his favorite stories.

But even with his tireless energy, Jim's magnetic therapy products had stopped selling and he and Phyllis were falling into debt. They could no longer keep up with hefty mortgage payments on their condo and yacht. It is a common story in pyramid selling. Markets become saturated overnight. Salesmen can't find new leads and money gets scarce. The intricate network founders and slips beneath the immutable sea of party nights and lush promises. Overnight hundreds or in some cases thousands of salesmen are scurrying like rodents trying to climb aboard fledgling networks promoting new products with their feasts and bonding sessions, their spirited promises of opportunity, residual income, the sweet life.

Most of the money Jim brought in from signing up recruits went to the guys above him in the corporation called up lines. In network marketing, executives profit directly from the start-up fees and sales of everyone in the organization below them; it is a grand joyride for these men when things are going well. With business down, Jim's bosses were afraid he would leave them for another marketing network with a new product line and more attractive recruiting incentives; it would spell the end of their rosy days. Jim's top guys—he referred to them as his best friends— offered him cash incentives to keep him traveling to meetings, selling their magnetic braces, mattresses, and blankets, hosting parties on his breezy terrace. It was the only way to siphon large sums up the massive network.

Jim's up lines were conference-calling him two or three times a day, probing for good news from the trenches, but meanwhile they made conversation about their gym visits, families, and illness, titillated one another, and Jim, with insider talk of payoffs, fancy new cars, and pathetic flings with aging lady "down liners" who were trying to claw their way up to the golden circle. Everyone was selling success while keeping a nervous eye on a plummeting market.

Jim no longer mentions these treasured friends, which is reasonable for a man making a fresh start, but it rubs me the wrong way. I cannot help myself. I roll out their names, Jack, Roy, Chet, Leon, as if they were the greatest fellows on earth. Occasionally, reluctantly, as if they were robbing from a sacred inner core, they had stolen time from golf games to come fishing with us for grouper or king mackerel. While Jim and I put out the lines or reeled in a fish, they sat inside talking about money or playing boisterous gin rummy, clobbering the table and scribbling tallies on a pad. That was fishing. They were profane men who aspired to little else besides ostentatious spending. Their lack of taste was stunning. But Jim urged me to take a longer look until I recognized them as the same royalty my dad had courted: cheating, whoring, usurious, and glittering brightly like strip joints they frequented or cheap motels on the edge of town. (In tacky clubs my father drank Jack Daniel's and laughed along with his rep friends until his teeth were rattling around in his mouth. The aging salesmen still envisioned young women and seven-figure deals that made them giddy and solemn in turns. Each of them made a show of grabbing for the check, but my skinny dad almost always got it, which made me proud.) Now I am stirred by their memory. Their garishness feels like my own hand. I want, no, I need for my friend to cherish them again, especially now as he moves into a life he and the girl would scrape clean of all wounds and history. I prod Jim to straddle sensibilities and time as she frowns in our direction. I am speaking to him urgently, pulling him back into the mud, and he is nodding, yes, as if I were Marvin Gesler.

Now Jim is grinning at the memory of some shady business maneuver or maybe the panorama of a thousand whorey deals, and Mara has become tight as a drum. She feels out of control when she's not directing every single moment. She feels accused. And she is correct. I am playing this song, at least in part, for her. I drive in the needle whenever I see an opportunity. Of course, Mara can do certain things very well.

13.

When she was living in the country with Jim, Ava's questions and self-doubts seemed fixable as the old barn. Jim knew how to do it all. She was so proud whenever he made a big deal about her "being right on target" buying the property—he adored her and that seemed enough for Ava. But there was more. He coached and complimented her every little endeavor. Soon she was even getting food onto the table. After fishing in their own stream Ava insisted on cleaning the trout herself, using her fingers to pull out the guts, the way he'd showed her, although she always made a distasteful expression that he found charming. He needed to hug and kiss her.

Jim was her meaning, her identity. He would teach her to take care of the farm, to fish, to cook, and they'd make babies. After all, he was thirty-five, she was twenty-six; it was time. He swore that their lives would be great. He swore it many times. He washed away her doubts with kisses. She believed him, again and again. If only he could have stayed with her on the farm, their story might have turned mundane but also lovely and long-playing. She often thought that.

But as the summer wore on, Jim began to feel restless and dissatisfied. He would recall early years on his grandfather's farm, watching his dad standing outside kicking the dirt and staring out to the horizon. Jim tried to shake it with long hikes in the woods, fishing, and spending time with Ava, who was lovely and trying so hard to cook, it was very touching, but he had this need for Marvin. Jim got sweaty when he thought of their late-night talks about making it big, scams beating against one another like windows in a big blow. All this good life was making Jim feel like a dead man. It was curious that Marvin Gesler, without scruples or subtlety or appetite for the art of living, was the gateway to Jim's deepest hopes and needs.

Ava knew what was coming. Marvin Gesler had taken over Jim's mind. One sunny afternoon he was pulling out of the yard, waving back at her from the front window of one of his sedans.

Marvin and Jim flew to Nassau at Jim's suggestion, their second visit to the islands. Jim loved the clear warm ocean, although Marvin barely noticed where he was. They talked all day on the beach. Marvin was dressed in Bermudas and a gaudy Hawaiian shirt. He was fatter than ever, the unhealthy whiteness of his skin beginning to blotch from the sun, a hairy chest, heavy jowls that suggested an inner burden. Jim walked beside him with the grace of an athlete, tanned, terrific looking, but entirely engrossed.

At night they continued in their favorite restaurant, Lord Rum Bottom's. Marvin gulped down his fresh seafood while expounding on the fortune to be made from manufacturing metal houses. But who would want to live in such places? Marvin waved off Jim's questions or remarked gruffly, Not now; hold it! For a day and a half Marvin couldn't stop talking about metal barns and houses. He needed to convey what they would cost to manufacture, their strength relative to load and wind, profit margins, the gauge steel required depending on the climate, under-the-table opportunities for chiseling. Marvin licked his fingers or absently pushed them into his underpants. When Jim thought it would never end, Marvin's mind suddenly veered to a factoring scheme involving diesel engine parts, an easy 20 percent a month, then some real estate scam that Jim didn't understand at all—accounting gimmicks, beating the government in twenty ways, franchising health stores, weight-loss clinics, offshore accounts, all in numbing detail. When the partners returned to Canada there were marathon brainstorming sessions driving in Jim's cars or sitting in cheap diners that Marvin favored. Marvin described chains of donut stores and muffin kiosks stretching across the provinces. Franchising was the key. Almost anything could be franchised, he claimed. He had a farfetched idea about prospecting for diamonds or gold in the Brazilian jungle where labor was virtually free. Then his mind arced back to constructing houses, churches, and bowling alleys from metal. On his most creative days Marvin was buffeted between ecstasy and intense frustration and pain, because most of his ideas were destined to be stillborn.

Jim once commented to Ava that instead of going to business school, a smart young man could make his fortune by taking Marvin to a cheap restaurant, buying him a glass of wine, and then devoting his life to virtually any scheme that Marvin tossed out. Surely some of Marvin's greatest business ventures went out with the leftovers.

He often complained to Jim of being overloaded with ideas, afflicted by a hurting brain. Sometimes he would remark to Jim or no one in particular, Why can't I just forget? Marvin needed to talk, or eat whenever the impulse struck. His desires were like physical protuberances. In the middle of a sentence he had to get out of the Chinese or Italian joint fast, feeling trapped, real fast, and walk it off, and Jim, who had been trying to catch up to Marvin's meaning, was sitting with his food in front of him, untouched. Marvin was up from the table and waving off Jim's incredulity. Walking and talking. Marvin's ideas were often implausible, given their resources, but brilliant. Jim began to see that Marvin was utterly helpless. Without Jim's considerable talents, Marvin could spend his life talking to himself on a bench.

Jim picked his moments to coddle Marvin, eased him back to the pyramid deal. They had hardly scratched the surface. Why move into something different when they knew pyramid selling? Marvin nodded his head. He had a file inside about exactly how it should work. Marvin described the vast glassy showrooms they'd build in a half-dozen cities, coupons that looked like ornate diplomas of merit, the financial intricacies of ever-expanding levels of payouts; they'd pay off the cops for two years, maybe three. Then they'd get out of this business and franchise muffin kiosks or maybe weight-loss clinics. Jim agreed. Marvin calculated the profits in his head. Jim made practical choices and kept Marvin on point.

By the fall of 1964, Jim and Marvin were soaring. In Montreal they had opened a deluxe eighty-thousand-square-foot store called International Furniture and Appliances that would quickly become a model for megaoutlets throughout the Canadian provinces. Marvin's marketing ideas were so clear and resonant it was hard to believe that selling appliances had ever been done differently. There were splashes of color everywhere, high-gloss hardwood floors, bright track lighting such as you'd find in the best museums showering flash and glamour onto washing machines and varnished dining room sets. Big stereo speakers pumped out sexy music. Marvin's vivid signs dropped from high like mobiles making it easy to find color televisions, bass boats, or fishing rods. The store had an attitude, a pace, and a carpe diem message: seize the opportunity, buying well is moving ahead in life. Shopping there became a Montreal event like theater or the circus.

Jim boasted to Mara that the store was his idea. This was mostly true. Jim had pressed Marvin to design a huge physical plant with a chancy Vegas atmosphere. Within a year of opening, Marvin's glitzy showcasing of products and sales efficiency were copied by other new mega appliance stores in Cleveland and Detroit. Boston's enormously successful Lechmere Sales was a knockoff of Jim and Marvin's Montreal retail operation replete with glossy packaging, lighting, and color schemes borrowed from Marvin. For Jim, their large modern building was proof of making it big, a trophy he could bring home to Ava or tell his mother about on the phone. But quite likely people would have flocked to their operation if Marvin had stacked the vast and varied merchandise into a dusty airplane hanger. Shoppers thronged to International to buy a dream. They stood on line to collect Marvin's coupons printed with florid script and abstruse explanations of the business bonanza ("a dynamic multi-leveled partnership" was Marvin's catch phrase) that would make them wealthy. Marvin's coupons were a masterstroke.

Most of the innovations in the store came from Marvin, who rudely waved off suggestions from Jim and occasionally from Ava when she came into the office. Jim begrudgingly admits this today, although he dislikes giving credit to his partner in front of Mara. Jim was a great salesman, of course, but his other contributions to the business were more difficult to describe, usually involving questions of emphasis or ways to motivate Marvin, some of which weren't conventional or so lovely. Quite possibly, Jim saved Marvin from a life of wandering destitution and madness, but how could he explain this to the Israeli girl? Despite her improving English, Mara was a straightforward young woman who was impatient with complications and nuance. She was impressed with a big flashy building crammed with shoppers. She enjoyed hearing about the tremendous white circus tent they set up once a month in the parking lot. If her concreteness and annoyance with subtlety was a limitation it did not register as such to Jim.

The monthly events were spectacular and they changed men's lives. How he wished Mara could have seen one with her own eyes. I was leaning back in Jim's war-torn La-Z-Boy, scribbling notes, when he glanced my way helplessly. It was such a long way from the wonder of that first store in Montreal to this impoverished room. He was worried that he couldn't do justice to the spectacle—he stuttered and worked his way in while Mara tried to imagine it.

There were crowds outside waiting to get in, powerful spotlights that crisscrossed the Montreal sky creating the draw of celebrity and opportunity. Inside, banners were blown by invisible wind, just the perfect selection of music to make the older folk—they were the ones with money—feel that the capacity for romance was still alive and stirring, a dozen wondrously packaged specials up front piled high on massive racks, they were flying off the racks, Jim, handsome Jim holding the microphone, and feeling all of life rippling through his powerful shoulders; if she could have seen Jim onstage with the golden future spilling out of him, long-legged women walking the aisles taking cash in exchange for coupons. Jim picked the women, he always picked the women for their businesses; the girls collected thousands with their promising smiles (Marvin insisted on that and went into a rage when they didn't smile) while handing out coupons for last-moment shoppers who didn't want to miss out; no one wanted to miss out on this night that presaged so much. The word was out around Montreal: People were making a fortune. This was better than any stock tip you'd ever hear in a lifetime. Get on board before this one disappears, because everything good in life disappears in a moment; although Jim rarely needed to mention life's abiding tragedy by name, people knew, they weren't stupid. He explained the deal without pushing—actually, it was the very same pyramid redemption scheme Marvin had employed selling irons, except in the store there was a broad range of products to choose from, each yielding coupons and a chance to make a lot of money.

Jim explained that for every fifty-dollar coupon you would eventually collect $1,260. For buying a comfortable two-hundred-dollar armchair you get four coupons and stand to make $5,040. Enjoy a terrific chair for the ball games and, if you like, invest your profits or some of your profits in televisions, boats, or bikes, things you need. Keep investing in more coupons if you want and make thirty thousand or a hundred thousand dollars down the road. Or take your profits home. Don't buy tonight. Jim shrugged, knowing that in sales you mustn't push, and particularly when your customer is already free-falling with desire. No problem if you didn't buy in, if you wanted to sit on your hands and enjoy the night air, the girls, the music. This deal didn't take any sales pitch; that's how good it was—Jim was selling free money. A lot of people were taking home money each month. Although no one knew exactly how much money was going out or staying in the house except for Marvin.

Marvin pumped profits back into new buildings and a few side ventures. He became annoyed when he heard that a group of men were mimicking their operation on a much smaller scale in western Canada, including weekend sessions in a party tent. He considered retaining an attorney, as if pyramid marketing should remain his alone for all eternity. Marvin thought of himself as an original thinker, a visionary entrepreneur, and he was fiercely protective of his creations. His ideas were like his innards. Yet as their business expanded and streamlined he became even more cranky and dissatisfied. His ideas were so much bigger and more arresting to him than what went on in their circus tent or ten such tents. Marvin saw himself as a Henry Ford but on a grander scale.

———————

Within a year Jim and Marvin had four more stores opened, one in Edmonton, one in Saskatchewan, one in Calgary, one in Toronto. Jim was always racing off to another city, another motel night, preparing for a weekend spectacular in one of the branches, prepping the girls, shaking hands. His phone calls to Ava on the fly were full of the life of the party. How could she blame him for not being on the farm? He was making their future. He didn't have time for her despair, her identity crisis, or whatever it was. He was hard-charging down the boulevard of his youth.

Ava began studying herself in the mirror. She held her large breasts in her hands, lifted them a little. They wouldn't stay where she wanted them. She discovered a stretch mark. Where had this come from? Jim must not see this, she thought, feeling ashamed. The mark obsessed her, and she rubbed it with cream until the skin became red and irritated. She couldn't get anything right. And there were wrinkles at the corners of her mouth and on her neck where he loved to kiss her. She was twenty-seven years old and her flesh was sagging. For hours she looked into the mirror. She hadn't dressed and it was afternoon. She was drinking way too much. Her thighs were heavy. Jim had always loved her legs. It was no use. She looked into the mirror and saw her decline spooling out.

She tried to ready herself for Jim's visits, whenever he came. She went to a food shop to buy ingredients. She walked down the aisle with her list for roast duck with sausage and apple stuffing. She wanted to impress him. Ava examined a few tins of spices and then, on an impulse, she slipped them into her pocketbook. She knew how to do this. She left the store feeling focused and tight as a cat. Then she wasn't thinking about roast duck or Jim's next visit. She wanted more adventure. She walked across the street and entered a small department store. She selected rejuvenating skin creams and nail polish and put them into her pocket. Ava looked poised and irreproachable leaving the store. She felt like a player. He played and she played. One evening she slipped a radio beneath her bulky overcoat. She wanted to tell Jim about her adventures but decided they should remain her secret. They gave her an edge, an inkling; following these minor larcenies she looked forward to returning to the farm, taking a shower.

Later she sat on the cool planks in the barn, drinking straight from a bottle as warm well-being spread through her limbs. Ava sometimes invited Grushuna, a Polish lady who did chores on the farm. The girls handed the bottle back and forth. Grushuna had a full bawdy laugh. She reeked from animals and perspiration, but when she walked across the yard or worked in the garden she had a grace of movement that made Ava feel emotional. She once described the Polish lady to Jim as legitimate. He wasn't sure what to make of this remark.

After a year of running himself into the ground, Jim began to hear Ava's distance on the phone. He started visiting the farm every second or third week. The hints of his wife's considerable burden were deflected by newly cut flowers and the smells of baking bread, her mom's recipes—Ava tried so hard for him. The first night back he usually took her to the little drive-through hamburger joint. They sat in the convertible eating and making out. Jim was fresh from huge victories. Everything he and Marvin touched turned to gold. She enjoyed his sundry tales about ugly Marvin, food spilling from his mouth. It really was a fairy tale, because her handsome Jim and this monster were making impossible sums of money. Jim promised he would soon buy her a palace, no more rickety farm. It would be the most beautiful home in all of Canada. She giggled. After breakfast, Jim rushed outside and swooped the projects of the farm into his strong arms. Thirty-six years old and he was on top of the world. There was too much of Jim to embrace—what to do with all this man? He crowded out any room for her spooks and remorse. They talked about the child they would make, even played with names and decided on Michael.

Ava brought out champagne in the evening. He was so pleased that she'd planned a little celebration. Jim applauded Ava for each tiny step, but he had no idea where she was heading. She held his glass of champagne while he drank. They made love and afterwards he told her that her legs were beautiful and she believed him and when she looked in the mirror her legs were shapely and youthful. He kissed her feet. She wanted to drink more, tried to coax him, but Jim was feeling sleepy. He was snoring on the sofa and she was sipping champagne and watching *The Tonight Show*.

Jim went back to work feeling energized. He had smelled the woods and country air. Everything was breaking Jim's way. He was making a lot of money. The farm was pumping with life. He could have it all.

Jim gave a few directions to the Polish lady, although he never paused to look at her. Ava noticed, but that was okay. Jim was Jim. She had her own game.

Jim encouraged Ava to come to their gala Saturday meetings in Montreal. It would be just like old times when he and Ava had hawked irons in the tent. The first night back onstage he gave her a hug and above the din he promised Ava a new car, something sporty. For a minute or more, Jim waved to the crowd with a radiant smile. They believed in him and he soaked in the adulation. He said to her, Do you know what this feels like, Ava? But she seemed to be somewhere else entirely.

They were on a stage that could have accommodated a good-sized dance company while twenty-five hundred customers settled into folding chairs waiting for the money. Ava was wearing a low-cut black dress and stylish heels. Jim held his arm around her as though showing his girl all his hard-earned glory, but also he was showing her off like a bosomy plaything. (He could feel Ava drifting. Okay, he'd pull her along.) Meanwhile, love songs floated on the night air and the tremendous storage rack was emptying like an hourglass. The whole setup manufactured a cogent urgency, and Jim never had to pressure or beg to sell his wares.

Ava stood at Jim's elbow, dreamy and alluring, while he introduced big winners from the past. Some of these men and women had taken home really large sums, twenty thousand dollars, as much as forty-five thousand dollars. Jim asked them how their lives had been changed. Customers came up to the microphone and talked about buying summer homes and elite cabin cruisers to explore the Great Lakes. Many people were counting on Jim and Marvin's coupons to build a big future—they were banking on it.

The thing is that Jim really believed he was doing good and true work. He always believed in his deals.

Marvin never factored in honor. He calculated dollars. He understood perfectly that his pyramid operation was a dying comet. As more and more people bought into the pyramid, the deepening levels would splay out into longer and longer numbers and it would take more time for consumers to complete levels and get payouts. In a matter of months, time lags would kill off the enthusiasm of eager shoppers. Party-time Saturday nights would come to an end, and furious investors would be left with their overpriced merchandise and worthless coupons.

Marvin understood that the key to success was buying time, dragging out the weeks of the operation. He prepared a simple but effective distraction. After a half year of monthly Saturday events, he added a lottery to these sessions, a one-hundred-thousand-dollar cash giveaway that was open to all shoppers in the store. It was basically a smoke screen, a way to pump out money to customers, slews of money that promised much more to come. Free money—

who cared if it came from coupons or a lottery? No one could be sure exactly how long it would take to make their fortunes, but good faith was abounding and customers felt confident their coupons were gestating like savings bonds. After all, there were winners every Saturday session to go along with inspiring testimonials about the good life from earlier investors who had come up big. As Marvin expected, with the lottery in place everyone continued to enjoy these celebratory nights about promise and winning. Marvin figured the deal could go on for another year, maybe a little longer. Then he'd shut it down, sell off the buildings, and leave with millions.

One Saturday night the legendary comedian Lenny Bruce showed up at their monthly event. Bruce had been doing his dark monologues for peanuts in Montreal after-hours clubs called black pigs. After a number of highly publicized arrests and obscenity trials, owners of the big stateside clubs would no longer risk hiring him. It was a shame, because by 1964 Lenny Bruce had redefined his comedic form and was a revered cultural figure, a Jack Kerouac or Charlie Parker. But he was frozen out and falling into despair.

Bruce could barely believe what he was witnessing. Consumers were in a buying frenzy for big-ticket items they didn't need or even desire. Lenny was a scam artist himself and he smelled something special. Years earlier he had supported himself and his wife, Honey, by dressing up in the stolen vestments of a Catholic priest and going door-to-door raising money for a fictitious leper colony. He listened to habitués exchange savvy remarks about the best deals for coupons, what products yielded the most coupons for the money. Products were marked up 20 percent or more from what you'd pay in Sears, but the built-in profit potential from the Saturday events made this premium trivial to shoppers. The deal seemed to be a bonanza for everyone involved. People spent their savings and some even borrowed against homes to accumulate coupons. He noticed the beautiful sad, sexy woman onstage, part of the operation but also way outside it.

The scene he'd stumbled upon was Swiftean and hilarious, the endgame of capitalism. Bruce immediately introduced bits and snatches of Marvin's business scam into his comedy routine in one of the local clubs. The comedian riffed on love and money with obsessed pig farmers buying color televisions they didn't need. They drooled over a stacked sad-eyed lady held prisoner in a billowing tent, forced to give away free money on Saturday nights. A few of Lenny's Montreal skits were recorded and still exist today. He wanted to develop the routine into something larger that he could use on television, if he was ever invited back on television, or even in a movie. But first he needed to learn more about what was going on.

14.

From the early years of my friendship with Jim, when Mara was still a small child playing in a dusty kibbutz in northern Israel, I feared losing him. I could see him spinning off into new deals and associations with hardly a glance back. This feeling became much more pronounced after he took up with the Israeli girl and cast aside all trappings of his former life; I would soon become another nameless and forgotten "bub" along with a thousand old customers, salesmen, and cronies whom he once loved. Unexpectedly, the fear went away when I began writing "the book."

Each visit to their place I learned new details of the story, colors, smells, minor characters; now and then I coaxed a secret. I already knew parts of his life, but when I pieced it together the panorama was a revelation. Imagine discovering that a friend of twenty years had once been an accomplished concert pianist or even a violent criminal or, in Jim's case, both, because his secret past encompassed vast dramatic and ethical terrain. My friend's youthful heroism saving his starving family might have inspired a nineteenth-century novel, and later on his moral drift was equally compelling, shocking really. For so many days he and I trolled together in the Gulf Stream, played gin rummy until dawn, drank beers at the Blue Moon. Jim was just Jim.

Writing pages about him had another effect that I hadn't anticipated. The more I learned, the more I became tender and protective toward the younger Jim, so much so that I found it somewhat painful to leave my character for visits to my actual friend in Florida. At first I found this split screen amusing, but then my mood hardened. Now that I had Jim on paper, I wanted him to have room to breathe, to be himself. I didn't want my character trifled with. It annoyed me to have my friend edit his younger self crudely, exaggerate his victories or take out awkward moments, to impress the girl. When Jim asked me about "the book," I could feel myself tightening up. I didn't want to talk about it. I ducked the question.

But I still needed to learn many things about him and I couldn't finish without his help. This made me extremely nervous. A writer's material is his wealth and future or at the very least his sustaining illusion. Writers suffer gold fever over story lines. In my work I sweated to write honest sentences, but when I visited Jim I turned into a salesman. I was smiling and glad-handing, offering bribes—dinner at the Italian joint or maybe a case of beer or I found myself telling Mara she was beautiful or, worse yet, that she was extremely intelligent, while Jim beamed at us, yes, yes—I said whatever I needed to get him talking. I became an operator. I just wanted the story. I wanted to hear about Jim's years in the jungle. He could have the girl. By now I didn't really care. I needed to write my book.

Lenny Bruce became an issue between us. It suited Jim's purpose to brag that the great comedian had been a habitué of his store. It was like professing his friendship with Sammy Davis Jr., the sort of name-dropping I'd grown up with around my dad and his friends, all of whom had boasted about drinking nights with their Vegas buddies Sammy Davis and Sinatra as if these stars had nothing better to do than hang out with reps. But when I asked Jim for details about the comedian he clearly didn't want to discuss the subject around Mara.

When I couldn't get things from Jim or sensed he was aggrandizing for the girl, I began looking to other sources. I spoke to Jim's up lines and salesmen. I telephoned two of his lovers from years earlier. I called his mother in Canada. I talked to Phyllis numerous times. I traveled to San Francisco and spent three days with seventy-year-old Ava—that revealed astonishing back roads. Jim knew that I made these inquiries and often asked what I discovered and then looked a little dislocated or melancholy. He gave me phone numbers and sometimes made introductions. We both recognized that there were two stories—the story of his life and the story he was telling in front of Mara. Usually the stories converged but not always. He and I were now motivated by different callings. Then there was the reality of our friendship apart from the stories. Getting back to that was harder for me than for him, which, frankly, surprised me.

When I spoke to Jim from my home in New York he said to me that he was just barely surviving, spending the last of Mara's savings and begging his elderly mother, Sally, for money. Nothing was happening about the Wow Card. Maybe it was dead. He was hoping Phyllis would let him have two paintings to sell; actually, they were signed Monet prints he and Phyllis had saved from their Canada house. There was no longer any jump in his voice, no big deals about to break loose. Jim worried about sustaining this new life with a girl he barely knew. What if it registered to her that he was old and broke? What if the whole thing unraveled and she dropped him? What then? At night there were strangers ringing up from Israel speaking Hebrew. What was she talking about to these people? Who were they? Every few days she asked him, When can we get married, Jim?

Soon, real soon, baby.

Jim was promising big things all around. Sometimes he sneaked off to a phone booth and called Phyllis. He needed to hear her voice so that he could continue running away. But she was also broke and scared. He assured her he would soon have money to take care of her in style, like always. He'd buy her a little house on the water, and they'd remain best friends. She could count on it. He didn't mention that he'd stopped paying the premium on his life insurance. Phyllis had been the beneficiary. What would be the point in telling her? he asked me. Maybe he was right.

I tried to close my eyes to all of this sorrowful news. His candor and pathos were making me nervous because I had been writing about a man who won or lost on a big stage, a phoenix. I was in the thrall of Jim and Marvin as they rose to the top in their unlikely fashion. I wanted to write a novel with a grand sweep. In my life, Jim, Ava, and Marvin were eclipsing Jim, Mara, and Phyllis. I was afraid his present circumstance would turn off the faucet or perhaps shake my resolve. So when Jim came across as pathetic or crotchety I wanted to erase him like a father who had been a failure and humiliation to his kids. Sometimes I didn't think about him for long stretches of time, although I was writing his story every day, or I found myself judging my friend, but increasingly I regarded him as a function of the book. What present turn in his life would make a better ending? Would it be better for the novel if my friend succeeded or if he failed?

I kept expecting Jim would phone me with the news that Mara had gone off with someone younger and wealthy and that would inspire my ending, but no. She was in the background, happy, humdrum, speaking Hebrew with her kids, or she might pick up another receiver and say something to us in English, very saucy, or she might ask him if there was a football game tonight—they had started watching the games together and he enjoyed teaching her the rules and telling her gossip about the players.

When Mara came on the line, Jim became playful and energized. One afternoon she was impatient to leave with the kids for a street fair where there was a large trampoline at the end of the block. They'd have pizza and the kids would jump. By then I had grown immune to Jim and Mara's moments of tenderness and I wanted to tell him that Jim would never settle for crumbs. Jim, the one that I was writing about, would have been appalled by such a wasted day. But the surfeit of her youth washed all over my friend and made him high. They'd go to the fair and do all of the mundane things a young girl wanted. They'd burn the hours, why not? It was still early and she was already inciting him with little jokes about tonight, dares and touching. He couldn't focus on finding work and he cared about money only to please her. Jim's days were pacing toward their cluttered bedroom. Nothing else mattered really, except to pull down her white tennis shorts and begin kissing her neck and under her lovely arms until she was giggling and he wouldn't stop. He turned her back to him and felt her wetness with his stiff fingers, while she made the word *yes,* silently like a bubble, and he explored more deeply. Jim glanced to the narrow mirror and watched his penis rise and thicken, begin to quiver. Her flooding smells and her strange unquenchable ardor intoxicated him. Their sex was an enduring feast, a miracle. He would do anything to keep her.

After months of cajoling and begging, Phyllis agreed to sign the divorce papers. It was the one thing she had left to give to him and he was so excited. She nodded and made her broad daffy smile. They drove to the courthouse together and signing the papers felt like a little celebration, as if they were getting married. He kissed her sweetly, and they went back to her apartment and shared a glass of wine and reminisced. She felt good about doing it. She would do anything for Jim. Before he left to go home he told her that he loved her and promised to take care of her.

That night, Jim didn't tell Mara the great news. It didn't feel clean, not then. He would wait a little longer.

I think Phyllis believed some angel would pluck her up and save her. She often lapsed into the positive-thinking palaver she and Jim had used during the last sinking years of their marriage; I'm terrific or I couldn't be any better if I was twins, she'd say on the phone to one of his old rep buddies, or to me.

Once a week she spent a reckless amount to lunch with four or five of her old girlfriends, all of them divorced from wealthy husbands during the past dozen years. Dressing up for these rich meals always brought a surge of well-being. The girls usually chose an upscale restaurant by the water. They wore wide-brimmed hats and watched the cruisers pass along the Intracoastal Waterway. They spoke about lavish dinner parties and animal rights, none of them with more ardor than Phyllis. Old habits don't die easily. Over the years she had raised thousands for wayward animals. The girls knew that Jim had left her for a young woman—they'd all been through it, although when Phyllis wasn't around they gossiped about the fifty-year age difference between Jim and Mara as though it set Phyllis's shame apart from their own.

She couldn't tell her friends that she was broke, fearing she would be left out of the club, or that she still adored Jim—even now she wanted to please him. The girls wouldn't be kind about this.

She shopped for the perfect little presents for Mara's kids and pictured Jim's delight when she next had the chance to pass them on to him. She greatly looked forward to the trip she and Jim planned to take to California to tell his daughter about their separation. Phyllis would help him through this awkward meeting, whenever he could somehow scrape together the airfare. They would be together again for a few days and she would savor their little jokes and old habits. She would treasure their time and help him in little ways that only a wife could know about.

PART III

15.

On the big stage Ava was sexy and whimsical and she was available, or so it seemed. At the end of Marvin's Saturday events men usually came on to her. For hours she had been onstage with all these products until she also became a product, the best of them. In the winding down of a night of coarse desires, men felt like they had the right to say hello to Ava, to nudge her or touch her shoulder or hip, some little intimacy. There had been a physical bond created; it had been purchased in fifty-dollar increments. She accepted this as a facet of her work or perhaps even an expression of her essence. Some nights it amused her a little or saddened her, but mainly she took it for granted, like the heavy night air.

Lenny Bruce couldn't take his eyes off her. One night he tried to speak to Ava. She brushed past him, trailing after Jim, but Lenny had had a whiff and he couldn't get her out of his mind. He went back to California and thought about her innocent teacher's voice and sumptuous body. Lenny slept with a lot of women and had a worn attitude, but she'd struck a chord. Two weeks later he returned to Montreal after working a one-week gig at the Elmwood Casino in Windsor, Ontario. At the end of the lengthy session, Ava was standing at the foot of the stage, talking to a few men. She didn't mind if they brushed against her or touched her arm. She was exquisite and tarnished.

My name is Lenny Bruce, he introduced himself with a trace of a chuckle. You've heard of me, maybe, the comedian. She shook her head no, never had. Ava was looking past this edgy guy, wondering about hamburgers after work with Jim. She was sweating from her long night on the stage, and Lenny suddenly felt unsteady. She had the same large breasts that sagged a little, same height and dark auburn hair. Even the clean smell like watermelon. He closed his eyes. She was the essence of his ex-wife and he'd never gotten over her. Now and again Honey would still call him from a street corner somewhere in California, his milky-voiced lost beauty stoned on heroin always promising she'd get straight and come home. He was needy and a little out of control. He was leaning toward Ava, pathetic really. He wanted to touch her, just touch her arm, and she wouldn't have cared, which was maddening. He wanted to be charming and worldly, but he stared at her with dark hollow eyes from years of shooting up and great expanses of sadness.

It must be hard to make money telling jokes, she said, filling a space. Ava had mastered the art of making awkward men feel on top, at least for a few moments. He smiled at her. She had no idea whom she was talking to, figured he was a small-time party comedian.

No, no, I do pretty well. I make money in nightclubs, all the best spots. Las Vegas, you name it. No response. Sure you never heard of Lenny Bruce? She shook her head and he could feel the breeze from her hair. They were standing in front of the stage as it was coming apart in planks and swaths of dirty rug. Workers were dismantling the racks and sweeping up torn coupons in the dim light. Ava was greeting a half-dozen guys who'd stayed to say hello.

Listen, you never saw me on *The Tonight Show*? I've been on the front pages of every paper in the country because of these trials.

She looked at him quizzically. She didn't know about the trials. He wanted her to understand that he was famous, and she wasn't listening. Ava was doing her work, if you'd call it work, pleasing each of the men with a handshake or a lingering remark.

Lenny was rocking on his heels. Everyone knows about me. Except they keep throwing me into jail because they say my routines are obscene. But they aren't obscene. Do you know Norman Mailer, what he said about me? Saul Bellow? No, she didn't know these men. Lenny wanted to tell her that famous writers had championed his causes, they considered him a genius and a visionary; but it was no use. She didn't know about such people.

He was so touched by her in this darkening theater of dreams where coupons promised a splendid prosperous future. Lenny's own future was gone beyond redemption, except, and it came to him right then waiting his turn on line with a half-dozen losers, maybe she was his chance. What did he have to lose, an old junkie who couldn't get a job and was nearly broke from defending himself in the courts? Ava was craning her neck for Jim, almost ready to drive off to a small forgettable life, cheap frayed curtains, and much remorse that would go unnoticed. Lenny really had no idea how she lived, but he wanted in. Badly. It didn't matter that she was married. He swatted away the idea. He'd leave Los Angeles and move here or he'd bring her with him. Preposterous. He was a big star and she wouldn't understand his world, but that's how he was thinking. He was swept away by this woman. She started to move away and Lenny grabbed her wrist, which surprised her.

He shook his head, don't go, and then he eased his grip, fearing she'd bolt or call out. No words but his crazy energy spewed all over—sent her reckless needs and such a deep tunnel of emptiness until she was staring at his torn-up face. And Lenny felt Ava's urges. He could fit in, fit right in.

I have to see you again.

It's impossible, she said. I'm a married lady.

I don't care. I have to see you. Just for a little while. I love you—ridiculous to say these words standing in line with this beaten-down group of men. Lenny chuckled a little. They were all waiting their turn as if Ava were the prize of the carnival and they'd bought tickets tonight to win a rapturous moment.

She laughed.

Listen, I could help you, he said. I could do everything for you. Just give me a chance. She looked at him quizzically. Just give me a chance, will you? He was so excited and heartbroken.

She was embarrassed by this talk and didn't know how to turn him away. But also, she heard something. Ava scribbled her number on a piece of paper and then turned to three men who had been waiting patiently.

He called her on the phone from California and the talk came out like jazz; now when he had his act together he was getting turned down at the clubs that once loved him, even the dives and strip joints were saying no; Lenny was writing a book about his life in exile, he was going to put Ava into the book. Lenny had written pages about his reckless attraction for Ava in his notebook. She laughed, and he promised she'd go into the book, you'll see; he read sections to her about his ex-wife, who had been a stripper; but Ava was even more beautiful than Honey Harlow; how wonderful and instructive that Jim and Marvin were scamming people with coupons until no one cared anymore about furniture; objects had been replaced by pure greed—capitalism was showing its true face; Lenny wanted to play all this music for her so that she would understand; understand what? Ava had never heard of Charlie Parker, Monk, Coltrane, George Shearing; she'd barely heard of capitalism. What was it? No matter, he would teach her. He would be her teacher and lover. She had to give him a chance. She said, Impossible, but he was insistent and charming. He would bring her records of Billie Holiday and Sarah Vaughan; he'd hold her in his arms until she began to feel it. They'd dance together and she'd soon begin to love him. He would crawl into her heart. Gerry Mulligan and Chet Baker, she must hear them playing "My Funny Valentine"; it was heartbreaking. They'd dance slow to Frank Sinatra. She'd heard of Sinatra. Jim loved Sinatra. That's good; that's good. She laughed at the pure rush of Lenny. When was Jim away traveling? He'd come to the farm and visit when Jim was away. He begged her. He hit every note.

In October of 1964, Lenny started coming to the farm every second or third week. He barely noticed the animals or bucolic view—he might have been visiting Ava in the South Bronx. For long stretches he stared at her, kissed her cheek or held her hand, and imagined her alone in this isolated place that he began to call the Sad Palace. Lenny was at the very end of his rope and he strained to find every dark connection with Ava. Almost from the start, he'd decided she was his last chance. In his Los Angeles house he was shooting up in his bathroom with four locks on the door so he wouldn't feel paranoid about the police bursting in on him. For months he'd been enhancing heroin with methedrine for extra kick. But in Montreal he rarely used anything and it didn't hurt so much when he was with Ava.

They got drunk each night on cheap whiskey or wine and talked and talked. She could say anything to Lenny. But it went beyond that. This strange guy pulled intimacies from her guts. She told him when Jim was away she'd walk into stores and slip things into her pockets. She knew how to do this. She'd walk out feeling as though the luck had turned her way. Some evenings she'd go to bars and drink and flirt with guys she didn't know; these tawdry episodes quieted her demon and she was able to go home and continue life, such as it was. She looked at Lenny's face and he smiled. No rebuke.

Ava admitted she didn't know what to do with herself. When she was a little girl she had carefully prepared for the great banquet that was coming. Now most nights she ate by herself in the lonely farmhouse.

They watched *The Tonight Show* together and he told her about Sinatra and Tony Bennett; he knew all the famous ones. He gave her titillating gossip about the stars and when the comics came on he told her which of them was borrowing his material or his timing, which of them had something special and the ones who were just going through the motions. Ava watched the comics carefully to learn what Lenny did. Meanwhile he stared at her serious face until he couldn't stand it any longer and he gave her a hug or kissed her cheek or raised her skirt and fondled her thighs. Lenny, why do you always want that? she'd complain.

Lenny was impatient with the animals and bugs, everything but Ava. He wanted to steal her and make a big life together. He had these big silly notions. Lenny told her she was born to be a showgirl or a singer. It wasn't too late and he would show her how to do it. He'd get her bookings. He'd take her around the world to see things she'd never dreamed of. They'd perform together. Ava let him say whatever he wanted. She was giving him a reason to live. She was filling him like a muse—it made her feel necessary. He was a really famous guy.

Their lovemaking was soft and dreamy and usually unfulfilled because Lenny couldn't quite do it anymore. Even that was sweet and informed by hurting and she'd hold him for a while and say, It's okay, Lenny; it doesn't matter. On Jim's fancy victrola, a present from Marvin Gesler, Lenny played her Joe Williams, Goin' to Chicago, sorry but I can't take you there; she felt it deeply and it made him so happy; in an hour he'd be trying to make it again, full of ardor and curiosity. He tried to please her, best as he could, but mainly he wanted to possess every inch of Ava, every capricious little smile, kissed the creases beneath her heavy breasts, rolled her over and opened her legs, searched; You know me better than my husband, she joked; he nodded seriously and loved her little fatnesses and cracks and smells, put his ravaged face on each mole, looking for clues, maybe about what was missing in himself, tried to fill it in with her taste, her sweat, and even her menstrual bleeding. She let him. She let him eat her alive until he was sated, his face dripping with himself and her—she quickly wiped it with her hand—before he began to kiss her deeply, long stretches of ardent schoolboy kissing.

She'd entirely opened herself to this man from the moon. He hardly ate food. He fed on her flesh and shadows. She allowed him. Then he'd pace around, talking about the Constitution and First Amendment law, and Ava tried to follow his ideas until her brain ached. He was so intricate and moody and his jokes weren't exactly funny. They were mazes of commentary and sarcasm. With Jim she was the arty mystery girl, but she wasn't in Lenny's class. She was just holding on. Then she would become frightened. How could she stay with this guy? He was in a different league. When Ava thought of Jim she felt appalled and lost, a fallen angel. She and Jim were going to make a baby. Jim brought the freshness of the woods and physical strength that lifted her spirits. He pushed aside her demons. Lenny called her to march alongside him in darkness. He surrounded her with his scrawny junkie arms and ideas that made her feel stupid. What was she doing? I'm not on your level, Lenny. It won't work. Whenever she took a little step back Lenny geared up and won her back with big promises, Fame, Mystery, and decadence that frightened her but drew Ava ahead as if this shady path were fated. He'd tapped into the primal Ava. Nothing was obscene, he told her. He wanted to know every secret urge. He wanted to watch her make love to another man or maybe they'd make it together with another woman; she tittered. He wanted to unleash the impulses she held back. Ava didn't understand Lenny, but he moved her.

Lenny appealed to Ava's ego with his tape recorder. Since the first obscenity trial he had taken to taping many things in his life: conversations with friends, testimonials on his work, the trials themselves. He turned on the machine and asked Ava thorny questions about her family life, her first sexual experiences; the worst she could say didn't make Lenny flinch and he'd make a little motion with his fingers, Give me something more. His questions had a thematic direction and she got caught up in his pace. Ava stopped being self-conscious and she could feel her life stitching together like a tapestry. He wanted it all on tape for something special he was working on in California. He was going to make her a star. Then he'd turn off the machine and he needed her kisses like a kid, an empty kid. He'd earned them with all his questions and the small machine that was taking in her life.

Even if Lenny was quiet a moment Ava felt his mind working and she tried to watch his eyes and feel his direction. Anything could trip him into laughing or falling into one of his routines, looking at her face for approval. Maybe I'll try it on *The Tonight Show,* he'd say, and she'd nod yes or no, so seriously, as though she were making America's cultural choices. Then he'd tell her how great she was or that she had soul or she understood things deeply. Her problem was confidence. She didn't understand how fine she was. He was always pumping her up. Believe me you'll do important things, you're still young, and Ava was half-believing she could be great at that nameless something, maybe a model or a performer; he could get her club dates, everyone needs a leg up; she actually bought into it. If she doubted for a moment, he turned on the tape, the tape of her life. And he took notes in the little black notebook as though she were a star. She was a star. She was Lenny Bruce's girl.

16.

When I got to Florida I went straight to Jim's. After dinner we had a few minutes by ourselves on the tiny patio. That's when he told me that Mara's ex-husband had arrived from Israel. Shimon had rented a small apartment a couple of miles away. He missed his kids and wanted to visit, she explained to Jim. But this was a strange situation. Shimon was thirty-two years old, handsome, and with a bodybuilder's physique. He was coming by twice, three times a week to pick up the children. He and Mara spoke Hebrew in the tiny kitchen. What did they say? How would Jim know? It hung between us, the chance there was something more going on, a secret arrangement or rekindling of their feelings. Jim had so little to offer Mara. Their great plans were stalled by no money and Jim's reluctance to leave her side. He didn't say this, but I could read him. His need for her had absorbed everything else in his life. It was a scalding need. She listened to his dreams and made him lusty. For years he had forgotten how that felt, what a beautiful supple body felt like against his chest and heart that pattered un- evenly or sometimes raced ahead. But what was the risk weighed against a young woman's breasts and arms, how they felt? Just to kiss her neck. Made him forget how old he was and how the luck had turned against him. That was enough for him; just to kiss her neck or fine arms was enough. He could not give that back. Even if she made love with her husband, it wouldn't be so terrible, if there was enough left for him, something for him. As long as Mara stayed with him, listened to his stories and promises. But he had to marry her, immediately, before she disappeared into a new life. Jim had stalled Mara about the marriage. Maybe he'd played it too cute. She might turn him down now and laugh in his face. He was sopping with fear. It didn't matter if Mara and her husband were setting him up. More time with her was everything to Jim. He needed to buy time. Something could still break his way. It was a good deal, good enough, because he would never find her again. For his remaining ancient days he would search for her.

I couldn't decide if Mara graced or degraded the remains of my friend. This physically slight, uneducated woman had eclipsed his great factories and showrooms, his glory days in the jungle. She had become Brazil, but Brazil had devolved into the most rudimentary needs and deceits. And still, Mara would occasionally look at me in a lingering way as though she was making a calculation: Would he be better for me? She was so audacious, preposterous, presumptuous, and yet I wondered, Could I resist her? I don't know. Mara was a calling, something way beyond herself.

I asked Jim about Phyllis and he hesitated before answering. His silence told a lot. Whenever Jim stalled like this, I knew he had done something wrong or, more to the point, he believed you'd think he'd done something wrong and he was figuring how to cover up. He's always had a very pragmatic relationship to guilt. After he coughed a couple of times, he said to me, Remember the paintings? Well, she changed her mind and decided to give them to me. She wanted me to have them. And I'll tell you something. She did the right thing. I picked out those paintings twenty-five years ago. She told me, You should have them, Jim. He seemed emotional about Phyllis's change of heart—that's how he tried to sell it. But I knew he was thinking about selling them, giving Mara something, and having a couple of thousand left to take her to Orlando for a few days after they were married. It was a chance to make her believe in their lives together.

Even when Phyllis could no longer pay the rent on the one-bedroom apartment, she had remained stubbornly in place. Jim had coached her, You can stay for a long time after they post the notice, months and months, sometimes years. No problem, she said to me in that chipper way that his salespeople had reassured one another while they were going broke. No problem. No problem. She stayed on until the day the sheriff came. It was August and very hot in her twilight rooms because the owner of the condominium had turned off the AC three weeks earlier in a guerilla tactic to force her out. While the tall man waited with crossed arms in the kitchen leaning against the wall, sweating through his khaki shirt, she tried to reach Jim on the phone. He's not home, Mara said curtly, and hung up. Phyllis stuffed things into four matching pieces of luggage and carefully took down the ornately framed Monet prints from the wall and admired them for a moment.

Phyllis hadn't envisioned actually leaving her apartment. She was an optimistic girl, and she didn't like being rushed about making her choices. She had stayed on in the swelter of summer expecting things to turn her way when the cool weather came. Network marketing always picked up in the fall when men and women turned down their air-conditioning and once again began to feel like going door-to-door. As she hauled the suitcases to her little black Nissan, she felt tipsy, as though her head weren't sitting exactly on her body.

Phyllis hadn't called Vivian in advance. Anyhow, what could Phyllis have said on the phone with this sheriff standing in her kitchen, wanting to get on with his police work.

She tried to remain peaceful, as if this were just another

happening in her week. The steering wheel of the Nissan had its familiar spongy feel. But she was misty-eyed and thought, if only she could have reached Jim, the whole matter could have been resolved differently. What a shame.

She rang the bell of her friend's house and looked through the glass door into the high vaulted living room; beyond that she could see through the open sliding glass doors to the small canal where Vivian's young boyfriend's ski boat was tied to the little dock. Vivian had come out of her marriage wealthy but also deeply wounded, and Chris filled a void. The girls had decided that this young man was good for her.

It was Jim's kind of house. They had come here for parties and Jim would sit on the tan leather sofa smoking a cigar and holding court with his favorite stories. It was an odd coincidence, one night Jim had discovered that more than twenty years earlier Vivian's boyfriend, Chris, had known Jim's son in Toronto. This news quieted Jim while Chris looked on with an over-the-top caring expression.

It was early in the afternoon, but Vivian smelled of alcohol. The friends embraced and Phyllis tried to keep it cheerful but had to dab her eyes with a tissue. She told her friend that she was feeling a little out of balance and needed a place to rest. For a short while. Do you know what I mean, Viv? I don't like to feel this way. She circled her finger next to her tilted head, to say "cuckoo," and managed a smile.

Phyllis liked things to be comfortable and attractive. It was too crude to say she'd been thrown out of her place and needed a bed to sleep. She didn't have forty dollars to her name besides the valuable prints in the back of the car. She'd left the family photographs behind in her apartment along with the sectional from the Canada house and some of her best clothes. She'd been rushed and hadn't made the wisest choices. She couldn't say to Vivian, Everything is gone. Desperation was outside the orbit of their friendship and so

Phyllis used psychobabble language to make her situation acceptable. She had to regain her equilibrium. She needed a place to rest,
she said to her friend. Then she'd be fine. Except Phyllis was gulping for air like a fish on the deck. Vivian nodded, but she seemed
unsettled or cross. Maybe it was from having to right herself from
a stupor.

Vivian was one of the girls Phyllis went out to lunch with on the
waterway. If Vivian thought about it at all, she would have believed
Phyllis had money, at least enough to float from good restaurants to
parties, cooling down at night with a drink beside the pool. All
these women were trying to paint themselves back together. They
had money from their settlements but were bracing against demise
with a bottle or a younger man. They drove fast cars and looked in
on one another with tenderness and shared regret. In the first weeks
without Jim these friends had been Phyllis's lifeline. One of them
had a grand yacht and had offered to take Phyllis and the others up
to Cape Cod for a week. The nights on the water were gay with
karaoke singing and sipping wine beneath the stars, meals you
couldn't imagine. But this afternoon at Vivian's, Phyllis knew she
had passed out of their circle. She was falling very quickly.

Vivian offered her the little garret above the garage, which was
separate from the main house. Phyllis smiled as if things were already much better. The room was put together with two-by-fours
and plywood, a rough storage space that was much smaller than the
maid's quarters in Phyllis's Canada house. She pushed Vivian's
luggage, bikes, and knickknacks aside to fit a cot. Phyllis smiled
and said it was perfect, just right to catch her breath for a few days.
She also shoved aside Chris's distaste for her visit. She wasn't staying here forever. Phyllis had resources, plans for her life, an artist's
eye, people said that about her; she had taste and convictions, and
that didn't go away because Jim had found a new romance. He'd
had other women before. He liked women. But he cared for her and
always would. They were a special couple; a thousand times she

had heard this from his customers: Jim and Phyllis. She became teary and shook her head at Vivian's question. Nothing, just feeling a little sentimental, she managed.

Whenever they spoke on the phone, Jim told her he loved her. Now she was crying and tried to wave it off. Jim would take care of her when his new deal came through. It was an arrangement they had. He'd promised her a house by the water and a car when he made his deal. Jim couldn't explain this to his Israeli girlfriend with her middle-class aspirations and plans for every nickel. It was Phyllis's secret with Jim, and she relished this intimacy. It became her castle. She couldn't tell her plans to Vivian, who would have snickered. But Phyllis knew Jim would take care of her.

It wasn't a comfortable visit. During the month she lived in the little garret, Phyllis found out things and she put them aside, one after another, because everyone was tarnished and holding on, she'd come to that with her changing fortunes; and it wasn't in her character to make trouble. She tried to carve out a place with a lighthearted manner. Cooked dinner, washed the dishes. Went to bed early. She had known Chris before from Vivian's dinner parties. He played folk guitar and had seemed a little depressed, a wounded guy who became teary when alluding to his father's years of rebuke.

Vivian was a big drinker for years, but now she was a drunk. When she came down for breakfast in the morning with a throbbing head, Chris handed her a Bloody Mary. He gave her refills until she couldn't stand and then he guided her upstairs into bed and tucked her in with a glancing kiss. This happened most mornings. Phyllis was appalled by his contemptuous smirking face except when he filled Vivian's glass, and then he oozed with graciousness and concern. You had to live with them to see his malevolence and snickering at the edges of a room, or from the upstairs landing, coarse laughter when Vivian stumbled or vomited on the patio. Vivian never noticed, she was so far gone.

When the girls called, Chris often said that Vivian was under the weather and couldn't come to the phone, as though he wanted to keep her numb and wrapped up for his own designs. He drove a new red Mercedes convertible, a gift from Vivian. Phyllis considered mentioning their way of life to the other girls, but then she thought better of it.

It was an arrangement that Vivian sanctioned, Phyllis reasoned. He was a young guy and was giving her pleasure in the same way that Mara was servicing Jim. Although Phyllis had a theory that scared her and she couldn't get it out of her mind: When the time suited her Mara would kill Jim with her love. He would die in her arms straining to be a young man. It would be so easy and no one could accuse her of anything. Mara was the devil. Phyllis couldn't tell this to Jim any more than she could warn Vivian.

Phyllis had to find her own place and leave this mess, but meanwhile she couldn't help noticing and she felt sordid standing by. While Vivian slept it off Chris would drive away in the sporty car and a couple of times he came back with a girl, a young blonde with a stripper's body. Phyllis watched from her garret window. He acted like it was his house. He ordered Phyllis with his inflated airs, Take out the garbage; mop the Florida room. But for the most part, he ignored her while he played the king.

Phyllis wouldn't have made trouble, except one afternoon she happened to be inside the house while Vivian was passed out beside the pool and Chris was on the phone upstairs talking to his brother in Canada. Why do I end up with such a pathetic hag when there are so many good ones down here? Chris had said, and then he narrated the ups and downs of managing an older woman with booze while Phyllis listened from downstairs. She'll give me anything, he boasted. Vivian had signed the papers and now they owned the waterfront house together. Chris was a millionaire. Vivian would do what he asked if he nagged her, or sometimes he did other things until she gave in with a shrug. He fed her alcohol and she staggered around a little but mostly stayed in bed and he lived his life. He invited his brother to come down to Florida and find an old lady, as though this sick arrangement were a laudable career.

That evening, Phyllis sat out back on a lawn chair next to her stuporous friend and began to discuss what she'd heard. She pushed into it but had trouble getting Vivian's attention. Vivian was bemused. What was this about? Yes, it was true, he did own half the house. Phyllis wanted to get all the girls together and talk about Vivian and Chris; an intervention was what she had in mind. The girls would find the right solution. It would be okay.

Solution for what?

Vivian, you'll have to stop. You know what I mean. There are lovely places to go.

Vivian's eyes narrowed and Phyllis understood immediately, but it was too late to pull her words back. Vivian didn't want to hear about rehab and her boyfriend's evil designs. She wanted to go back inside for a drink.

The following morning, Chris came up the stairs with the fury of a man about to lose everything he had worked for. He shoved open Phyllis's unlocked door and he grabbed her arm and pulled her out of bed. He held her by the shoulders, real close, shouting and spraying saliva. He wouldn't let her get dressed or grab her clothes. He chased her down the stairs to her car. She was crying and his rank smell was on her face. Her shoulder hurt and Chris was cursing her and smacking the closed car window with the heel of his palm.

She didn't know where to go. Maybe drive to Jim if that woman was off with her kids. Tell Jim what had happened. Phyllis stopped and called him collect from a phone booth. Mara picked up the phone. Jim wasn't home. Click. She wasn't letting Phyllis get through. This was not acceptable. She'd have to talk with Jim about it.

Chris must have become nervous about keeping Phyllis's things, afraid she would call the police. A couple of hours after Phyllis drove off he phoned Jim and said he was putting her clothes out on the lawn, Jim could come and get them or they would go into the garbage the following morning. It meant Jim would have to drive an hour to Miami fighting the traffic, and he had plans with Mara and the kids. It would ruin their day. Mara was disgusted, which always put him on edge. But he decided he'd better go.

Jim picked his wife's clothes up from the lawn; a few soiled underthings were in the bushes, and he stuffed them into garbage bags that he had in the car, a pathetic situation. Then the two men walked upstairs to the little storage room where she had lived and Jim collected the two Monet prints. Chris never said a word, but he looked on with a supercilious expression. Jim thought, even a few years earlier he would have beaten this guy to a pulp, left him quivering on the lawn. But now he didn't dare. Everything in his life was hanging. He just wanted to get back to Mara and what was left of the evening. Jim was planning to give everything to Phyllis when she next called him—that's what he told me two weeks later when I arrived in Florida.

After driving aimlessly, Phyllis had stopped by a park where she and Jim had gone Rollerblading on weekends. It was a beautiful cool spot bordered on one side by the waterway. She sat inside the car watching the boats pass on a Sunday afternoon, tried to collect herself. She was barefoot and wearing only a black slip. She recalled that Jim had said she looked lovely in that slip.

A few hours later, she drove to the house of another girlfriend. Phyllis stood outside Janice's door wearing next to nothing, but she still talked in her pleasant dreamy way. She told Janice she needed to stay for a while to get back on her feet. She was having a hard time. She tried to say what she had learned about Chris and Vivian, but Janice raised her hand. Not now, not the right time to talk. Phyllis needed some place to catch her breath, just for a few days. Janice looked at her feet. It wasn't a good time for her, she said as though she were having issues with someone who was waiting inside.

Phyllis nodded. I understand.

Wait a minute, Janice said, and soon came back to the door holding jeans, a blue work shirt, and some old running shoes. She kissed Phyllis on the cheek and closed the door.

None of the girls would have her—Phyllis was frozen out. Vivian was making calls to each of her friends and complaining that Phyllis had made trouble in her life with Chris. He was feeling depressed because they had invited Phyllis into their home and she'd stabbed him in the back with lies. Phyllis was making trouble because she had been jilted by her husband.

Phyllis waited three days before calling Jim again. She hated asking him. Because he and Mara lived in a tiny house with two kids. Phyllis hated to impose. Also, it scared her that he might say no. But she didn't have any money, besides a few dollars in change. She was sleeping in the little car in a parking lot behind the Publix near her old apartment. Jim was sympathetic, but he didn't invite her to come by. There wasn't enough room. He wanted to, he said, but Mara wouldn't understand. We're trying to make a new life; you can understand that, Phyllis. How would it be for her if you were in my house, sleeping one room away? Jim leavened this tough news with the possibility of their intimacy; the chance was still alive to him. She could imagine his grin and she answered with her own smile. There had been so many sweet embraces. Jim always gave with one hand even while slipping in the dagger. And he always left wiggle room for returning home. Don't you worry, he said to her. Soon he'd have money; not too much longer and he would be able to help out and she'd be okay, more than okay.

Then he cleared his throat and he told her about the phone call from Chris. She shouldn't be concerned; Jim had driven over and packed her clothes into plastic bags. He would meet her someplace and bring them and he'd try to scrounge together a few dollars. The crazy son of a bitch had strewn her clothes across the yard. Jim had found some of her underwear in the bushes. What a bastard. Jim had also brought home the paintings, as he called them, but when he hadn't heard from her he took them to a gallery in South Beach.

Phyllis understood now, and the rest of what he said didn't matter.

They were beautiful, she managed to get out the words. From our lives, I was trying to keep them, trying to . . .

She cried pitifully and Jim said he was sorry. He needed the money to feed his kids and pay the rent. There was nothing else to do.

What else could I do, Phyllis?

Jim, how could you? How could you? They were mine. All that I had left.

He insisted the paintings were his more than hers. He had selected them twenty-five years ago. Don't you remember, Phyllis?

You had no right, no right at all, Jim.

Anyhow, what do you want me to do about it now? They're gone. I can't get them back.

She cried bitterly. She might have rented a little place with the money. Now she had nothing.

You had no right, Jim. I've given you everything and you did this.

She had forgiven him for the years in Brazil. She didn't say that, but she was thinking it. She had taken him back and healed him.

You had no right, Jim.

They kept going back and forth like this, Jim insisting the paintings were his. He needed the money to keep a roof over their heads. They were tugging back and forth about whose they were. She kept putting quarters into the phone until they were all gone. Then she took a deep breath and said she forgave him. Jim was her only chance. He was all she had left. She had nothing else but his promises. You wanted them so badly. Maybe it was for the best that you took them, she said firmly.

17.

Jim was boxed in between Mara's impatience and Phyllis, who tormented him, especially in his dreams, where he couldn't shut her out. And he had to deal with me. I asked him, What happened then? What happened next? He asked me, What should I do about Mara? Who should I trust? He and I were tuned to different channels. For years I had enjoyed my friend's salon of extravagant stories and schemes with its constant flow of needy glad-handing recruits and pompous up lines. My visits to Miami had been like dipping back into childhood. Really, they were priceless. I'm sure that Jim thrived on my admiration, particularly as he had grown older and was mainly chasing success. The girl had changed everything. Yet it would come to me in painful spurts that Jim and I could put it back together again.

One afternoon we were able to get away from her for a few hours. He and I pulled out of their driveway with its tragic pile of cheap bikes and battered plastic toys leaning against the flaking stucco wall of their bungalow. We were escaping like kids—Let's get the hell out of here. We drove nearly an hour to the south end of

South Beach and pulled up to the Blue Moon, our favorite spot for drinking and sharing daydreams.

We were both thinking about old times here, the adventures we had plotted. Jim had always ordered Pellegrino to start while I declined and asked for regular ice water. We would watch the yachts powering offshore from Government Cut and indulged in a favorite fantasy about the sixty-foot sport-fishing boat we were going to design and build. He would get rid of his trawler yacht, which was slow and ungainly for fishing. For years it had sat beneath his condo on Brickell Avenue, a prop for his selling more than a real boat. But someday soon he and I would ride the blue swells together on the great bridge of our new boat and travel to unexplored islands. We could taste these thrilling days trolling our baits in virgin waters. More than once, I admitted I would never have the money for such a splendid craft, but Jim insisted that he would put up my share and make me an equal partner because we were buddies. Then we'd have a spirited argument about the configuration of the staterooms and the color scheme. I always picked up the lunch tab while Jim stared out the window, considering the bigger picture.

Jim and I tipped glasses—maybe he could still get away from her; that's what I was toasting. She never let him out of her sight. He needed her permission to go out for the paper. Really, it disgusted me. I didn't want to drive him back to their dump in Homestead. But Jim pushed away from the table: it was time to go home so Mara wouldn't get nervous. Please, she turned him into an old house pet. I wanted to keep him here, at the Blue Moon, where the big picture still seemed possible, so I launched into our version of confessing the truth. The game was a legacy from my youth, when friendship and sharing intimacies were more urgently important to me than anything else. Jim and I had played more than a few times in the early years of our friendship but not once since he'd taken up with Mara. If either of us prompted the other with a serious question, the other had to answer honestly—it was a test of our fidelity and a kind of dare—putting aside any and all jockeying for advantage, all hype and salesmanship, and in my case, considerable inhibitions to respond fully with the truth.

The question jumped from my mouth like a living thing. Jim, did you ever kill someone?

He looked at me with a little smile and I leaned in close. Come on, it's just the two of us. . . . Although it wasn't just the two of us. The restaurant was packed, elbow to elbow.

I know you had a bad time in Brazil. There were different rules in the jungle.

He nodded, yes.

Yes, what? Did you ever put a gun to a man's head? Or maybe you used a knife? I had a sense for the couple next to us leaning our way, listening while they ate. But I was feeling high from drinking beer and saying these reckless words. I was way out in front. He could have laughed in my face.

Did you? And then maybe you walked back into your normal salesman's life again . . . like nothing important had happened. . . . You have to answer my question.

He nodded yes to this, slowly, and one side of his face tightened like leather. It made me nervous and a little giddy.

You killed a man? A woman?

I was whispering way too loud, making a mess, but I couldn't take my eyes off him, because now Jim had raised both hands and put them gently around his throat as though he were adjusting a scarf and then he began tightening it around his throat. He held this pose for a few seconds in the busy restaurant.

18.

With jarring frequency Marvin Gesler would hear about the grand opening of another pyramid operation in western Canada. Almost always they were virtual clones, a big store with a circus tent outside.

Marvin's bold dream-selling enterprise that even the great Lenny Bruce had lauded for originality was becoming common fare. The final insult came with news that copycat operations were flourishing in Detroit and Columbus. Marvin had pushed to open in the States, but Jim had been concerned about being undercapitalized. Now there was competition on all sides and savvy customers were traveling for better deals.

In the last disheartening months, before they put up the real estate for sale, Marvin was frantic, sending Jim racing to a distant store or calling him back hundreds of miles because he needed to have dinner and a talk. Jim was never at home, and if he even mentioned driving to the farm to visit Ava, Marvin flew off the handle. He couldn't accept that Jim had a retreat that gave him pleasure.

Marvin was beset by an urgency that seemed pointless and chaotic. His business musings were replaced by gluttony and lusty thoughts. He asked Jim to introduce him to girls. This seemed laughable and grotesque, but once Marvin seized upon an idea he wouldn't let it go—he asked Jim compulsively. Whenever Marvin was around any good-looking woman, he wanted to touch her. He didn't accept normal social limitations. He didn't understand how he looked. He knew what he felt. Whatever Marvin coveted was essential and irresistible, and particularly now when he was afflicted. He attempted awkward lurching seductions. Jim watched at a late-afternoon office party while Marvin cornered one of the secretaries, a twenty-year-old redhead with freckles and a zesty laugh. He lumbered ahead like an old wrestler. He felt her breasts and began kissing her neck. He was the president of the company and his power conferred lurid appeal along with dread.

Jim wondered where all of this would lead. As the business unraveled, alternative lifestyles came into his mind. He enjoyed a stolen day or two with Ava. He felt the itch to move on to something new.

But at the same time, Jim recognized his limitations. He could close a deal with the best or he could torque up the energy in a lazy room. Jim could even inspire men's lives, but Marvin was a creative force. Jim never lost sight of this, and their relationship had a daunting and persisting autonomy. Marvin was profane, but Jim worried that on his own he would be banal. Marvin could bestow the wealth of Solomon. Think about it. How much would you be willing to give a man who could give you many millions in return? This bribe was at the center of their lengthy partnership.

It was sealed with a nod that Jim would find Marvin women. Marvin wanted this from Jim as if it were a key clause in a new contract. Jim had to digest this new responsibility and decided, finally, that helping Marvin with girls would be hardly different from feeding him or listening to his rants. It might even be amusing and it would get Marvin off his back. With their tacit agreement Marvin felt greatly relieved and was able to close one door a little and open another.

The partners spent a week driving cross-country brainstorming. Jim's great spirit for the road inspired Marvin, who was soon holding forth on money schemes and sports minutiae. The world just looked brighter with Jim at the wheel driving toward unnamed pleasures. Marvin's ideas were swelling all through him again as if someone big had pulled the switch. He kept coming back to franchising, which was still in its adolescence in Canada. Put a man deep in debt, he said to Jim, and he is more likely to make you money. Marvin walked into roadside restaurants with a new bounce and jauntiness that was a little silly for a man of his heft, but he didn't care. He had emerged from defeat with unexpected optimism.

The opportunity to go into an entirely new venture spurred Marvin into a flow as if all his myriad schemes were linked to a common line of reason; the particular commodity or service hardly mattered. He said as much. Muffins, credit cards, weight loss clinics—they'd all suffice. In this respect, why was business any different from music or art? Whether a master artist rendered a barn or a smiling woman, the painting would still have his energy, his stamp. They would all work; virtually any business idea could work. This made sense to Jim, although he found it curious that his partner was making references to music and painting.

Marvin was content to talk endlessly. He was stirred by his ever-shifting notions and abstruse refinements. One fine October afternoon, they were on a country road about a hundred miles north of Toronto, passing herds of long-haired black and white cows, meadows bordered by little forests of rust colors that filled Jim with a restless feeling. Six years earlier, heading west along this road for a thousand miles, Jim had sold Bibles and then months later he'd come back and sold the same farmers waterless cookware. He knew all the turns and knolls and the tired smiles and wary hesitations of a thousand housewives. In his new Cadillac Jim had delivered the tonic for bleak lives. He had silver spoons and stories to stir desolate souls; sometimes passion was key, but just as often he aroused them with the sorrow of our passing lives. To succeed, Jim needed to crawl into hearts, which wasn't hard, because he was moved by his customers. Jim really wanted to connect and he believed that he was delivering the goods, whatever the product. He loved each of them, if only until he walked out the door. Marvin didn't understand the puzzle of Jim's selling because he mainly cared about ideas, making profits, and hoarding money.

They were on the top of a hill, just south of the town of Bracebridge. Ahead was a vista of lush farming territory that stretched west and north for thousands of miles. And then on the downside of the hill Marvin began pointing at something and his voice was sharp as a fisherman spotting the big school. That's it, Jim, that's it over there.

What are you looking at? Jim answered. It was just more farm country. Jim drove down the road a quarter mile until it angled closer to a small dairy farm. Then he stopped the car.

Marvin was gazing across the grain field. He stepped outside the white convertible and stood against a barbwire fence pointing toward a covey of structures, including a lovely red gambrel barn, a classic.

Is it the barn?

No, no, look at the one with a domed roof. Marvin was pointing at some kind of old storage shed fashioned from crumpled rusty metal like a giant inflated accordion lying on its flat ends.

What is that?

Never saw one before in Canada, Marvin answered. There are some in the States, shipped there from Europe after the war. Marvin was admiring this shed or shanty that was squat and unsightly and so out of place in this timeless Edward Hopper farm vista that it suggested Marvin himself standing in a room of handsome, understated people.

Jim, that's a gold mine, he said. That's so much money over there you couldn't spend it in six lifetimes. Most anyone would have taken this for empty blather except Marvin was entranced, so Jim stared at the ungainly building and he strained to imagine the magic that Marvin was seeing. But all Jim saw was a big piece of junk.

On the drive back to Toronto, Marvin gave Jim a short history of these unusual structures. At the onset of the Second World War the U.S. Navy anticipated mammoth problems creating shelter for troops and the wounded and storing untold amounts of ammunition, food, and supplies. They needed a design for an inexpensive, lightweight, portable building that could be constructed rapidly by untrained people. The navy took the problem to the Fuller Construction Company in Quonset Point, Rhode Island, and within sixty days two very smart engineers had designed a structure in which ribbed galvanized steel sheathing was placed over a frame of steel arches. The whole thing came together with self-tapping screws. It was so simple to put together that virtually anyone could do it. The buildings, called Quonset huts, could be erected on a concrete base or even a plywood floor. By the end of the war more than 170,000 of them had been produced. But the design itself proved to be far more durable than anyone had imagined. The components worked in unison, making them virtually indestructible. The domed roofs did not collapse beneath the weight of a blizzard of snow or the pounding winds of hurricanes.

Marvin recognized that, despite their homely appearance, staunch inexpensive buildings had a tremendous market in rural Canada, particularly for farmers. Gesler Sheds—he named the new company on the spot—would be perfect for storing grain, machinery, and livestock, but really they could be used for just about anything. They could be insulated and partitioned into rooms. You could use them for houses, churches, or hockey rings. They went up like giant Tinkertoys. A man and his wife could put one together in an eight-hour day.

Marvin envisioned millions of his squat sheds changing the face of Canada.

19.

Ava offered the great comedian respite and a degree of pleasure he could not have imagined, but Lenny Bruce couldn't shake off his demons. By the time she met him, pain and degradation had taken over his life. When Lenny was feeling confident about Ava he wanted to show her the whole misery. It was a test. Several times he pressed her to come to his hotel room in Montreal, although she was uneasy about these visits. The sparse room seemed to resonate with bad encounters.

One night he hadn't bothered to hide his works—he wanted her to see—and she tried to avert her eyes. He wanted her to try smack. He'd made the suggestion before, but that's where Ava drew the line. He badgered her. He took her hand and tried to pull her balking like a mule into the bathroom. Okay, okay, then watch me, at least. Lenny's voice turned unctuous and pleading: Honey liked to watch. It turned her on. Lenny imitated pumping the syringe in and out as though it were sex. Ava didn't know whether to run or stay. She followed him like a ghost.

Sitting on the toilet in his underpants, he looked sickly thin, and his skin was green and pasty in the dim fluorescent light. He was frantically jabbing his callused veins for a hit. She turned away trying not to gag. Just give it a chance, he whined, looking back over his shoulder. Lenny was so out of whack—how could he think she would like this? Afterwards, there was blood spattered on the tile floor. His lips were turning blue and the needle was still hanging from his vein. Ava pulled it out. She threw some towels down on the blood while he stumbled into the bedroom.

She wanted to drive back to the farm, but Ava waited until he came around. He didn't want her to go. It was too late to drive thirty miles. And Lenny was pining for her as though she were his mother and his lost wife, and all of his regret. He was so raw and pathetic, no holding back. Manic bursts of ideas came out, tears welling up, maybe for his junkie wife wandering the streets. Ava hadn't seen him like this. Whole dialogues and different voices came out of Lenny, shards of old routines, and she laughed and cried, but she couldn't touch him. Then he drifted off, nodding to dreamy jazz. He started humming, but she didn't recognize the tune. Do you get it, baby? he whispered hoarsely. Do you get it? Do you get it? She wasn't sure. Do you love me? He opened his eyes a little and tried to find her. Do you really love me? She nodded sadly. He'd put the whole mess on the table. His eyes were set way back in dark tunnels. One of them wasn't focusing and the whole right side of Lenny's face was slack. He seemed to be asking, Can you handle this?

Okay, not forever. Not forever, he said. Nothing is forever. Promise when I come back from Los Angeles you'll be my girl. Promise that.

She looked back at him and said simply, I promise, but she was thinking.

I know. I know, he said, becoming agitated about what he'd done. He wanted to reach across to her. He couldn't find her in the dark. Lenny was slurring his words. It was Stan Getz, he said.

What?

We'll get married. We'll make a baby. What you say?

She shook her head.

We'll make a baby. Lenny couldn't back off, though all this was too much for her.

A baby. Ava was holding her hands against her ears. Lenny, don't talk about such things. I'm a married lady.

Don't tell me. Don't tell me, he said all red in the face. The veins in his neck were bulging. Don't decide what you won't do with me, okay? Okay? We'll see. We'll see what happens with us.

Two days later, Lenny Bruce was back in Los Angeles, thinking of Ava. She was always in his mind and he couldn't work or even make his phone calls. For the first time in three years, he was scheduled to appear on *The Tonight Show,* but it didn't seem important. He had a trial coming up, but when his lawyer called to talk strategy Lenny couldn't follow the arguments. He was scribbling about Ava in his notebooks. He felt such remorse at pushing her to watch. It was pitiful. Lenny knew he was wretched and couldn't help himself. She had become his whole world, his only chance. He thought of her framed against a doorway of the farmhouse, her face touched by a shadow of sadness, her features flushed and gathered around a darkness so charming and sublime that it was burning him up. The expression of Ava's lostness and hurting possessed Lenny and he couldn't help himself; he was back on a plane to Montreal, flying to her. He had to see her, talk to her. He had to tell her all his ideas, convince her to stay with him. He wouldn't take no.

20.

Gesler Sheds was the most extravagant and enduring expression of Marvin's profuse genius. By the spring of 1966 Marvin had sold the retail stores and put most of the money into constructing the first of four mammoth sheet-metal factories, altogether nearly two million square feet of manufacturing space. The partners would in fact change the face of Canada's farming landscape, and beyond that they would rapidly transform the manner and upside potential of agricultural storage throughout a dozen arid countries in Africa and the Middle East.

At this most prolific time in Jim's life, he didn't know anything about Ava and Lenny Bruce. Jim first learned about their affair nearly four decades later, when he and Ava met for a whimsical and affectionate evening in San Diego. (Some of this history came directly from Ava, during our visit, but many details I discovered myself at the Princeton University Library, where Lenny Bruce's notes and journals are archived. There were nearly a hundred fervent handwritten pages about Jim's wife and the meaning of love as seen through the comedian's dark and improbable lens.) Jim readily acknowledged to me that if he'd known about them in 1966 it wouldn't have mattered very much. He was working fifteen-hour days assembling and training a national sales team and looking after Marvin. He didn't have the time to placate his wife with her considerable sorrows. Jim was racing for glory and the dreams of his father. But I could imagine my friend pausing a beat to pawn his wife off to the great comedian, absolving guilt with his extravagant salesman's largess. Jim was always working the angles.

It was also in the spring of 1966 that Ava had made her decision to move out to California and become Lenny Bruce's second wife. She was biding her time for the right moment to tell her husband. She still cared for Jim, but he was no longer in the front row of her concerns and dreams.

Ava hadn't yet told Lenny she was two months' pregnant with his baby. It felt exciting to be sitting on so much power. She imagined his ecstasy and the way his life would change overnight. He hadn't visited Canada for a month, but they talked nearly every day. She didn't want to tell him on the phone. She found it pleasant holding back the news.

Ironically, Lenny Bruce was never so highly revered as a performer as during this period when he was holed up in his California house, not working a day, because the clubs wouldn't hire him. Following his second LA trial more than eighty prominent figures, including theologians, scientists, entertainers, novelists, playwrights, and critics, a virtual Who's Who of American intelligentsia, had signed a public protest against his legal persecutions. They described Lenny as a "performer in the field of social satire in the tradition of Swift, Rabelais, and Twain." Many cultural luminaries wrote letters to Lenny ruing his suffering and extolling his art. For the most part he didn't answer this correspondence.

Lenny was dead broke from not having any income and paying lawyers for his frequent court appearances. Since curtailing his visits to Ava, he had stopped taking care of himself. He was surviving on junk food, diet soda, smack, methedrine, uppers to study, and downers to sleep for an hour or two. Lenny was paranoid about the police breaking into his Hollywood home and taking his drugs from the medicine cabinet, so he paced his rooms with syringes, vials, and pills jiggling in his pockets. He was putting on weight and his ankles and feet were achy and swollen with edema.

Nonetheless, Lenny harbored the hope of winning back his reputation in the courts and salvaging his career with something new and bold. For a few hours in the morning he studied law books, listened to tapes of his past trials, or sometimes jotted ideas for routines or notes about Ava. Their white-hot love affair had been more obsessive and delicious than any man could imagine, but winning Ava's commitment had changed the experience almost overnight. Lenny wrote in his notebook that it was a relief not to feel such wrenching desire. This huge love had been a distraction and now he felt drawn back to his old habits, and if they shortened his days on earth they also brought back his artistic hunger. An old friend of Lenny's, television pioneer Steve Allen, was guest hosting for Johnny Carson on *The Tonight Show* and had invited Lenny to make an appearance. Lenny was looking forward to this first gig in months.

He began writing pages about romantic love with the notion of developing ideas into a book or perhaps a screenplay. Ava would be the gorgeous centerpiece while Jim and Marvin's flashy business hoax would be the metaphor for critiquing an unethical economic and legal system that pillaged men's lives. "Ugliness and beauty, who can tell?" Lenny wrote cryptically in one of his journals.

While Ava was dreaming about a new house and a baby in Hollywood, Lenny was turning her over in his mind, examining his attraction and doubts as closely as he examined her nude body when they were together on the farm. He still got horny when he thought of her arms, her neck and breasts, but it bothered Lenny that he cared so much about the way she looked. If she weren't a stunning beauty in the manner of his ex-wife, maybe he wouldn't like her at all. It was hard to gauge the wisdom of an exceptionally beautiful woman like Ava. Probably he loved her because she made him feel young and alive. His little black books had pages of such musings. Perhaps it wasn't Ava he loved but an image he'd created? Maybe she was hardly more than the projection of his desire. Lenny became obsessed with this idea that Ava lived in his head and that loving her was mostly loving himself. She was just handy.

Lenny was thinking about these ideas incessantly. What is love? he asked Ava on the phone after sharing some thoughts about the new project. Lenny's mind was filled with the taped sounds of her life, her darkest urges and needs. He thought of her more now as his model and muse than a lover and he wanted to share each bratty caustic irony, except her deep silence stopped him short. The question of her value apart from physical beauty had tortured Ava ever since she realized that first-place trophies in beauty pageants were the way to her father's heart. But more immediately, she was on the verge of leaving her husband to come to Lenny. She wasn't feeling like a muse. She was nauseous in the morning, pregnant with his son, not that Lenny knew this. Ava was confused and upset.

Lenny tried to mask his mistake with fast talk and gaudy promises. But he got off the line feeling disgusted and out of control. Then, for a moment, he saw it clearly: they were both scrambling to grab onto something, two big losers. He loved her, or he needed her, what did it matter? She'd wanted to come to him and he'd tortured her with insipid conjectures. He wanted to touch her, call her back, explain everything, but he was too sick and weak. He was trapped in a bottle. He tried to pardon himself with junkie excuses: he couldn't help himself; he'd call her back later. He went in the bathroom and took out the stuff. He watched himself grinning into the mirror.

Ava was late turning on *The Tonight Show* and host Steve Allen was nearly finished with his introduction. . . . he's more than a comedian; Lenny Bruce comments on the world with the genius of a philosopher. Here he is, the great Lenny Bruce. . . .

When Ava saw him on the grainy little black-and-white television her heart began flapping in her chest. She had no idea he would be on. Lenny was seated on a stool, twenty pounds heavier than the last time he visited Canada. By the way, I'm not proud that I'm divorced, he began hesitantly, as though trying to fathom the routine. Lenny's eyes were swollen and spooky and one of them hardly opened. Ava knew the look. It's a failure, you know, and it's a hang-up, being divorced. Especially if you're on the road. He spoke slowly, mumbling his words, occasionally spitting one out like a bad seed. But once the material caught hold, Lenny smiled to himself and delivered the routine in a restless, searching manner all the more affecting for his obvious discomfort.

Society has made up a lot of dirty words that actually hurt me as an individual. Now, I'm on the road, and it's three o'clock in the morning, and I meet a girl, and I like her. Supposing I just have a record I wanted to hear, or I have a good painting, an original Degas, and I want to relate to her, just talk to her. There's no lust, no carnal image there. But because where I live is a dirty word—at three in the morning—I can't say to her, Would you come to my hotel? 'Cause "hotel" is a dirty word at 3:00 A.M. Not the next day at two o'clock in the afternoon when the Kiwanis meet there, though—then "hotel" is clean. But at three in the morning . . .

So you start to think. You know you can't say "hotel" to a chick, so you try to think of what won't offend. What is a clean word to society? "Trailer." Trailers are hunting and fishing and outdoors. You tell a chick, Hey, you wanna come to my trailer? there's nothing dirty in that. Okay, uh, where is it? "Trailer" is clean and so she'd be happy to come there.

I met a chick I really dig; I'm crazy about her. I met her in a circus tent where she tries to entice guys to buy coupons with her looks; because she's really stacked, everyone wants to touch her. Me too. Is that dirty or clean? Maybe it's dirty, but it seems clean to me. She's in this tent selling coupons. Buy a coupon and you get a dream. An expense-paid trip to the Caribbean. Or money for the rest of your life. They sell big dreams in the circus tent. People are spending hundreds for coupons that are probably worthless, unless a dream is worth something. Apparently it is, because I told this lady I loved her, right there in the tent, and she laughed at me. He must be a dirty old man, says he loves me in a tent. He wants it. He must be dirty.

My girl is so beautiful, reminds me of my ex-wife. Maybe that's bad, to fall for someone because she reminds you of someone else. I'm not sure if it's good or bad.

Anyhow, she lets me visit her on the farm, whenever her old man is away, which is probably wrong. But it feels right. I call her place the Sad Palace. It's sad because this chick, she's so beautiful and stacked, she thinks she's ugly. The Sad Palace turns things upside down. My girl can't stand her arms, her legs and breasts, as if someone told her they are dirty. They are beautiful. Legs and breasts aren't dirty. I always tell that to judges when they haul me into court for obscenity. How can legs and breasts be dirty, c'mon! That's what the farm does to her, confuses ugly and beautiful. In the Sad Palace, beautiful is ugly and ugly is beautiful. She looks out the window at the trees and thinks the view is ugly. This place makes you wonder, What is dirty? What is clean? Maybe what you think is dirty, Steve, is different from what I think. I keep saying that to the judges. Maybe what's dirty for you is clean for me.

Ten days later, Lenny called Ava on the phone and was just barely coherent. He said that his ex-wife, Honey, came over to the house and they shot up together, very strong shit; he collapsed on the floor.

Ava missed some of the words, but Honey was all through it. Honey was worried he might die. She couldn't get him standing. He was too heavy. Honey and a friend brought him around by holding ice cubes against his balls and then they forced him to drink coffee and walk around the pool. Honey fed him uppers so he wouldn't fall asleep. She said she wouldn't do smack with him anymore because she couldn't lift him up, he was too heavy.

Lenny insisted he was okay. He didn't sound okay. He was back seeing his wife. Ava told him then, blurted it out that she was pregnant with his child. Lenny, do you hear me? I'm having a baby, your baby. You wanted this baby. You hear me? His answer was incomprehensible. Then she heard a shuffling sound and he was off the line. She tried to dial back, but no one picked up. She didn't know anyone in Lenny's California life to dial. She was shut out. There is nothing about this last conversation in Lenny's notebooks. There is no telling whether he understood what she was saying about the baby.

Three days later, Ava was in the kitchen having a sandwich when she heard on the radio that Lenny Bruce had died of an overdose in his Hollywood home.

21.

Nine months had passed since Mara had introduced herself to Jim at a recruiting meeting in Israel. They were seated on a torn sofa that smelled like old dogs. She was now his wife. They had taken their vows in a civil ceremony with two witnesses selected at random from a small group of people milling around.

Mara was absently turning through yesterday's newspaper and glancing out the window at her kids playing in the backyard near the rusty swings. He called her name, but she didn't answer. He waved at her playfully, hoping for a smile. Jim sat back and stared out the window at the kids.

He couldn't sell this one small woman who had become his wife. He couldn't convince her that things would turn his way again. He couldn't make Mara believe he would lose twenty pounds or that he would have the check next week from Peter—his youngest brother occasionally sent Jim a check for thirty or fifty dollars—and they would be able to go out to an Italian dinner in the mall. She had a resistance, a thickness he could not penetrate; perhaps it was petulance or the arrogance of youth. He couldn't make his words stick. He couldn't close it.

Jim's focus had narrowed to her smallest impulses and re-
sponses. All his selling had become devoted to currying her favor.
When Mara was happy and especially if he made a remark that
captured her interest or made her smile, he felt as if something
very large had broken his way. Immediately he wanted to build
upon it, make it forever. If she made a caustic remark or turned off
to him completely—she had been doing this more lately—he felt
like a spurned adolescent. He rarely thought about his daughter or
his ninety-five-year-old mom, who was still living in Canada in the
house he had bought for her in 1975. He tried to squeeze Phyllis
from his mind, although she had saved him from many jams and
shared his aspirations for more than two decades of marriage. They
had lived in spectacular homes and shared thousands of delicious
meals. Now Jim didn't know where she was sleeping or eating or
whether she was eating at all. He wasn't even curious—this was
proof, he reasoned, that Phyllis was no longer alive to him and hadn't
been for some time. This was his justification, his righteousness.
Mara was living in his skin. She was lurking behind every miscel-
laneous thought.

Trying to find work seemed pointless. Who would want to hire
an old man? Also, the history he was narrating trivialized the sorts
of jobs that might be possible. Jim had once tamed the jungle. How
could he take a job in a shoe store? Even the Wow Card seemed
pitiful. Jim endeavored to please her with yachts, trophy homes,
new offices, business finesses, even Marvin's sordid love life; he
served the past up to this petite woman he did not understand very
well.

Of course anyone could see that she was drawn to her ex-
husband. There was unfinished business between them, also something raw that Jim could not compete against. Some afternoons
when she went off with her kids she didn't answer her cell phone
for hours. Jim felt desperate and weak; his heart fluttered. But later
that night, or the next day, she leaned back his way, peeled away

her fierceness. She said to him, I like to make you happy, Jim, and he smiled like a grateful boy. Mara touched his face and he shivered. Perhaps at such moments she saw her own father, whom she had adored. She'd lost him less than a year before she came from Israel to live with Jim. He could accept this. A salesman worms his way in from any angle.

And their passion was a magical potion. It left him feeling alive and young, absurdly young, and giddy with hope. He didn't wash himself afterwards so he'd remember their smell when she drifted away again. He liked to think about her little sounds, most of all her urgency. No one could pretend like this, he said to me a dozen times when she was out of the house and he didn't want to think where. Maybe he could still beat it back, whatever was taking her.

Making love and fleecing each other—that *was* the deal, but Jim didn't understand or couldn't accept it. He pressed for a longer, bigger contract. He rolled out his best of times like my dad's aging salesmen friends who had squeezed out the last drops of glory in shabby Jewish delis and cheap hotels in Miami Beach. He regaled her with opulent stories (as he had once filled Ava's life with every gift under the sun), although it occurred to him that someday Mara would know all of them and they'd be looking at each other in these terrible rooms with the two kids pestering them in Hebrew like hungry chickens. Not yet.

Jim's voice was a little reedy. He wasn't feeling energetic, but he wanted to capture her attention. Mara, dear, I lived like a king. Jim sometimes forgot the names of his children, but he could envision every detail of the magnificent house he had built on the lake. Mara, he repeated gently, until she looked up. He paid $5 million for the property alone, forty-eight acres of rolling land that narrowed to a peninsula with stretches of sandy beach. That's where he and Ava built the main house for an additional $2 million and more. What did it matter?

Jim had insisted on ten-foot ceilings with broad antique beams, and Ava nervously turned through a dozen magazines and eventually settled on custom knotty alder cabinetry to go with limestone flooring and Brazilian granite counters. A barge hauled in huge rectangular stones to make a picturesque seawall. But the main house was angled out over the seawall so that you could not see it from the rooms.

Every Friday, unless he was traveling, Jim brought home a large brown paper bag with their spending money, fifteen thousand, some weeks thirty thousand in cash, play money. Jim urged Ava to buy things for herself, for the house or for their son, Michael (the strange boy was her secret whom she tended like a precious garden), but she couldn't keep up the pace. She tried but found it exhausting to spend all the cash Jim brought home. Whatever they couldn't use immediately he stashed in a safe.

Winter nights, the lake raged like the stormy Atlantic. They ate caviar and sipped Merlot pretending they were on the bridge of a liner. In July and August, it was mostly calm and the water lapped against the retractable dock, with Jim's two Chris-Craft speedboats at rest in the shade of the house. In the evening light the property was exquisitely restful, like a Wordsworth memory. On the hill behind the house, a small herd of Irish sheep grazed. He could still smell the bloom of Ava's cut flowers in the summer. He could almost place all of it in Mara's arms, almost.

Mara was more attentive when he described things she could imagine, the beauty creams and perfumes, cooking aids, exercise equipment, cashmere sweaters, hunting jackets, and despite the sweltering heat of August in Florida, Ava's lustrous fur coat appealed to Mara, as well. But as Jim grew increasingly more wealthy and flagrant in his buying for Ava, Mara lost her focus. He had lived so far beyond her petit bourgeois dreams. Mara could barely imagine Jim's wealthy past and it made her feel agitated and angry she was missing her only big chance in life. Her youth would be gone in a minute while she was living with an old man in a house wreck.

Why should she care about Ava's third-floor penthouse studio that Jim had built lavishly for her new arty life with a marble fireplace and a golden travertine floor to match their alder kitchen cabinetry, or the twin greenhouses, and why the hell did he need Irish sheep? Now, while Jim was waiting around for things to break his way, the four of them were eating chicken wings unless they splurged for burgers at McDonald's. Jim was sweating each nickel. You promised me gymnastic lessons for the boy, she repeated bitterly every few days. You promised me, Jim.

Nineteen-seventy was a banner year. Grain prices were up and farmers had capital to buy machinery and they needed storage. Jim and Marvin were planning a fourth plant to service the western provinces. Mara, please look at me when I'm talking. He could still taste success. He wanted to surprise her with the little white BMW she dreamed about. The best had been effortless for Jim; just drive to the dealership and write a check. Jim believed that money could buy love or at least something close enough. The money washed back and forth through time; it was confusing for him. Every week they could have thrown thousands off their balcony into the waves and it wouldn't have mattered. If only he could shower Mara with toys, she wouldn't leave him.

No good. Desperation is pathetic in a salesman. Jim had seen the play in New York in 1975 with George C. Scott playing Willie Loman. He cried throughout the last act. Walk away from the deal, but never plead: he taught this rule to every one of his men. Except he was in a terrible position now, boxed in by old age and poverty with no redress. Did she care about him anymore? This question raged within him. Since their marriage, something had changed, that's for sure. Probably had to do with her ex-husband living nearby. Jim could feel her disgust as if he'd suddenly turned old, with varicose legs and a hanging belly. He shuddered, piled on the high life. More and more cash had accumulated in the safe in Jim's study. He started betting on football games; fifty thousand each weekend, soon it was a hundred thousand. Ava was so beautiful while she tried to save herself, no more makeup and sexy dresses, peeling down to find the truth, and men yearned for her all the more; she was the dream of every man. Jim's brown bags of money only deepened her confusion and sorrow. She began to collect fine art. She was slow, painfully slow, making her choices, and this irritated Jim.

Many nights there were phone calls from Israel. When Mara spoke in Hebrew her voice turned harsh and even ruthless. Shimon, her ex-husband, continued stopping by at least twice each week. The children were gleeful with their dad in the house. Jim tried to be cordial or matter-of-fact around the younger man, but it wouldn't have mattered, because Mara's ex treated Jim like furniture. She made it clear she didn't want Jim around for these visits. After Shimon left she seemed satisfied or resolved. Jim was afflicted by movements and plans beyond his reach. A few times he asked her, What's happening? She shrugged or changed the subject. But soon she smiled at him and became very sexy. If anything, she was even hungrier for Jim. He told himself that it was his stories, his grandeur, that roused her appetite.

After they were married, time had seemed to tighten and become more jerky. Her gentle moments quickly gave way to rebuke or more often indifference. Whenever he displeased her (if he happened to speak to Phyllis on the phone, if his brother was late sending the check, if Mara became frustrated by his stories) she withheld. She pushed back with emptiness. With her glance or no glance at all Jim was enfeebled, wanting, reaching, pitiful. He felt old and oddly sapped of the vigor and youth she had bestowed only the night before or two nights before, the power she had given to him. Then for no apparent reason Mara smiled and well-being and gladness filled him like a beaker.

But they danced in ever smaller stretches of shared space. It occurred to him that they had stopped listening to music together and holding hands. When he turned on Sinatra she stood up and left the room.

Sometimes he implored her pitifully. Mara, I love you. I need you. She nodded his way but with an expression so coarse that she might have been a junkie or a whore. He shivered.

He pushed back in the only way he knew. He tried to close the deal. He was sure that he could win her back with money, with glistening mahogany speedboats from forty years earlier. I sat in the tattered chair with my notebook while he gave her imported furniture from the Canada house, piece by piece. He watched her become more frustrated by what she could not have. He saw it, but he couldn't stop talking money.

22.

Something about the building business focused Marvin Gesler's restless mind, and he dug deep and found the gold. Perhaps it was the squat Quonset buildings themselves and Marvin was like a man who fell in love with a dog that looked like him, or maybe it was the skillful way Jim played Marvin, kept him satisfied and aimed at their astonishing enterprise that kept growing every which way and made them both very wealthy.

Marvin's petulance and his insufferable childlike neediness gradually became more muted. Jim noticed other smatterings of civility. Marvin stopped spitting into his hands and lost a little weight. Maybe it was just that he was becoming more streamlined for success, Jim thought. During their wacky brainstorming dinners Marvin came up with so many angles, large ones that made millions and clever side deals.

Jim did hire several lovely executive assistants for Marvin. What was the harm? The girls seemed to tolerate him like an hour of inclement weather, nothing worse, from what Jim could tell. The first of these hopeful, needy girls sat with Marvin in his large swivel chair and allowed him to kiss and touch her. She was new to business and wanted to make her way. In the morning he brought flowers for her and little presents. Marvin discovered his heart and he quickly gave it away. He dreamed about the girl. He had never known such feelings. After three months the twenty-year-old felt guilty about her boyfriend and she quit the job. Marvin was disconsolate and distracted until Jim introduced him to another assistant and feelings began to stir again as if he had taken a potion.

Jim glimpsed his partner's evolving person, an unexpected romantic bent, his absorption in books, but this was not a reflective time for Jim, who was doing the work of many men.

I didn't have time for Marvin, he said, looking up with exasperation.

I noticed Mara's expression at that moment, red in the face, impatient, exasperated herself, as Jim had been while trying to manage his partner's love life over the phone from London or the plant in Caledon. Jim and Mara were drowning in his torpor and introspection about a storied life that had been defined at every turn by remarkable energy, moneymaking, an unquenchable drive for success, big balls. Jim had sold more sheds than all the other salesmen combined—he'd been a tidal wave. One great salesman can do the work of a thousand. I've seen it firsthand. (My own father was such a salesman for nearly ten years until he became sick.) But now Jim was trying to make sense of the whole picture. He had made so much and lost it all. How had he gotten to this point in life where he was sitting around on torn furniture with this impatient, secretive girl who was everything to him?

Mara was made for the younger Jim—it was all over her face. She wanted the energy, his scams, money, charisma, power without apology. Mara wasn't Ava. Perhaps Ava might have accepted this more reflective slower Jim.

In 1976, Gesler Sheds had nearly three hundred salesmen working mostly in the eastern half of Canada, placing ads in local papers and farm journals, responding in person to leads, mainly from farmers. The sales force, trained by Jim, brought in almost a hundred million in business that year. Their growth was so spectacular the company had difficulty keeping up on the manufacturing end. Jim had the energy of six men, traveled the country hiring and coaching new men, worked with contractors to build additional factory space, and every year he made hundreds of calls on farmers because he loved selling door-to-door. Meanwhile, Marvin was scheming for every dollar, reconfiguring the operation, and whittling at the edges as if it were a deepening conceit. He rarely left the Toronto plant. That was the year he implemented his franchising idea. No one else in the Canadian building business was leasing territories to salesmen, but Marvin was convinced that a man would work a whole lot harder if he owed money on his own business.

Most days Jim was crisscrossing the country. He spent one week each month in the Toronto factory that was only a forty-minute drive from his house on Lake Ontario. Each morning the partners had breakfast and caught up. Jim spent much of the day meeting with farmers who regularly stopped by the factory to get brochures and price lists.

In 1976, a basic Gesler fifty-by-one-hundred-foot retailed for fifteen thousand dollars, which was a large expenditure for a poor man. Most farmers worried whether they could afford a shed or should make do without. Jim understood that the lives of his customers were filled with toil and unattended needs—they could barely imagine another way of living. With such men it was a mistake to ladle on the easy life. Shared pain was Jim's foot in the door. He recalled his own mom's sixteen-hour workdays on his grandfather's farm. She never took a single holiday. Hard work was the only way the family survived. With the farmers Jim was patient and respectful. Soon a conversation was trickling back and forth.

Jim asked about the application for the steel shed, because it was a big move and he didn't want to steer a workingman the wrong way. If it was potato or onion storage they would need special access ports. If it was machine storage Jim suggested adding a small partition for a little heated workshop. Maybe the farmer could put in a radio. It would make a comfortable little workplace during the frigid months, a simple retreat that even a stoic farmer might envision. Sure, it was an awful expense, but his machines wouldn't rust in the rain and snow. He'd get more life out of them.

Finally, reluctantly—because Jim preferred the talk of planting and tending animals—he agreed that he could save the farmer some money. This was always a serendipitous and emotionally charged moment. Jim happened to have a shed already fabricated; it had been on order for someone else, but it hadn't been picked up. It was five thousand square feet, just what the farmer needed. If he could use this one and move quickly, Jim could save him four thousand dollars. Now, the farmer couldn't believe his luck because his neighbor had just bought the same shed for fifteen thousand dollars. Four thousand dollars was a fortune. Jim would throw in the partition for the workshop because he and the farmer had talked about it. He'd let the shed go for eleven thousand in a private cash deal, a handshake, no contract. But it was an arrangement just between the two of them, a onetime favor.

Marvin choreographed these cash-and-carry deals that made the partners a fortune. There was no expense, as steel suppliers were always "gifting" rolls of steel to Marvin as inducements for future orders. Besides him, no one knew exactly how much raw steel was coming in, and with tens of thousands of finished sheds rolling through the factories each year they could always sell off six or seven in a week and pocket the money tax free. "Tax free" became an inside joke between Jim and Marvin, who knew every loophole and created his own. He could have written a book. Jim's insider deals with farmers were where he got the cash to bring home to Ava.

Three or four days a week there were boxes and packages arriving at Jim and Ava's house on the lake, knickknacks mixed in with Jim's pricier acquisitions from wherever he had traveled for Marvin. Some mornings Ava tore open a few, but mostly she stashed them in closets or carried them down to the basement.

Ava could buy virtually anything she wanted, but their newest surge of wealth made her exhausted. She was the caretaker of a massive junk heap of finery. That had become her primary career, a bitter insight for Ava, who felt like an ornament herself. She couldn't explain this to Jim, who was either selling or spending, buying more appliances and gadgets, shipping home cases of French wine, buying a new Mercedes, pressing Ava to spend thousands in tax-free cash.

Jim was mostly away, but just having Ava within his orbit kept him balanced and gave him energy to succeed—that's what he told her during his few days home, along with runs of goopy adoration and praise of her beauty that she tried to ward off, please. Increasingly, Ava was afflicted by doubts. What was she doing on the lake? She brooded that Lenny Bruce was right; she was eye candy, hardly more than a vehicle for a man to love himself. She was mortified by the idea. She began wearing simple clothes and eyeglasses. She studied lists of words, gave up her charming Southern accent, as if the real Ava would finally emerge.

Mostly she wanted to be with Michael. She listened for the sound of the boy playing downstairs. He sat in his room for hours looking at books about dinosaurs, learned their habits and names. He liked walks by the water's edge, skipping rocks or stepping on small crustaceans, or he wandered through the meadow behind the huge house imagining a triceratops or stegosaurus lumbering down from the hills. She liked to think that she and Michael were both studying and becoming wise. She began looking at fine art and photography in books and reading the papers, particularly political columns, so she could teach him.

Ava felt so powerfully connected to the boy that it unnerved her. She wanted to kiss and smother him with mother hugs; he was irresistible to her and she worried it might be wrong, particularly after reading in a magazine that a mother's excessive physical affection could be harmful to a boy. She wanted to be a good mother. She tried to gauge how much time together was too much. Ava turned her face to the side when Michael tried to kiss her, but sometimes the little fellow burrowed in and kissed her neck. She allowed it for a moment, giggling, and then pushed him away as though a line had been crossed. Ava worried about the urges that appealed to her most, How much is too much? Lenny had preached that there are no lines worth the price of banality. After she spent an hour or two in the studio, tinkering, ordering something from a catalog, it felt more acceptable to go to the boy's room, invite him to walk on the beach or, better yet, to ride in the new convertible. Michael came alive when she stepped on the gas and gravel shot out from behind the Rolls, the big engine roared. The skinny boy grinned broadly at his mother's wild ways, people staring from the street as the gorgeous creamy convertible burst past screaming, MONEY! Ava drove fast for him, her scarf blowing, and the boy reached up and felt the wind with his hand. He must have thought he was manufacturing all of this commotion and high life.

After an hour of riding, the boy became sleepy. She loved him so it made her teary. Ava stopped in front of a roadside tavern she knew and wiped her eyes. There were four or five bars she visited; the closest was a safe half-hour drive from their house. Every few days the urge would build to come to one of these places. She wasn't sure if her visits were a renegade form of expression, legitimate in Lenny's terms, or a slow self-immolation. In a minute or two she would walk through the door into the room, blinded by the dark, but she would feel every man in the bar turn to look at her. With a soft smile and a few lingering words she could change the direction of a man's life. She raised the convertible roof of the car and closed the windows, leaving a crack. She touched the boy's forehead and placed a book in Michael's lap. If he woke up, Michael wouldn't be afraid. She double-checked that the car doors were locked. When she returned she would find him reading or looking out the window.

When he was a baby Michael had scrambled after Jim, but as a young boy he gradually lost interest and then he began to look at his father critically, as if Jim's selling manner, his manipulations and glad-handing, were ugly. Michael didn't warm to Jim's salesman cigar-smoking buddies who came by for all-night gin rummy sessions and football talk in the game house on the beach. The boy made damning judgments and wanted to find every answer for himself. Jim loved Michael and kept trying to discover the right door inside, as if the boy were a wily customer, but Michael was something else entirely. Curiously, when the boy addressed Jim it was in dry, careful sentences without any name reference, neither "Jim" nor "Daddy," as if Michael were talking to a stranger.

Unless the kid warms up to people, how will he ever be good in sales? Jim once commented.

I don't want him to be a salesman, Ava responded acidly. The problem is you, Jim, not Michael. Why don't you try being honest with him for a change?

Ava was intent on cultivating her son by herself and would not tolerate Jim's values and critiques mucking up the works. In the afternoon, she read Michael poems by Robert Louis Stevenson and she played the West Coast jazz she had come to love. Ava sang to Michael the Joe Williams classic "Going' to Chicago, sorry but I can't take you." The boy became teary at this bittersweet homage to leaving the nest. I don't want you to go, Mommy—Michael read to the heart of her longing. She laughed and hugged him close.

Ava educated herself with an eye toward teaching the boy. Jim was impressed and he backed off and accepted her primacy in this area of their lives. Jim adored Ava, rebukes and all. From the first day he was attracted to her surprising choices and canny intuitions. He seemed to rediscover Ava each time she was tempted to leave him. He wanted to fill her with love, and her dark excursions, or what he knew of them, inspired his own conviction about their lives. He held her in his arms and kissed her. When Jim discovered that his wife had had a brief affair with a young salesman of his, he desired her more than ever.

Their rapprochement was sweet and passionate. She was touched by him, maybe she loved him, and Jim, well, he was ecstatic. He was inspired by Ava but also by his own depth of caring. During their raw times, she allowed him to love himself. After remorse, tears, much coupling and hugging, she said to him, Jim, it meant nothing, NOTHING. She released him to embrace his work with even greater fervor. Jim rushed back to work at the top of his game. Ava's elusiveness was surely a part of her astonishing appeal. She was a Cracker Jack salesman's top prize, and that Jim could find her, bring her back home again and again, was proof of his greatness. He felt as though she bestowed his life back to him, hurled him back out for a new run at the stars.

There were layers of insult and Jim knew only the surface. Ava allowed Jim to think her sins were manageable, but she was gravely wounded and mostly covering up. She led him to believe that the boy was his flesh and blood. Jim didn't know about the bars and bathrooms, cheap motels. She was desperate to touch herself. For Ava debasement and catharsis had become one and the same.

23.

One day when Jim was visiting the new plant in Toronto, he noticed boxes on the floor of Marvin's office. Jim was intrigued and pulled out a dozen old books. They were literary classics. Fitzgerald, Mann, Poe, Balzac, Baudelaire, Milton, Tolstoy. Jim hadn't heard of these writers and was surprised Marvin was doing so much reading. He mentioned the books to his partner, who shrugged and turned the conversation to business.

In 1977, Marvin was focused on foreign markets. His desk was crowded with brochures, periodicals, and financial data about third-world countries, along with novels. He was always studying, making remarks to Jim about crop yields, water tables, foreign tariffs. This was the year that Marvin established two shadow companies in England that saved the partners millions in taxes.

Marvin worked at his desk coming up with unusual applications for his shed and designing add-on features such as a forced-air cooling system for desert applications. Often he called for his secretary, Pat, PAT, PAT, like the house was burning down, though all he wanted was a cup of coffee or an envelope. His face grew flushed from shouting and you could hear him all the way down the hall. But Jim also observed moments when Marvin seemed to lift out of himself and became cordial or concerned. He asked his secretary about her husband or listened when a salesman complained about his home life.

Many days Jim and Marvin hosted customers from around the world, Englishmen, Nigerians, secular businessmen from Iran: supporters of the Shah who dreamed of golden palaces amid aged cypress and aspens on the outskirts of Tehran. There were also Islamic fundamentalists who loathed the Shah's Western leanings and were trying to raise millions to unseat him. Jim didn't know where Marvin found these contacts. By the same token, Jim hadn't a clue about how or why Marvin developed his impressive reading list. One afternoon Jim walked into Marvin's office and he was reading a book called *Death in Venice*. He closed it abruptly, as if he had been caught at something unclean.

Gesler Sheds was becoming an international player. This kept Jim away from Toronto more than ever, which was bad for Ava. He knew that, but he was closing the biggest jobs of his life. In the new company jet, Jim flew to Nigeria, Morocco, and frequently the Middle East, tiptoeing through social upheaval while working on contracts that Marvin initiated.

Jim was Marvin's eyes. He came back to the factory describing their galvanized storage sheds dotting the lush storied countryside outside Cambridge and Sheffield. He reported clusters of doughty sheds replacing the rotting dockside storage buildings of the Nigerian port cities of Lagos and Calabar. Africans favored them for keeping rice, beans, and various grains. You could store anything in these structures powerful enough to stand against the steady blast of a typhoon. Marvin dreamed of his sheds rising like cities in the desert. Already there were more than two hundred thousand of them spread across the verdant fields of rural Canada.

———

Marvin spent long stretches in his swivel chair reading financial journals, or after the office closed he hunkered over a first-edition volume of poetry or a novel. For Marvin, who grew less inclined to take walks and drives with Jim, the office in Toronto became his world—except his reading took him to places he could never have imagined. He became a night stalker through works of Nabokov, Kafka, Gide, Greene. He favored stories about obsessed men who explored side roads and dark pleasures. Marvin identified with many of the characters and became emotional reading tales of unusual personal discovery.

Marvin enjoyed sex in the late morning, when he was most energetic, sometimes sitting up in his chair. His third girlfriend taught him how to be a lover and Marvin cherished her. He gave Francine fancy gifts and all the money she wanted. It didn't matter to him. After a year he bought her a home just outside the city. She was tender with him and had become a source of inspiration and energy. Marvin's thinking had never been sharper. In a way she had replaced Jim.

Marvin conducted business meetings from the same chair, or he talked to Jim, who was putting on salesmen in Paris and Tel Aviv. Marvin liked the familiar office smells of his cigars and fast food. He often slept on the sofa. He fell asleep listening to classical music while considering ways to refine the steel arch of his shed for additional strength or how to beat the government out of taxes— he didn't want to pay a single tax dollar and believed this was possible.

The mystery of the books began to irritate Jim, who could not connect Marvin to poetry. How had Jim missed this side of his partner? Soon there were oil paintings coming into the office, Degas, Renoir, Chagall, and a few contemporary abstract canvases, although Marvin favored the impressionists, particularly delicate line drawings of women or lovers. Marvin was as brusque about fine art as he had been about the literary classics.

Jim was comfortable with the Marvin he knew and was slow to recognize that his partner was changing. Many of us are like this, making boxes for the ones we love, stuffing them back inside. Jim wasn't a reader and could not imagine the pleasure Marvin took from books, nor the depth of Marvin's discoveries and how they turned his head.

At this remarkable period in their business lives, Marvin was growing impatient with Jim. There was no shared language to express Marvin's late-night reading delights and it felt unclean to describe the romantic feelings that inspired his days, so Marvin cut Jim off in mid-sentence or occasionally showed him the same old Marvin or an even more uncouth and dissolute Marvin.

Marvin recognized that his new English and Nigerian accounts were puny relative to the marketing opportunities in Iran. Despite its inhospitable climate and vast stretches of desert, Iran had near-limitless potential for farming growth, according to Marvin, because of its ingenious underground system of ancient channels, or *qanats,* that conveyed water from aquifers in the highlands to the lower levels by gravity. There were 170,000 miles of these channels crisscrossing the country like an underground sprinkler system. Marvin became obsessed with Iran. He said to Jim that with improved affordable crop storage the Shah would push for a modern farm industry and the desert country would soon bloom into a farming colossus ready to exploit nearby export markets. Our sheds will be everywhere, Marvin predicted.

Jim traveled to Iran. For six weeks he introduced himself to bureaucrats and businesspeople; one new friend led to another who was better situated or knew just the person Jim needed. Eventually, he gained an introduction to Ahmadi Mashid, Minister of Agriculture, an international figure in his own right and an intimate of the Shah. Jim made his case for the easily assembled Gesler Sheds as a sturdy cost-efficient storage solution for small farming communities in the desert. Soon, Jim had established a more personal connection and the men began meeting for drinks and dinner. It was Mashid who introduced Jim to Tehran's unusual nightlife. By the time Jim returned to the States, he had brokered an order for an astonishing five thousand steel sheds.

24.

Jim returned to Canada a conquering hero. The Iran trip augured a different realm of financial success for the company. There were many desert countries in need of staunch portable storage. But for Jim it went beyond money. He reveled in the hushed silence when he walked into the weekly sales meeting packed with a hundred reps. All the men knew Jim had traveled to Iran cold and came back with a $50 million order. Every one of them was thinking, How does he pull it off? What is his magic? Jim couldn't restrain himself and was grinning ear to ear. The truth was that he could sell more in a year than the rest of them combined. He was that good.

A week after Jim's return, he happened to be visiting in the accounting office and overheard one of the girls muttering about Marvin, who had come and gone minutes earlier. Marvin had written a check to Cash for five thousand dollars. As Jim flipped back through the pages of the large checkbook he discovered that his partner had been writing sizable checks for nearly a year. Some were made out to art galleries or auction houses specializing in rare books, others to cash; probably to support his girlfriend, that was Jim's guess.

Marvin had never mentioned these checks. Had he been taking money from their other accounts as well? Jim began to sweat. How stupid to trust Marvin with the money, all the money. Jim didn't begin to understand the finances of their expanding business. He was a traveling man. Was the company worth $20 million? Fifty million? Jim didn't even know the names of the financial institutions where Marvin invested their money.

But maybe there was a more innocent explanation, Jim thought, thumbing through the check stubs. After all, the checks were in Marvin's handwriting for anyone to see. Marvin considered everything in the factory his own: the heavy machinery, the huge rolls of steel that were delivered twice a week. Marvin was the master of this universe, after all, while Jim was an outside guy. It was likely Marvin had used this account simply because it was handy and stealing from Jim had never entered Marvin's head. Marvin was a spoiled child who needed to have what he wanted when he wanted it.

But it was stealing nonetheless. Jim shouldn't allow it to go on, but he felt weary at the thought of confronting Marvin or, worse yet, trying to coax or coerce him. Jim was still awash in the aura of Tehran's grandeur, its palaces and secret clubs, the dusty evening market that smelled like olives and lamb simmering with curry. Tehran had been the apex of his career and Jim allowed it to play over again in his mind, the victories and glory. He had been courted by men in the highest places. A $50 million order was agreed upon with a handshake, not even a formal written contract. Jim was feeling his own magic. Marvin's checks, so what? So what if he grabbed a hundred thousand or two hundred thousand? Marvin was Marvin. Maybe Jim shouldn't say a word, just live his life as before. They were making millions every month. He reasoned with himself that Marvin needed to deceive and chisel. He told himself they were making a fortune and he should keep his mouth shut.

But he couldn't get past the insult. Jim was unnerved by Marvin's new manners and his secret reading. He stormed into his partner's office and slammed the door, started shouting, and smacked one of Marvin's first editions down on his desk so hard he cracked the binding.

Marvin calmly folded his hands and said, So, what are we going to do, Jim? He never raised his voice or got red in the face. Would you like me to apologize? Okay, I'm terribly sorry. Marvin addressed Jim with a dry, controlled sarcasm he'd never heard before.

No, that's not it, Marvin continued, nodding slowly. You want to call the police? Okay, go ahead. Call the police. Here's the phone.

He pushed it across the desk to Jim.

Go ahead, Jim; dial the police.

Marvin never once pounded the table or made the pleading, petulant expressions of their early years. Jim was doing all the screaming. Jim had only empty threats. Marvin knew where the money was.

This affront would have driven Jim to madness—fraud enhanced by Marvin's great books, his love, his new direction, whatever it was—but there wasn't time to reflect. Easy money was breeding on itself like a disease. Almost immediately Jim needed to fly back to Iran. Jim had hardly seen his wife in three months, but there just wasn't time. Marvin's sheds were creating a revolution in desert farming. The partners weren't speaking, but they were making millions and everything else bent to that.

25.

Jim, we eat soon! Mara called from the kitchen. She was preparing a feast, baked chicken, potatoes with onions and chicken fat, an Israeli salad, challah, two bottles of Merlot sitting on the table. For the past week they were drinking wine every night with dinner, as if there were an ongoing celebration. For Jim this was odd and a little unnerving. There were just two of them in the tiny house. The kids were taking an extended visit with their father, who was living a few miles away. After dinner, she had been serving Jim rich desserts. Tonight, it was a moist double chocolate cake.

Jim's brother in Canada had sent a check for five hundred and Mara had spent most of it in a week. In a few days it would be gone, and there was no one else to ask. Jim had used up all his favors. He even considered calling Marvin Gesler, who as an old man was now living in Cincinnati, running a prefab-building business. But asking Marvin for help was too degrading, and Jim couldn't make the call. They hadn't spoken in more than twenty years.

He felt a little dizzy when he stood up quickly, and he needed to steady himself on the furniture. His feet hurt. He should monitor his blood pressure and watch his diet, but the stronger impulse was to please her, eat whatever she served him, try to be young for Mara. He could do that if the world stayed away. If her ex-husband didn't visit, with his weight lifter's body, Jim could still settle into the fantasy. He liked to imagine himself as he looked at fifty walking softly in the jungle beside Ribamar. During the Brazil years Jim's face had been lean and he'd had long flowing blond hair, a flat belly, and tan powerful arms.

Even now Jim wanted to be beautiful, but he was off base with his vanity. Mara was impassioned by the winter of his life, perhaps for conflicting reasons. She had been very close to her stout, difficult father, particularly at the end of his life when he was sick and furious. Every day she had traveled a hundred miles each way to visit him in the hospital. When he died Mara had fallen into a paralysis of despair. That was a half year before she met Jim in Israel. Really, Jim knew very little about his new wife. He knew that she'd been repeatedly abused by an uncle when she was seven years old. She told Jim this story in a matter-of-fact tone, as if she hadn't been touched deeply. She had been in the Israeli army, where she strip-searched female Palestinians. He knew a few other things, but not much. She didn't like to talk about her past and he could accept that. Even more, the darkness on all sides of a few events intrigued him and gave their feeble world mystery and thunder.

In their bedroom, Jim was a stallion with swollen ankles and a racing heart. His increasing infirmity seemed to incite Mara. Every night they made love. She was fierce about their sex and their sessions had become frantic and mercenary: Could they do it again? Could they complete it? She pushed him. Jim could no longer fuck her from behind because he quickly lost his breath. Even with her on top, Jim's heart raced and skipped half its beats while Mara twisted from side to side and made a strange loud keening sound. Maybe she was feeling desperate about losing her Lion Heart. He preferred to think this, but perhaps it was another motivation, as Phyllis had once speculated. She was certain that Mara would fuck Jim to death and then after collecting her green card she'd remarry her ex-husband unless someone came along who was a better bet. Who could ever prove a thing? Phyllis had said to me. But even if Mara was already planning her future after Jim, when he considered it this had been an honorable deal. He had made much worse. More likely, Mara's course wasn't a steady one and her strategy changed with the slightly altered circumstances of their days, with the expansiveness of Jim's salesmanship, and perhaps even Jim's story factored into her whimsy.

Sex came after chocolate cake, but first Jim pushed on with his story. On this night he courted Mara with her own part of the world. She hadn't realized that Jim had spent so much time in the Middle East. With the children out of the house, she could concentrate better, or maybe she was captivated by the palace of gold and a larger-than-life monarch and his empress. In school Mara had learned about Shah Pahlavi, king of kings, who had been a friend of Israel and President Nixon during the time of the Yom Kippur War, when Israel was threatened by a circle of enemies. She was impressed that Jim did business in this elite inner circle.

We were the biggest in Iran, Jim said with his voice gathering strength. We peppered the country with our sheds, although for the first year very few people knew the name of our company. Jim paused for a moment to make a simple line sketch of a Quonset hut. He said a few words about the ingenuity of the design that allowed for a building without columns that could be easily disassembled and dragged around by nomadic farmers. For the first time, she seemed interested in his sheds, maybe because he was speaking about her part of the world. Jim was so happy that he had her attention. It meant everything to him.

They were using thousands of our sheds over there, but we

weren't looking for publicity, at least not at first. It was best to be behind the scenes. There were so many people making money, really large amounts. We charged about fifteen thousand for one of our larger buildings, but after everyone got a piece, all the ministers, it went up very high; the buildings ended up costing the government nearly forty thousand. And no one cared. There was so much oil money in 1978. The Shah was a celebrity all over the world because of the oil. Mara, when he walked into a room, people shivered. The Shah had many palaces, seventeen as I recall. Some of the palaces he never visited. He owned three thousand cars. Yes, three thousand. Twenty Rolls-Royces.

How do you know this?

I'll tell you how I know.

On September 16, 1978, there was a major earthquake near the city of Tabas in eastern Iran. At the time, Jim was in Tehran, more than two hundred miles away, and the aftershocks could be felt there for two days. The first news on the radio reported five thousand deaths; then it rose to fifteen thousand. It was a terrible tragedy. Hospitals were destroyed along with most of the city and surrounding villages. Thousands of wounded were lying in the rubble or in dusty fields. The phone lines in Tehran were jammed with calls, but somehow Marvin got through. It was a very brief conversation, because at this point in their history the partners were barely speaking. Give them away, Jim. Do it. Do it today. That was all that Marvin said.

Despite his rancor, Jim never doubted Marvin's craft. In the city of Birjand, less than fifty miles from the disaster site, their company had fifteen hundred sheds stored on pallets, awaiting shipment to potato farms on the eastern border near Afghanistan. Within twenty-four hours Jim had arranged to have them trucked to Tabas, where he met the convoy and rapidly assembled work crews. On the outskirts of the devastation, a city of sheds was erected in five days and nights, hospitals and shelters for twenty-five thousand wounded and homeless.

When Jim returned to Tehran, a close-up of his exhausted sun-blistered face was on the front pages of all seven daily papers. In a second picture, a man in attractive Western clothes—again it was Jim—was shown toiling in a field with a dozen bereaved peasant workers. This was a powerful visual image. In the weeks following Marvin's public relations brilliancy, Jim was treated like a hero. He did TV and print interviews. Government officials, large landowners, and scores of *bazarris* from all over Iran lined up to order corrugated Gesler Sheds that had suddenly become a symbol of friendship between Iran and the West. Jim graciously wrote the orders.

In November, he received an invitation to dine in the storied Green Palace with the Shah and his beautiful wife, Empress Farah Pahlavi. What a smart, lovely woman, Jim said to Mara, while recalling Farah's sharply sculpted face. The empress was worldly, with a broad knowledge of government, literature, and art, but also she was fun-loving, curious, and fine-tuned to the moment.

The Shah was ten minutes late arriving. He came through the door wearing a striking tuxedo and flowing blue cape. He had a fine, majestic, and deliberate manner. He sat across the table from Jim and the empress and motioned a greeting to his Canadian guest. The emperor's smile was evocative and charismatic. Farah Pahlavi was dressed in a simple sheath gown with long white gloves, in the style of Grace Kelly, except she wore a sparkling diamond necklace and broach that was worth millions, probably many millions. They were an arresting couple, eternal somehow.

The empress quickly put Jim at ease and they spoke of many things. Jim described his home beside the lake and a little about how he had arrived there from the poverty of his youth. When Jim mentioned his wife's art collection Farah Pahlavi flushed and clasped her hands. Art was her passion. Jim inquired about the dozens of richly colored miniature paintings that adorned the walls of the room. She had great knowledge of ancient Middle Eastern art and explained that the miniatures were from the Safavi style of the fifteenth century. The theme of these naturalistic works was the splendor and grandeur of the royal court. They portrayed the handsome faces of nobles in sumptuous garments at banquets, beautiful palaces, scenes of battles. Indeed, the entire opulent spectacle of the Shah's court presaged the enduring legacy of the Persian monarchy.

Even while the party played on, Jim imagined how he would bring the event to life for Ava. He would tell her of thirty-foot chandeliers reflecting an intricately carved golden ceiling and brocade curtains tailored for a regent who considered his grandeur and legacy comparable to what Cyrus the Great achieved for ancient Persia. He would mention Farah Pahlavi's adoring smile for her husband, while he gave an after-dinner talk highlighting Iran's burgeoning economy. The Shah predicted that within five years his country would have the economic and military heft to join the elite superpowers of the world.

Jim would later reflect on the tiered ironies of this night of celebration. The empress, the caring wife, had been quietly encouraging a coup against her husband. For some time—Jim read this months later—she had been co-opting left-leaning intellectuals and constructing a government in waiting. If she had been more decisive and moved more rapidly, the empress might have won the great prize. We'll never know. The resplendent Shah, who bragged to the world of the broad support of his people, was both mortally ill and politically feeble. Within eight weeks of the splendid party in the Green Palace, the Ayatollah Khomeini would drive the Shah and his beloved from their land. For the next year, until he died, the empress cared tenderly for her Shah while he suffered with cancer. Despite his megalomania and her own imperial designs, she loved him.

After returning from this last trip to Iran Jim couldn't pull Ava back. She had fallen too far from his fantasy. He tried to be fatherly and gentle. He lectured to her about her health and the happiness they shared. They had such a special life. He held her in his arms and described the things they would do next year. They'd go to Paris, wherever she wanted. Ava reeked of booze and had stopped brushing her hair. He'd been away too long. She wanted him to drink with her. She begged him and then she became sarcastic when he refused. She slurred her words. You're a salesman, she said as though this were contemptible. What are you? You're a salesman. He didn't know what to do with her. Her smell made him nauseous. She doesn't know what she says. She'll come around.

One night Ava was standing nude in the upstairs bathroom when he walked in on her. Without saying a word she undid his pants and made him hard with her hand. She turned her back to Jim and pulled him inside her as if he were a stranger in a hallway. Ava was leaning on her elbows on the bathroom sink with her head down. Her ass and thighs had grown heavy and she had a belly that Jim held on to like a handle. They fucked savagely. When she rose up her hair was stringy and her face had become coarse and a little puffy. She looked into the mirror at his straining face staring back at her. Jim, look how ugly we've become.

He didn't know this woman. He shouldn't have stayed away so long. He told himself this a thousand times. In Iran Jim was a hero. He'd wanted her to know. He never got to tell her about the palace. He couldn't bring her back. She drank vodka like water. She couldn't stand up. When she wasn't numb with alcohol, she knew she had to get out. She must leave this gated home, this ugliness. But where could she go? The beautiful people are so ugly, Jim. He didn't understand such talk, and this frustrated her even more.

The waterside estate had become her jail. Their strange boy had become afraid to sleep in his bed. Michael had gathered all of his clothes into tall piles. He slept on the floor amidst columns of neatly folded clothes as though they were icons to protect him in the night. Michael's room felt like a burial ground.

One night when Jim came back from the factory, Ava and Michael weren't home. He read the newspaper and paced around. It was almost eight o'clock when the phone rang. The police had found her Rolls-Royce convertible parked in a dark alley. There was a frightened boy in the backseat. Michael had been sitting there for four or five hours. He was okay. They were keeping him at the station house.

Jim took a taxi to the police to retrieve Michael and the car. When Jim returned to the house, Ava was sprawled on the sofa holding a bottle of whiskey, her skirt hitched up on her white thighs. He could see her underwear and it disgusted him. Ava couldn't stand up or pronounce her words. She'd gone to a bar and then home with someone. She couldn't remember his name. Just some guy, Jim, doesn't matter about him. Michael was listening to every word, but she was too far gone to notice or care. When I left his place I couldn't remember where I'd left the car. No idea. She described it all reasonably. She had called a cab, fallen asleep in the backseat. It was humiliating in front of the boy, but she wouldn't shut up.

She reached out, wanted to touch Michael's face, but she couldn't stand. She drank more from the bottle. It didn't mean anything, Jim. Never means anything. She glanced at the boy, and Jim shivered. We're both so ugly, Jim, she said, choking on her drink. Her chin was wet. We're awful. She drank some more.

Jim walked into the bedroom and returned holding his .38 revolver. He pointed it at her face and she shrugged as though she'd been preparing for this. Jim had always loved her face.

Michael was pleading, Daddy, don't kill her. Daddy, please. Don't do it. Please, Daddy, don't. Don't. Don't. Don't. Don't. Michael was kneeling beside him, pulling the crease of Jim's pants, begging, Daddy, don't, Daddy.

Finally, Daddy, Daddy. Jim had waited years to hear this. That's what saved her. Daddy, please. Jim caressed the boy's wet face and he put the gun down.

Okay, Michael.

Jim left them in the house and spent the night in a hotel in Toronto. The following morning, when he returned, they were gone. He didn't care. Or the next day. Then he cared. He wanted to see her and talk it over. He imagined the perfect arguments he'd make, rehearsed his lines. He sighed over and over again. He wanted her back, even now. It didn't matter where she'd slept. It didn't matter if there had been thirty guys. He didn't know where to look. He burned for her. Every day he believed she'd come home. She didn't. He began to search. Walking down streets in Toronto, he looked at each shapely woman. He chased after women to see their faces. She was gone. Wholly gone and yet wholly within him. He had no phone number to call. He no longer cared what she'd become. He'd take her back. He'd throw everything out of the house. Give up the house of his dreams. They'd live a little life together in some dive. If that's what she wanted. They'd live together in squalor. Fine.

He didn't care about the business. Marvin was off on his own, chiseling the government out of taxes, flying to Paris with his secretary. Then one of the salesmen told Jim that Ava had moved in with the seventy-year-old father of her first husband. Jim took this as good news. She was broke and desperate to do such a thing. He had hope all over again. Surely she would listen to his arguments. He tracked down the phone number. He was greedy for her all over again. Ava hung up at the sound of his voice. He left pitiful messages. I want to see you. I want to talk. I need you. He left this message ten times, more. She wouldn't return his calls. He went to her apartment and watched the front door from across the street like a stalker. Jim couldn't accept that she wasn't feeling the same as him.

The last of that winter was raw and miserable. Jim no longer traveled or went into the factory. He wandered through the rooms of his estate, lost and homeless.

Mara looked unsettled by this tale of ruined people. It felt too close to her own life of squalor with Jim in Florida. Mara was not a patient girl. She didn't know about the developing arc of a good story.

Why do you tell me this, Jim? she asked with exasperation. She looked as though she were about to bolt for the door. She had been drawn to the powerhouse Jim from earlier in his life. She might have stayed with that Jim.

Wait, he said, grabbing her wrist and forearm with two hands. There's more.

Mara was taken aback by Jim's wry grin. She sat back on the torn sofa.

PART IV

26.

The Brazilian city of Manaus is surrounded on all sides by the Amazon jungle, although on its eastern border the forest is kept at bay some miles by the Negro and Amazon rivers that sideswipe each other, creating a broad stretch of unique waterway traversing the continent from northeastern Brazil to the western coast of Peru. In the summer months when the water is low, standing on a massive granite wall looking thirty feet down one sees an expanse of bog covered with filthy sewage, pop bottles, old tires, junk of all sorts. A gangplank leads across this smelly muck to the brown water and a ragtag fleet of passenger, fishing, and cargo boats headed off to places like Tabatinga and Leticia.

Day and night, there is a bustle of commerce here: heavy sacks of strange-looking fish, some of them huge, pulled from the river to feed the swelling city; other sacks are loaded with pineapples or a coarse flour called *fainha,* a staple in Brazil; also filthy bags of charcoal are coming ashore from the rickety boats. The wild jungle nurtures this city, which is an island. It also gives Manaus an urgency you can feel, particularly in the sultry night air.

Coming off the boats, mixed in with the produce, there is a

stream of exhausted men, small, wiry men, for the most part, some suffering with malaria, who are back from the gold mines in the south. There is also a sprinkling of beautiful women, strikingly beautiful. A stranger could wonder what they had been doing in the jungle. Although the girls had been traveling for a week or longer, sleeping outside on deck in the slow-moving riverboats, beset with mosquitoes, torrential rain, and sick workers seeking favors, they look lovely coming ashore and they smile at the men sitting on the granite wall.

In 1980, when Jim returned to Manaus from his first visit to the putrid mining camp half-buried in the rain forest, he discovered in himself unlimited energy for a new way of life. Of course, it was the excitement of first experiencing the jungle, dining on anteater and maggots while dreaming of gold, but also, Manaus itself was exotic and deeply inviting. Anything was possible in this city. Fortunes were won and lost here in a month or a violent day. It was a perfect place for a gambling man who was trying to come back from ruin and heartbreak.

Like Jim himself, his new city had a gaudy history of glory and calamitous defeat. In the early part of the last century, the rubber trade was born in the Amazon and Manaus quickly became the hub of the industry. The city's downtown area was lavishly fashioned after Paris and Lisbon; even a world-class opera house came to the Amazon. Rubber barons made kingly fortunes at the expense of thousands of poor workers who died in the jungle from disease and animals. But soon the rubber business in Brazil was outmoded, as agricultural farming techniques and better soil brought the trade to Malaysia. Manaus went into a lengthy depression; the palatial residences of new millionaires became chalky and cracked from the sun. Some rubber barons committed suicide while others lived hand to mouth as peasants.

By 1980, Manaus was back on top due in part to the government's decision to make the city a free-trade zone. This encouraged multinational industries to come to the city as well as shoppers from all over Brazil, who could save as much as 40 percent buying appliances. But probably the most intoxicating inducement to travel to the Amazon was gold. In the last quarter of the twentieth century, if a man dreamed of striking it rich prospecting for gold Manaus was the place to come. It was where you set up your operation, did your shopping, hired the people you needed, and came back from the jungle to rest and party.

Nothing was a sure bet in Manaus. The artifacts of victory and ruin were everywhere. Driving north through the downtown area, you saw fancy new hotels and skyscrapers going up, business burgeoning in each shop and spilling out onto broad, new well-lit streets. But when you crossed one of many small bridges and looked to the right or left there were impoverished towns of rotting shacks on the muddy banks of creeks that reeked of human waste. Prosperity in Manaus was running perpendicular to heartbreak and misery. People in the city were inflamed by chance. They lived fast and did whatever was necessary to slide through before the door slammed shut.

When Jim told me his stories about Brazil, he often referred to Luis Carlos. Luis was a short, thin man in his late forties with a dark, Indian complexion, yet his skin had an odd transparency, particularly on his cheeks and below his eyes, where purple veins showed through, giving him the aspect of a fragile or sickly person. On a daily basis Luis worried about his blood pressure and other diseases, but it wasn't clear to Jim if there was any real problem, as this very bright, nervous man avoided doctors and the bad news they might convey. I could have a heart attack making love, he'd say out of the blue. His anxieties arose from a dense web of musings about his several lovers, his lists of appointments to keep when he returned to Manaus from the mining camp in the jungle, a thousand phone numbers jiggling in his head because he didn't carry a book. For all his worry, he could walk in the jungle at a brisk pace for a week.

Luis was a man of unusual resources and he was at Jim's side practically from his first day in Manaus. Jim hired Luis as a translator and guide, but his responsibilities quickly broadened and he became Jim's right-hand man. Jim couldn't have said where they met or who introduced them. Yet he knew how he'd made contact with most of his friends and business associates in Manaus— merchants, gold buyers, cardplayers, airplane pilots, mechanics, gunmen, beautiful women—because it was almost always Luis who made the introductions. Jim, I know someone, he would say. I have a man who could do this. He will be perfect. Don't worry.

In this city where people typically arrived late for appointments, very late, or they didn't show up at all, Luis always seemed to know someone who could track down the phone number or street address.

When Jim returned to Manaus, from his first visit to the campsite, he was exhausted and elated. It would be more than five weeks before the second trip and all the while he had to restrain himself from rushing back into the jungle. He wanted to touch the gold again with his fingers. He was beset with anxiety because he would never get another chance like this. Someone could steal what he had discovered. Gold would be Jim's redemption. Even Marvin Gesler could never hope to achieve the wealth that Jim would soon dig up from the fetid mud. His fears and dreams were so compelling that it became physically painful to focus on practical details. In Manaus, Jim felt trapped in a quicksand of impediments, red tape, permits, and broken appointments.

Luis counseled patience. There was no point tramping back into the jungle without a crew, without machinery to build a functioning camp, and without a master plan. Jim needed to find a safe house for the city part of his business, and he must hire armed guards to look after the gold in Manaus until he sold it for the best price. Luis warned Jim he must travel everywhere with several gunmen or he'd be murdered or kidnapped for ransom. He needed to learn a whole new way of life.

This one is much too large, Jim said to Luis the first afternoon they looked for a house. Jim's yellow sun-bleached Mercedes sedan was parked outside an imposing gate. Through iron bars he could see a sprawling house set back about three hundred yards from the road. Much too large, he said.

Probably, Luis agreed with a world-weary expression, but please have a look anyway, since we've come so far to get here. They had driven on the only road leading north out of Manaus for about twenty minutes to the extreme edge of the city limits, the very point at which Manaus was stymied by the rain forest. Luis got out of the car, mopped his brow in the afternoon heat. He suffered greatly from the humidity, and when Luis was in the city he liked to shower four or five times a day. He said a few words to one of the men working on the property and the heavy gate swung open.

The main house was handsomely built with dark, aromatic native wood, Angelim rajado, that is resistant to rotting in the wet climate. This wonderful name seemed to evoke the grand house itself, which had fifteen generous-sized rooms, newly painted white shutters, and a large wood-paneled office that reminded Jim of his office in the house on Lake Ontario where Jim's new wife, Phyllis, was now living with his cook and chauffeur. Looking out the window from the office, Jim saw tiered gardens, and beyond that there were several connected man-made lakes, strung together by waterfalls and raised walking trails; the lakes had many strange-looking Amazonian fish, and ducks swimming around, and there were a few small baby black caimans that would some-day reach twenty feet but now lay harmless, sunning on the bank of the lake closest to the main house. All around the lakes there were apple, orange, coconut, and cashew trees and lovely flowering plants called *inga*.

Jim stood on the back porch for a time, breathing the jungle air and considering the sharp turn his life had taken from a tremen-dously successful business life and from everyone he'd ever cared about. Yet he didn't feel at all lost or lonely. He felt impatient, hun-gry. Jim turned back to the big house. Through the open shutters to the kitchen he noticed a young woman with dark peasant features and a lovely smile. She was Caboclo, a mixture of indigenous and European ancestry. She was cooking something and the smell made his mouth water.

The house was situated on twenty acres of property, all of it encircled by a ten-foot concrete wall painted light green to blend into the foliage. On the east side of the estate, just over the wall, Manaus approached with its open sewers and glistening corporate headquarters. The most intriguing facet of the estate was its west-ern vista: behind the house, servants' quarters, and past the lakes, the wall braced against the dense jungle that played out unabated for nearly four hundred miles. If you walked along the west wall at night you might hear the growl of a jaguar. The estate, presently owned by the wife of a diseased Mafia capo now living in France, was a buffer zone between conflicting realities.

The property was much more than Jim required but was very special, as Luis had said. Jim found himself lingering. From the front side of the house he looked out across a field of fruit trees, and the same kitchen girl was now taking a walk. She was very young, eighteen or nineteen, with long black curly hair. The girl was laugh-ing and picking fruit. She was wearing red shorts and was moving slowly across the dusty property alongside a boy of about twenty, one of a half-dozen workers who maintained the property; they walked through a stretch of cashew and *guariguara* trees, close, in rhythm with each other but not touching. The girl looked toward the house and saw that Jim was watching, but this didn't make her self-conscious. Jim wondered if she and the boy were lovers and decided they must be. The girl's walk was slow and rhythmic, as though drawing purpose from the earth.

Jim was about to leave with Luis when the girl came back on the porch holding a knife and a piece of fruit. Jim didn't know what it was, but she was offering him a cashew. He cut off a slice and ate the tasty fruit from the skin like a mango. Then he looked around for a place to put the rind. The girl smiled at him and offered her hand. She won him on the spot. She was intoxicating but utterly from another world, and much too young.

At the start of their drive back to town, Luis looked amused, but his mind quickly turned to something else. The following afternoon, Jim bought the property from the owner's widow for $140,000, nearly one-third of what he'd brought to Brazil for his new business venture. It was much more than he wanted to pay, but he reasoned, impractically, it was only a tiny fraction of what such a place would cost in the States or Canada.

When Jim returned to the estate two days later as the new owner, the Indian girl didn't seem surprised.

Jim had never built a business without Marvin Gesler's vision and prodding. He wasn't a business genius like his partner, nor was he a detail guy. Marvin's vulgarity and raunchy deceits had always cast Jim in a favorable light, and Jim had relished being the good guy. Now he wasn't sure who he was or needed to be. Marvin had always known the rules, or he made the rules while Jim brokered their deals. Jim felt Marvin's absence, to be sure, but he had found gold near the Rio Novo four hundred kilometers south of Manaus.

This simple fact quickened and thrilled him more than any lust he had ever known, more than any previous worldly success, perhaps more even than his desire for Ava, or at least it was enough to make him forget. The grains of gold in the *batilla* kept Jim on course. If it was the right course was a much larger question than Jim could resolve, not that he ever cared for abstract inquiry. Jim had no Marvin, limited cash, and scant knowledge of finance, but he had gold, or the chance for it, and he had Luis Carlos with his considerable quirkiness and personal magic. Jim had no desire to return to Toronto and the Quonset shed business. He didn't miss it or even want to know what was going on.

Luis guided Jim to a street lined with cantinas, maybe fifty cantinas housed in a four-block stretch of Spanish colonial buildings from eighty and ninety years earlier, when rubber barons had imported renowned architects from Europe to design the most daring, opulent residences on the entire continent. By 1980, they were long ruined from neglect and water damage. There were jungle plants sprouting through cracks in the floors as if the rain forest were trying to reclaim the land. The venerable houses smelled from hardworking girls and the sweat of an army of lusty *garimpeiros* back from the gold mines. Jim needed to learn about such places, counseled Luis while he mopped his brow and took Jim to see the tiny cheerless cubicles where girls worked on soiled mattresses for next to nothing. Most of them were very young; some were attractive, others fat; they did their work with dead eyes. Jim found these places depressing, but Luis urged him to stay awhile and take a look around.

During the next month, Luis introduced Jim to gold buyers, airplane pilots, gorgeous women. Luis introduced working girls with a touch of nostalgia or regret. Jim, he explained as a longtime connoisseur, many of these girls are sincere people, believe me. But on other occasions, Luis referred to them dismissively as bitches. He introduced the owner of a gun shop who sold Jim an arsenal of weapons, at a fair price, and then, within an hour, the white-haired shop owner had assembled a militia of thirty gunmen, each of them willing to risk his life for ten dollars a day. Luis drove Jim to meet Martha, a plump woman with an endearing smile who was a good cook and didn't mind working in the deep jungle; Luis brought the pilot Ramon Vega to Jim's estate.

Ramon ran his own jungle operation eighty miles east of Jim's camp. He was a handsome, powerful guy about Jim's height with a coffee-colored complexion and a contagious smile. Men and women were drawn to Ramon, who was nearly Jim's equal in terms of charisma and affability. He rented a turbopropped helicopter to Jim for two weeks to fly heavy equipment into the camp; after that, Jim bought two older planes from his new friend. When the two men were in Manaus they went to clubs with Ramon's knockout girlfriend, Iliana, who had studied geology in college and was presently working in the gift shop of one of the local hotels. Ramon entertained his friends with stories about the jungle life, ambushes, murders, animal attacks. He had a talent for finding the attractive or socially acceptable side of cruelty. Listening to Ramon was like going to the movies. His girl had a pleasant polished manner that you could almost take for softness, but she could turn on a dime. Iliana wanted a lot of money and would do almost anything to get it.

Jim questioned Iliana about rock formations that might offer clues to concentrations of gold on his property. She was attracted to Jim, even though he was twice her age. They were always fooling around, probing and tempting each other. Ramon didn't seem to mind. He had this manner: what's mine is yours. Jim enjoyed Ramon's largess and extravagant convictions about women and the predatory rules of the jungle, which he enunciated with deeply felt pleasure.

Whenever Luis saw Ramon and Jim together, he smiled, as if he'd known all along they'd become friends.

Luis seemed to grow in stature at the prospect of bringing people to meet Jim. These were Luis's Broadway moments. During the initial starburst of making introductions he was charming and well versed, verbally nimble about subjects one would not expect him to know about. He got people talking. He knew how to break the ice. But then he lost interest. Once he was past the stage of facilitating, Luis's observations became shallow or seemed ill-informed. The deepening levels of a subject didn't interest him. After fifteen or twenty minutes, he was looking off to the future, and he would say to Jim, I am like Cinderella. I have to leave now.

Over time Jim grew confident about his assistant's suggestions, even though it wasn't always apparent, with the language difficulty, where the quality of Luis's many acquaintances might diverge from his own considerable enthusiasm and charm. Luis became Jim's Jim. Of course, in their hardworking thirty-month history Luis would make some terrible choices. He'd wipe the perspiration off his face and make up for disasters with more matchmaking that was nothing less than astonishing.

He introduced Jim to Ribamar, a short, powerfully built man of about sixty with thirty years in gold mines south of Manaus. He had spent the past eight months living in the city with his young wife, Lu, and their new baby. No one understands the jungle better than Ribamar, said Luis, who became melancholic when he spoke of the older man. You'll need Ribamar to survive; you'll need him like clean water.

It was a hard moment for Luis and surely a reflection of his affection for Jim that he brought this new man into their world, because including Ribamar meant that Luis had to sacrifice some of himself, maybe the best part; whenever he was around Ribamar, Luis seemed undressed, cheapened, largely irrelevant.

Ribamar was a calm and serious man who filled a room without speaking. He sensed keenly, like the animals he knew so much about, and he trusted himself beyond all else. In their first meeting, Ribamar admitted to missing the jungle greatly. He had been away too long and was very pleased to hear about this new mining operation. Also, with a young family, he needed money.

Jim voiced his many concerns about the large task ahead while Ribamar listened patiently but also with a hint of irony or dawning conviction. His judgments were deeply held and he almost never shared them fully. Jim kept returning to the threat of jaguars because he'd heard that the area around his camp was infested with big cats. In the history of the camp, many workers looking for gold had been killed. How could they survive and run a business with jaguars slaughtering the workers? For some reason this grim question tickled both men and they began to laugh.

Finally, Ribamar answered that jaguars don't attack unless a man is alone in the jungle or the cat feels threatened. The jungle is safe, Jim, if you know what to do. *Garimpeiros* are attacked because they are reckless people. They think they can do anything they like. They feel tired and go to sleep under a tree. You must learn where you cannot sleep. The jungle is healthy. It can be your friend as well as your enemy. It will provide for you when you are sick. Men make the forest dangerous by stupidity.

Jim had many questions for Ribamar about gold mining, jungle animals, malaria, the right and wrong foods to eat, where to get drinking water. Is it true, he asked, there is a tiny fish that swims up a man's penis? It was an extensive list of concerns that Ribamar found burdensome. He put a strong arm on Jim's shoulder. Jim, the job for you is to know two things. The first is only to focus on small things, one at a time. The second is that all things are small things. Then he added, enigmatically, Listen to the sounds of the jungle at night, Jim. It's a great music. You need to pause and listen to the music or you are wasting your time here.

Jim nodded. He was greatly drawn to Ribamar.

At first, Jim felt uncomfortable being with the girl who was only eighteen and dressed for the heat in shorts and T-shirts or skimpy dresses that showed a lot. When they drove to Manaus in his Jeep or walked on the cobbled streets of the city holding hands, he looked like her grandfather and worried about being taken for a dirty old man. That passed quickly in this city where anything goes. No one cared about Jim and the girl.

During the first several months, because of the language, Jim never knew what Angela was thinking. He tried to imagine what she said to him or what was in her mind. In his pidgin Portuguese, he tried to convey that she should try to imagine what he was saying, that's how they would become friends, by guessing and making things up. They would create each other in their imaginations. They tried to do it and laughed. This was an appealing idea, to be utterly new and special and perhaps even invented for one other person in the world. And it was true that they never really learned many basic things about each other. But the girl was better at their game than Jim. She didn't mind not knowing.

The guessing sometimes heightened Jim's pleasure, but it was also frustrating. He wondered what she was making up. He would find himself listening for clues when she spoke Portuguese to one of the other workers on the property. Jim could tell that the girl was self-possessed and had much to say.

In their imagined language she seemed too good to be true. But he wondered sometimes if she had ever worked in a cantina, because sex was so comfortable for her and she knew a lot for her age; how would he ever know for sure? He decided it didn't matter. But then he couldn't leave it alone and he pressed her about the men she had known. He thought that she said he was her third or fourth; it seemed important at the time, which, three or four.

Oddly enough, the peasant girl did not seem to have large expectations or needs. When he took trips into the jungle, she wouldn't ask when he was coming back. She worked in the kitchen and in the gardens for the same modest wages Jim paid other workers on the property, and Angela seemed satisfied with her lot. When he was in the mining camp, he didn't think about her so much, because the jungle was a huge passion. Also, the girl had trained him. When he came back, she would be there, waiting, like the large rooms of the house made of fragrant wood. The girl never once asked Jim for extra money or presents. When he once brought her expensive red sandals from one of the hotel gift shops she accepted them without fanfare and put them away in her little closet, preferring to go in bare feet or in cheap native slippers. She didn't have aspirations like all the other women Jim had known. At first, he was suspicious about this and wondered if she had secret motivations, some devious plan, but eventually he took for granted her graciousness and lack of guile; it was part of his new life in Brazil.

Since Ava left him, it was over a year now, Jim had had trouble making love. For a week or so in Canada, before he met Phyllis, he had dated a beauty queen, Miss Alaska, and he couldn't have sex with her. It wouldn't work whatever she tried. With Phyllis, there were stretches of time when he was impotent. He never knew when it would happen. With the Indian girl, this problem disappeared.

He loved the taste of her, which was like sweet mango or cashew. He couldn't get enough of kissing her. The girl had great patience for this, but eventually she giggled and bit him gently on the lips, urged him with her voluptuous body and sweet manner.

When he began to have difficulty, she brought him back, patiently; she had a few ways that surprised him and he tried not to think about how she had learned. Finally, they'd fuck, very hard and fast; she had spirit and hunger that came from the jungle, where she had grown up—at least Jim fancied that was the explanation—until finally all of his life flooded out of him; it felt that way. He was empty and almost desperate afterwards, as if he couldn't reclaim himself. She offered him a piece of melon in the canopied bed, but he couldn't move. She laughed and fed him.

Angela didn't sleep the night in Jim's bed, although he invited her. When he asked, she smiled, as though she might, but in the morning she'd always gone back to her own little room. It had been her place for nearly a half year, since the day she'd come from the jungle to work in the large house. In her parents' small thatched hut, on the bank of the Igapo-Acu River, Angela had shared a tiny doorless room with three younger sisters. Having a room of her own was very important.

She was an unusual girl, Jim decided. She would fall into a trance listening to nonsense on the radio, jingles and such, and when he bought a television, she watched the soap operas. All of this was a revelation to her, a new universe. She didn't know much and yet she seemed to understand a great deal. Angela was very young, and though Jim lured her with his great salesmanship and a touch of the Manaus high life, she kept a big part for herself.

The first evening back in the camp, when it was only a small clearing, pitiful really, without so much as a hut or lean-to, Jim swathed himself in netting and climbed into the hammock. The air was warm and sluggish, laborious to breath. Jim hung between two skinny *açaí* trees, wrapped like a mummy, sweating, and hardly able to turn over. He would remain this way for the next thirteen or fourteen hours.

The night fell quickly and was darker than anything he had ever imagined. He could not see the hand in front of his face, nothing, and yet the jungle filled Jim's head with an ocean roar of insects heaped upon the bleating and screaming of parrots and monkeys, birds in crisis, predators and prey, that infernal racket drowning out logic and even conviction. There were menacing crashes beyond the clearing, calls and cries that were inexplicable and savage.

In time (but how much time? Hammock nights were restless and without end) the bedlam blended to a more predictable buzzing and chirping; it took on a rhythm that pulsed in Jim's head, as if there were a greater sense to it. He even found it appealing and it gave him something to lean against. Jim fell into the sultry mix of jungle sounds, memories, and sweating, gulping water, wondering, vaguely, if he had malaria. He went off into the night with his father, Nathan, searching for the farmer's cows, or tracked game with Ribamar. Sometime later (but when? Three hours? Was it almost dawn?) Jim dreamed about the girl in Manaus, or he thought of Ava. She wanted him again and Jim's desire spread into the jungle's mysterious urging.

The two camp dogs barked whenever something approached the edge of the clearing. Jim woke with a start. He could see the glow of Ribamar's cigarette. He was sitting nearby on a log, and he nodded solemnly. Or some nights Jim would hear Ribamar's soothing voice and he wasn't sure if he was dreaming or remembering yesterday when they walked together in the forest; many days they went hunting for game. Jim loved to watch Ribamar move quietly through the dense bush, with his elbow pushing aside vines and drooping fronds, letting them flow back in place as though they'd never been touched. He moved without a trace.

Jim, you mustn't wear deodorant, Ribamar reminded him gently. But Jim slathered it on every night because he couldn't stand the smell of himself for thirteen hours in the hammock. Jim, when you are in the jungle you want to smell like an animal, Ribamar cautioned. Deodorant is for the cantina, for the girls. If you wear it in the jungle, you make the jaguar curious. He wants to see who you are. Ribamar knew so much that he could say anything at all and it might be true; he could make it true with his will, his gravity, his amused and lordly conviction. In the hammock, it seemed as though Ribamar created the jungle. Still, Jim tried to guess what was really true and what was part of their gamesmanship. He decided it wasn't true about the deodorant.

When Jim sat up to ask Ribamar, the older man was lying on the dirt a few feet away, dozing. And yet when Ribamar had set up Jim's hammock he'd been careful not to allow it to even touch the ground lest ants and other bugs crawl into it and torture Jim through the night. Jungle insects didn't bother Ribamar.

In an hour, or three hours, when Jim looked up again, Ribamar was sitting on the log, smoking a cigarette. What about the snakes, Ribamar? Can you hear the cobra in your sleep? Ribamar nodded yes. Once or twice a week, a cobra, coral snake, or pit viper would crawl into the clearing. Ribamar, or one of the other men, would kill the snake with a machete or smack it with a log, and kick it back into the trees. With his ear on the ground, Ribamar could hear a snake coming out of the bush. He could hear a man approaching. Even without dogs, he could sometimes hear the jaguar.

What does it sound like, Ribamar?

Your body starts to tell you when a jaguar is near, the older man said. Sometimes you hear it moving through the vegetation, but usually it's nothing specific. You feel your death arriving.

Ribamar was smiling a little, but Jim decided he was telling the truth.

Go to sleep, Jim.

In the early light, Jim awoke with the conviction that he was saving his family. It was the remnant of a dream and he didn't stay with it for long. Jim rarely thought about the past, and when he did he felt impatient. Every morning he was newly born in hot rancid water. It still wasn't time to leave the hammock, another couple of hours before the mosquitoes mostly disappeared around mid-morning and Ribamar released Jim from this hanging hell where he ached and scratched his legs and belly drenched from sweat or from pissing on himself when he couldn't find the bottle in the dark.

Jim listened to the squeal of parrots and thought about his

plans for the day. He had flown in a dozen laborers from Manaus. There were four gunmen hanging around the clearing and more were coming. There were about a dozen *garimpeiros* living near the camp, beginning to dig for gold. Jim's tiny community was growing. There were no barracks yet and all of the laborers slept in hammocks slung between trees. In another hour they'd be working on the runway, hacking through the trees south of the clearing. It was so exciting. Big things were happening and mistakes were often not tolerated. Two days earlier a worker bathing in the river had been eaten by piranhas. There were many deadly creatures, and yet, besides the insects that teemed everywhere, you didn't see them. They were hiding in the trees or inside your hammock or boot, biding their time, protecting themselves, or waiting to pounce.

Jim didn't worry about animals or sickness. Ribamar watched over him, made Jim feel untouchable. More, the violence of this habitat excited him. He knew that he could win here. He saw it clearly while lying in the hammock. He could stay in the fire longer than the next guy. He loved constructing an empire from a puny clearing in the forest. He wasn't afraid to get his hands dirty. Many afternoons he dug in the mud with *garimpeiros* or swung a machete, clearing trees and vines. Jim knew a few words of Portuguese and gestured expressively, what he wanted and where. He urged his gunmen to lend a hand, though they were lazy men who resented labor, but eventually they also grabbed machetes and cut back the bush. Jim's enthusiasm was infectious and his men loved him. He gave them a hug. He knew just the right words to keep them going. He told them a little about the future. They were like his children. He knew the men would follow him and do whatever was necessary.

Garimpeiros were finding traces of gold, nothing to speak of. But the word was now on everyone's lips. More of these wiry little men showed up every day. Soon they would begin to build Jim's enormous sluice box. Each day, gushing wealth would wash down into his hands. Gold was the drummer's beat. Jim could hear it from the hammock.

After a few weeks the morning sounds had evolved to hammering and chain saws and you could no longer hear the parrots and monkeys. The rudimentary dorm and cantina were going up. The men were nearly finished cutting a landing strip into the tall trees. Ramon Vega's helicopter flew in each morning with a two-thousand-pound load slung beneath its belly. The Caterpillar had arrived in pieces and the mechanic was assembling it in the small clearing. Then two big diesel generators arrived. Soon there would be power. Lights and *musica* were on the way. They were creating a little civilization.

Some days Ramon Vega stayed awhile and looked over the camp while it came together. His own *garimpo* was eighty miles to the east. There was no gold on his land, he sighed audibly, but he had a cantina with six working girls and miners from nearby *garimpos* came to visit. Ramon cleared the equivalent of eighty thousand dollars a month from the cantina. He explained to Jim that once he began to export gold the most beautiful girls in all of Brazil would find their way to this impossibly remote place. They would walk out of the jungle smelling of French perfume. They would gladly give their gifts in the heat, amidst the poisonous frogs, snakes, and disease. Ramon and Jim bantered back and forth. They shared the language of gaudy deals and success.

Ramon explained to his friend, once the tractor had cleared the land and they were flying out the gold, Jim would need to roll heavy logs across his runway unless one of Jim's planes was taking off or landing, because bandits would try to take over the *garimpo*. This was another part of the life here. Gold meant bandits along with beautiful women. Jim should expect armed men to approach through the forest unless they tried to land in planes. There was no law here besides money, no police, no recourse other than fighting it out.

Maybe they'll come to you on a beautiful morning, Ramon said with a playful smile, a perfect blue sky when your men are feeling warm and lazy from a night with the girls. Jim, this is the moment to worry. When the jungle is golden from the sun and you feel relaxed. Ramon stretched like a cat. He relished these little *firefights* in the jungle, full-fledged hostile takeover attempts that were common in the region. In the gold business, camps such as Jim's were often overrun and there were terrible slaughters; but Ramon made treachery sound like manly fun, our guys against their guys. Ramon didn't worry. This was the life we were made for, Jim, and Ramon shook his fist. We'll beat them unless they beat us. Another laugh. So what! We'll live the life until someone takes it away. In the jungle, power was the soul of morality as well as the key to surviving. The two men pledged to help each other like blood brothers.

Jim had enormous appetite for this new flagrant life. It fired him like nothing he had ever known.

Every five or six weeks Jim brought the Indian girl with him. While the camp was still in its construction phase, Angela hauled water and timber like one of the men. She was comfortable here. She had grown up in a tiny village only sixty kilometers from Jim's camp. At night, in front of the fire, she told Jim, Ribamar, and Luis about her life in the small village on the banks of the Igapo-Acu River. She spoke rapidly, while Luis translated with a melancholic or agitated expression that seemed to mirror some internal musing of his own.

Angela's community of forty Indians was a world unto itself. The men fished in the river and did a little hunting. The Indians didn't need anything more than what they could harvest from the river or nearby fields and gardens. There was always enough to eat. The villagers considered themselves blessed to live their lives here. Their children fed fish to pink dolphins that appeared like magic in the brown water. The gentle mammals whirled around the legs of the children and their mothers washing clothes in the river.

On the south end of the village, the natives had cut a clearing where a small plane could land in an emergency, but this rarely happened. Most of them lived and died among their family and friends without ever once visiting Manaus. Angela's migration to the city had been a great surprise to everyone.

Angela had learned about farming from her mom, who grew pineapples in a clearing at the top of a steep hill about two miles from their thatched hut. Sometimes Angela helped her mom plant seedlings or haul the burlap sacks, but on most days she worked by herself. She liked working alone, feeling the cool afternoon rain on her wrinkled face, and when she was in the mood she took a swig from a bottle of whiskey and enjoyed a snooze.

Angela's mom was nearly sixty by the time her daughter left for the city. She was a small old woman with the muscled back of a man. For hours she hauled eighty-pound sacks of pineapples. Every night she walked home by herself along a little path through the forest. She had to be inside before dark or she could be killed by the cats. One evening, the old woman came across a jaguar on the path. She dropped the sack and held her machete in her right hand. She watched the animal while it paced to the left and right, back and forth, eyeing the old woman. There was only one way to save herself. She mustn't drop her guard for an instant. This went on for nearly twenty minutes, staring at the pacing cat, waiting for the moment to defend herself. Almost always, such confrontations turn out badly for a native holding a machete. The tension of watching the swift-moving cat while holding the heavy blade wears a man out and he needs to rest his arm, shake the pain out. Then, he is lost. But Angela's mother was fearless and her arm was powerful from working with the machete her whole life. Eventually the cat drifted back into the jungle and the old woman walked home with her sack of pineapples.

Angela's family and neighbors had learned to navigate the considerable dangers of their neighborhood. Mothers stayed close to their infants so they wouldn't be carried off the riverbank by a Royal Eagle. When one of these tremendous birds swooped down for fish, it casts a shadow like a plane. Mothers kept their kids out of the water during the dry season when thousands of starved red-bellied piranhas gathered in deep pools. Once the rains began in November, the vicious little fish glutted themselves on berries and swimming in the river was fairly safe for the next few months.

The locals stayed inside after dark. Nonetheless, the work of the cats was readily visible. South of Angela's tiny community, there was a narrow walking trail, leading hundreds of kilometers toward Pôrto Velho and the gold mines in the south. Beside the path locals found bodies of *garimpeiros* who had been trying to make it to the mines. The men had been killed by jaguars. Usually the local people would put up a simple marker without a name. Ribamar shook his head and reflected, once more, that *garimpeiros* were valiant but stupid men. They couldn't get it through their heads that a single man cannot survive in the jungle.

Angela and Jim slept together in his hammock. She shook her head, no, and smiled at him, yes. She pretended to be shy at first; it was her endearing affectation. She liked him to take her clothes off like gift wrapping. The night fell quickly and she fed him her youthful breasts and tousled his thinning hair. They made love, though Ribamar was always a few yards away, dozing or listening to the droning insects and jungle shrieks, or suddenly the forest lapsed into inexplicable and daunting silence but for their heavy breathing. Jim was inside her for hours as though humping the moist sultry jungle, her smell suffusing him, into his hair and fingernails. When it wouldn't work anymore he pushed his fingers into her and kissed her neck. Angela, sweet laughing Angela, what did she really know and think about? What was in her mind those rapturous nights? Did she think it would never end? How would it end?

In the morning he felt like a lion and headed off into the jungle with Ribamar. Jim promised that he'd take her to visit her parents and little sisters. Once Jim's runway was complete, they'd fly into her village and taxi up to Angela's tiny shack. She'd step out of Jim's plane like a princess bearing gifts; he promised her, but then he forgot. The camp, this great endeavor of his life, obsessed him.

27.

The little house in Florida felt barren, as if the spoiled furniture had already been moved out. Yet Jim and Mara were still lingering in the crestfallen place. Even at this late hour, the most basic questions hung in the air. They didn't have thirty dollars between them.

Why don't you call your rich friend Marvin? she asked with a caustic expression. Jim was jolted by the question, as if she had read his mind. He had been mulling over dialing his old partner and pleading for a few dollars. But what a humiliation after such a history of victories. Marvin knew nothing of Jim's recent life. He shook off her words and rushed back into the jungle.

He described the camp to her. At first, it was so little, hardly anything at all, and all around the clearing there was a virtual wall of trees with flowering trunks and branches that shot back into the ground and tangled with vines and bushes. How could you beat it all back? Jim was running out of time. It was the most passionate section of his life and he told her about it with a building excitement. During the early weeks, when the crew was still sleeping outdoors, Martha, the chubby cook, prepared meals over a big pit. Always there was an enormous pot of rice and beans and the smells of meat cooking on the pit carried into the jungle. Sometimes the miners couldn't resist the smells and walked into the camp to share a meal with Jim and the construction crew. Jim allowed each newly arrived *garimpeiro* one free meal. After that miners needed to pay to eat in the camp with his crew.

All the men enjoyed Martha. Her food was tasty, but eaten in this remote and difficult place it was beyond exquisite. Martha was the only woman in the camp. She had an endearing smile and wore little blouses that showed her cleavage. She was the delight of all the men and she soon had lovers and other suitors lined up. In the jungle camp Martha was irresistible, and it pleased her to no end. She had little interest in returning to Manaus, where she had been homely and ignored.

Months before Jim's cantina was in place, the news had spread to the slums of the city that there was a new mining operation and *garimpeiros* began showing up at the clearing. No one had to tell them what to do or where to go—this hard work was in their ancestry. Their fathers had dug for gold and their grandfathers had lived in the jungle tapping rubber from the trees. The men set up their hammocks and little tents in the jungle. They cooked rice and beans. They began digging in the earth. For all of the physical discomfort and dangers, it was the life they understood and valued.

And so Jim's business came into being. Even in the beginning, when no one knew where to look, the men found small amounts of gold, and they brought it to Jim in little leather pouches; usually it was an ounce or two of dust, but occasionally they found nuggets, even a few large ones, which sent a thrill through the camp. Yes, they all had come to the right place. Jim had discovered a vein of opportunity in the Amazon wilderness. He carefully and honorably weighed the gold and he counted out reals as if he were paying off in a casino. For the *garimpeiros,* gold provided the chance literally to rise from the mud, to move their families from the slums along the fetid slimy riverbanks in Manaus.

Jim was forever working the math in his head, calculating how much he'd pull in each month when he had three hundred men digging and sifting the earth, how much with five hundred men, how many millions he'd clear when the mammoth sluice box was in place; that was his dream, to build a sluice box the size of a lofty downhill ride in an amusement park; such an apparatus could do the work of an additional five hundred workers with shovels. Maybe more. The numbers were staggering.

His mind raced ahead. Jim might open a hotel casino a half mile from the camp, beside the river, a Vegas-styled temple of gold. He'd salt the mud along the riverbank with flecks of ore and let his guests dig a little to get a taste of gold fever.

Mara was subdued at first, while Jim laid out the basics, but soon enough the scope of his dreams and the gold, and the anticipation of gold, went all over her face. So much chance and even the potential for treachery enflamed his young wife. Jim had had his hands right up into the stars. This was what she wanted for herself. Mara had her own bold plans. But now, with her kids shipped out of the house and very close to making her move, she was stirred by him again. Mara no longer knew if she was staying or leaving, which was frustrating. (She was not a woman who tolerated ambivalence, and particularly in herself.) But couples are like this, of course, making meaningful life choices, crossing bold lines, and then reconsidering. Jim's story about the jungle—it was the last story he had to tell her—gave her reason to pause. Mara had known from the start that Jim wasn't a regular old guy. Even now, she would sometimes think that he was ageless and that he could deliver his whole life again; they could do it together.

Jim spent the better part of a week describing the jungle life to Mara. Often he went back to a scene several times because he wanted to taste it over again. He couldn't quite imagine that he had traveled all the way from the jungle to this young woman who was about to break his old heart. Also, Jim was trying to stall for time. But I don't think this was the main thing. The Brazil story had come on like a fever. There was no more guiding or burnishing the story for self-aggrandizement or political correctness. It gushed out of him. I was there for several of these nights. Jim hardly acknowledged me, except once or twice when she stepped out of the room he looked at me with a sickly expression and asked for a couple of hundred. I nodded but felt used and angry.

The story was Jim's passion or his curse and he had to push it all out of himself. If the milkman had come into the room Jim would have told him about the camp, the animals, treachery as common as malaria. Mara was riveted. She was a ruthless girl and she must have found the Brazil history instructive. Also, the story affected me in a way I wouldn't have guessed. Sure, I was greedy for details, but I knew much of it from earlier, beginning decades before on the bridge of his trawler. But Jim couldn't contain himself and it made me nervous. I felt like he could take the story outside and spill it onto the street, give it to anyone who would have it. He would tell the mailman or the fat sweaty guy at the pizza shop or one of his old down lines. By then I had been working on the book for more than a year and I had made the story my own. I wanted every detail, but I didn't want him throwing them around. Or even telling Mara. Not now. I felt like the story was getting away from me. I wanted him to shut up. This meretricious girl could take it for herself and sell it. Where would it leave me after a year of writing and imagining my own treasure? Maybe Jim's history of paranoia and greed had infected me—I don't know.

After two months of being cautious, Jim began jumping out of his hammock at dawn. This was the real life, just as Ramon Vega had said. Jim wanted to dive deeply into the pool. His great desire

spread out in all directions, and for a time he confused it with im-
mortality. He felt confident he wouldn't get malaria. He wouldn't
take a bullet. He wouldn't crash in the plane, although each landing
and takeoff was a close brush with tall trees at the end of the very
short runway. Animals couldn't get him. One morning Ribamar
grabbed Jim's arm when he was reaching into a hole. It contained
poisonous frogs. One bite might have killed him, but Jim was moving like a magic arrow.

Ribamar taught Jim where to step, what roots he must eat if he
got an infection. If he got lost, Jim learned to beat the trunk or the
massive exposed roots of a *sumaumeira* tree, and Ribamar could
hear the resonant thump two miles away.

Jim tried to adopt Ribamar's style of traveling through the bush
gently moving the vegetation aside. It was like swimming through
the greenery. In a month, Jim was moving at the older man's brisk
pace. Jim quickly devoured the signposts and mysteries of the rain
forest. Creatures were hiding everywhere. Ribamar showed Jim
small bats protecting themselves behind the drooping leaves of
trees. He pointed out lethargic armadillos burrowed into the ground
and a twelve-foot boa constrictor that was practically invisible
moving slowly along the leafy jungle floor.

Jim tracked deer, tapir, and wild pig for Martha's outdoor grill.
Ribamar sensed early on that Jim had a gift for finding animals; he
could see and feel them like an Indian. Jim had learned about tracking animals as a young boy in Canada. He would show Ribamar a
bent blade of grass, or the traces of an animal moving along a dry
riverbed. One time, walking along a tiny path to the river, they
both stopped at the same instant, sensing something foreboding
and powerful. They looked up, and just ahead of them there was a
black jaguar crouched on a tree limb. They grinned at each other
and gave the cat a wide berth.

Jim was learning this world in huge gulps. At dawn in his
hammock he would think how his dad would have loved this life,

foraging in the wild for game and fortune. But oddly, he had Ribamar's face.

Jim stalled calling Phyllis for as long as he could. Every second or third trip back to Manaus, he reluctantly dialed his house in Canada. He'd quickly mention something about the jungle to appease her curiosity while feeling chagrined for tarnishing his experience with insipid conversation. Then he'd ask her to wire money so he could pay his men. Jim was beginning to sell small amounts of gold in Manaus, he explained, holding in his exasperation, but he was supporting a large crew of men and still had to spend thousands building the camp. He needed money, as much as she could get.

One day she told him Marvin had stopped depositing checks in Jim's account; there were problems with the business. He cut her off in mid-sentence. He didn't want to know about Marvin. After a pregnant pause he ordered her to sell her diamond engagement ring. Jim had spent thirty thousand for it. He needed funds to buy a water cannon. What is that? she asked him. Don't worry about it, Phyllis. Just sell the ring.

Phyllis was hardly more than a voice on the other end. He'd married her impulsively six months after Ava had run off. He didn't feel anything for Phyllis and didn't want to. He didn't want to be dragged back. He had been another Jim in Canada.

But it was hard to get her to stop talking. She insisted that he hear about his cook and chauffeur, a married couple who were still living above the garage, in the servants' quarters; they had stayed on even though Phyllis could no longer pay them a salary; they couldn't find work and had no place to go; it was a painful situation for Phyllis; he was jumping out of his skin listening to this. What did she know about hardship? She dressed like a party favor. She wanted Jim to understand that the manner of the cook and chauffeur had changed. She used the word "paranoid," although Jim didn't trust Phyllis's choice of words. It was painful listening to her. He didn't care about the chauffeur and his wife.

There was no sense or fairness to it. Phyllis had a big heart, and she was trying so hard and failing. She came without guile and without Ava's deep pool of regret. He soon began to resent Phyllis for this.

Phyllis dressed in gypsy outfits, all bosomy in the style of Brazilian women; she looked at pictures in books and tried to imagine her way into his life. She wanted to be appealing for Jim when he came home. Some of his Canadian friends considered her a duped woman, but she ignored them and pushed ahead bravely, doing his bidding. She told her friends she needed money for Jim's Brazil project; that's the phrase she used, as if he were constructing a majestic dam to save the rain forest and local Indians.

Mara scowled each time Jim referred to Phyllis. Even now, with his former wife vanquished from their lives, maybe sleeping in a park frequented by homeless people in North Miami where Jim had brought her two shopping bags of clothes and twenty bucks, three months before, even now, Mara held Phyllis in contempt. The story of Phyllis's struggle in Canada, twenty-five years earlier, disgusted Mara. It was something more primal than Phyllis's naïveté: Mara seethed as if his spurned wife were trying to worm her way back into their lives, into these last repellent rooms. Even while Mara was contemplating her separation from Jim, if you'd call it that, she feared being robbed by Phyllis. Mara wanted every drop that was left.

Phyllis was only twenty-six and young for her age when Jim had disappeared into the jungle in 1980. She was living by herself in the house he had built for Ava. Jim's monument on Lake Ontario was waiting for the next run of good times, with half the designer rooms unheated and the furniture covered with sheets. His game house on the beach was closed down like a chilly mausoleum. Phyllis believed that Jim would soon come back to her with a fortune and they'd amp it up again, the tennis parties and feasts on the deck with dancing lights spilling out onto the lake. She was keeping it for him. Phyllis appeased her anxiety and poverty with positive thinking. She could not imagine that Jim no longer thought about his dream house.

Usually he didn't call home for two weeks at a time, and during these stretches she was mostly by herself. Jim had never explained to her anything about Marvin's aversion to paying corporate taxes. But now with her husband mostly unreachable, government investigators sometimes referred to as CPAs with guns were all over Jim and Marvin's factories. Marvin's clever tax evasions had reached back years and amounted to tens of millions. It would prove to be one of the largest tax fraud cases ever prosecuted in Canada. Authorities had tapped the phones on Jim's estate as part of their investigation. Jim's business friends were alarmed about being implicated and didn't want Phyllis stopping by or phoning. She was frightened and in way over her head. Jim did not want to hear about any of it.

Then he stopped calling home. As the weeks passed, she decided he was punishing her for not sending money. Then she began to worry he was dead. Phyllis tried to stay positive, but how would she continue without him? She couldn't pay the bills. Not one word from Jim for three months. She began dressing in black and avoided seeing people, even her sister.

When he called, finally, Jim sounded distracted and tired. She didn't know how to respond. Was it right to be elated or deeply offended? So Phyllis rushed ahead breathlessly. She told him that one afternoon, out of the blue, Ava had rung their front doorbell. This had been a singular moment in Phyllis's life. She had never met Ava, who was Jim's great love and the wellspring of his existence. Ava was so monumental in his life that Phyllis had never felt jealousy. But rather, during her months with him, she was daunted by the specter of Ava. She understood from the start, if Ava changed her mind, Jim would install her back in the house and Phyllis would be out. Perhaps this was the moment.

When Phyllis opened the door, she greeted a battered woman. Ava's mouth and the left side of her face were scraped and bruised and she was missing a tooth. She had been pushed out of a moving car by her elderly boyfriend, the father of Ava's husband before Jim, who was also a drunk. Standing beside Ava was Jim's son with long stringy hair and a pasty, pimply complexion. He was clutching a little white poodle. Meeting Ava and Jim's son in one moment was a lot to take in.

Ava sat on the L-shaped brown leather sofa that she had once selected from an Italian furniture catalog. She looked around the living room and noticed the paintings unmoved from where she had placed them. She smiled.

Aren't they beautiful? Phyllis asked nervously. She had a feeling Ava saw more deeply than she did.

Ava shook her head, and took a breath.

I can't take care of him anymore, she said in a flat voice, gesturing toward the boy. Even all beat up, she was still beautiful.

Ava wanted to leave for California to try to salvage her life. She knew someone there. She'd hoped the boy and dog could stay with Jim.

The wives nodded.

Ava was trying to locate where she'd once fit in here, if she ever had. She shivered a little at the loneliness. And yet the house was more appealing to her now, in its repose. The great expanse of the lake was regal without Jim's noisy motorboats and glamour splashed all over. She had learned from him about taking chances to win big. Ironically, Jim had given her the courage to try with Lenny. It still seemed right.

Ava hadn't heard Jim was living in Brazil. She hoped he was happy.

I don't know if he's alive, Phyllis said helplessly. She was feeling so lonely. She thought about inviting Ava to spend the night or maybe even a few days. She wondered what Jim would think. Would it be wrong?

Ava was drawn to Phyllis's helplessness. She might have stayed if Phyllis had asked. That was in the air for a minute or two.

Ava made an expression of resignation. Her son was distracted and wild-eyed. Phyllis thought he might be on drugs. He was clutching his mother's white poodle. Phyllis gulped at the face of this monumental change in her life.

She rushed ahead with her story fearing that Jim would cut her off; it was so easy to misconstrue his silence on the phone from Manaus.

Jim, Phyllis said, Michael is cuckoo. He sleeps on the ground in his old room above the garage with piles of clothes all around him. The kid washes his hands and then goes to the sink and washes again, and again. You get what I'm saying? Peter and Susan, she said, referring to Jim's chauffeur and cook, have convinced him that I want to sell his dog or put it to sleep. I've told him, I would never do that, but he doesn't believe me.

There was much more to say, but Jim stopped her. He needed to absorb this news. Jim promised to call back. Then he was gone again.

Phyllis tried to accept the silence on the other end. She tried to feel the jungle. She wanted to be a good wife. She tried to be cheerful. She wanted to come there, but he'd made it clear she would be out of place. He told her to look after his affairs.

Jim couldn't quite envision Ava and the boy. It disturbed him to have Phyllis narrate the story and he tried to pick through it setting aside her singsong voice. He surely could have them back now; it's what he had wanted beyond everything else. Jim couldn't quite remember Ava's face. Even the ache of Ava disappeared into the warm, humid evening and the bedlam of parrots and insects. Jim was standing on the back porch of the large house outside Manaus watching Angela walk across the yard watering plants. He fancied that she'd grown from the land like her trees. Near the west wall, she had started putting in an area of seedling pineapple trees in the spirit of her mother. Angela was so confident and fulfilled. He liked the sight of her legs soiled with dirt from kneeling on the ground. He savored the smells of her cooking. He liked all of her smells.

Why should he want to go back? Jim had the jungle, the girl. He was king here. Gold was coming soon, truckloads. He loved it in the camp; all the men did. It is important to remember this in light of what happened. No one wanted to leave. The life was so exciting. The music at night wafted into the forest, calling the men camped beside the river. Every night Frank Sinatra invited the little miners. A cold beer in the jungle was the best a man ever tasted. In the city Jim's girls were attractive, but out here with the jaguars and snakes they were a dream.

Every key decision went past Jim, particularly for the first year. He decided how much punishment a man deserved and who got a seat out on the small plane. In most renegade mining operations in the Amazon, gunmen spent their time sitting around waiting for war. They flirted with the girls and drank beer. In Jim's camp he had them working on construction projects and later on they toiled over the sluice box. Even the two mangy camp dogs lived by Jim's rules. The mongrels barked whenever any animal or person approached the clearing from the forest, but Jim could not stand their yelping when he returned from walks with Ribamar or climbed out of the plane returning from Manaus. He trained the dogs to greet him with silent joy, wagging tails and squirming at his feet.

More and more *garimpeiros* showed up at the camp. They came out of the trees in bunches. Jim offered them a cold beer and a hearty pat on the back and Martha had her big pot of rice and beans and something cooking on the barbecue; often it was monkey, which the men favored. The miners came through the jungle flashing victory and tired smiles as if they'd crossed a big ocean in a little boat. Each month, one or two were killed by jaguars. Almost always they were men who tried to brave it through the jungle alone. Within several miles of the camp, there was an unusual infestation of little cats the local Indians called *jaguatiricas*. Likely, it was the smells of garbage and cooking that lured them close. These ferocious animals, the size of large house cats, attacked in small packs of three to five, and if a man survived he recalled the sound of whining babies, but almost always a single man was doomed. The small cats sprung out of the underbrush with thin devil faces and raced up a man's body, ripping and biting. Even these horrible creatures didn't keep the miners away. After a year, there were three hundred *garimpeiros* working on the land and selling their gold to Jim.

Sixty percent of Jim's men came down with malaria or dengue fever, which was even worse. Occasionally, an Indian dropped down, hemorrhaging, and died beneath the trees. Some of the sickest workers flew out, but most of them suffered for a few weeks and then went back to work. Men didn't want to leave. The life was so exciting and fraught with the chance for wealth and glory.

Luis was the exception. In camp, his expression was forlorn. He felt feverish half the time and was afraid to bathe in the river where there were too many things waiting to kill him. Luis couldn't distinguish between the heat, malaria, and worry. He was miserable without his wife and mistresses. In the camp he avoided Jim because he was embarrassed by his weakness, and he felt overshadowed by Ribamar. Luis hunted for shady spots to keep cool. He did a little construction work or waited around, wiping the sweat from his eyes until, finally, Jim signaled it was time to return to Manaus for a few days or a week. Then, Luis could emerge from the shadows and become, once again, the progenitor of business associations and intimacies, if he could only survive until then.

28.

At first the prospect of running a cantina had made Jim uneasy. But he was advised that he needed to have a place with music, drink, and girls or the men would become moody and go off to other *garimpos* to find gold. Even Ribamar agreed that it was so. The cantina was a part of the life here, a gift for the men in this harsh place; that's how Jim justified it to himself. There really wasn't any choice if the camp was going to run effectively.

Jim paid his girls 50 percent of their take. He might have kept a larger cut for himself, but it appealed to him to make poor women wealthy, as if the Lord had stepped in to change a woman's destiny. In a year working in Jim's camp, a girl cleared about two hundred thousand dollars. It was an inconceivable sum for a poor person from Manaus.

In return, the eighteen- or nineteen-year-old delivered her gifts in a tiny, hot cubicle only large enough for a small mattress and a washbowl to clean her men. She began each session with a kind of foreplay by dipping her thumb and two first fingers into the miner's narrow leather pouch and slowly withdrawing as much gold as she could hold in one pinch. The men loved this starter that proved their virility in the jungle, something that went beyond sex, and the girls were very impressed by what they felt with their fingers in the pouch and teased the men, took a little extra with the hint that what would follow would be indescribable bliss. Usually, it came to about three hundred dollars for twenty minutes of love in this wild outpost where greed and privation pushed desire to the limits.

The men were always falling hard for girls and would some-times pay a favorite fifteen hundred dollars for the entire night, as much as a man earned digging and sifting for two months or more. Men fought over girls. Jim stayed clear of these drunken battles, even when one of the men took out a pistol and shot another worker. This happened several times. But Jim dolled out harsh punishment if a man abused one of his whores.

It was true, all the men loved the cantina. Some *garimpeiros* made monthly visits as if taking a short holiday in the city. What a treat after suffering weeks of wretched mosquitoes and slinging mud from a hole. A few of the older men walked to the clearing two or three nights a week for conversation and a cold beer. Setimbrano was one who no longer visited the girls. He was a tall, imposing white-haired figure of about fifty with the gravitas of Ribamar. Jim liked to sit with him and Ribamar drinking beer like three old fishermen at the end of the day. The *garimpo* is a psycho-logical illness, the tall man reflected, and then he smiled, just barely, to affirm it was a malady that captivated him still.

Ribamar knew Setimbrano from thirty years earlier, but re-cently this impressive self-educated man had been working in a *garimpo* three hundred kilometers to the south where the gold was found by divers dredging in the Madeira River. The riverbed was called the big hole of pain because many workers got sick and died. For years the illness in the muddy river was linked to black magic, but eventually *garimpeiros* learned that the hole of pain gave them radiation poisoning along with gold nuggets. Nonetheless, most *garimpeiros* remained on the job, the river's peril heightening their gold fever along with the passion of cantina nights. The life here is an illusion, Setimbrano would say, savoring his beer while Ribamar nodded gravely. Each night men crowded into Jim's cantina as Frank Sinatra crooned into the dark rain forest.

After eighteen months, there were more than five hundred men camping out on Jim's land, digging holes; some of them were twelve or fifteen feet deep. It was hot, punishing work. Eventually, every one of the men walked into the clearing to sell gold to Jim for 60 percent of what it would get in Manaus and to book passage home in Jim's plane. There was no other way out. Even in groups, walking out of the forest was very risky because of animals and the likelihood of being killed by bandits for their savings.

To return home, a man put his name on Jim's list and waited around the camp until there was a seat available. It usually took four or five days. Meanwhile, the worker rented a hammock, ate Martha's delicious food. At night he drank a beer and felt intoxicated by the music, and the girls were so young and playful. Not just sexy, they were tender and caring. They asked about his hardship and great plans, caressed his face. Luis was right about the girls. How could a man resist, particularly a man who had endured the jungle for five months? A small lump of gold dust hardly mattered when a miner was bringing home a kilo. And just beyond the clearing, the jungle was saturated with more gold. It was like fruit. There were nuggets out there worth ten thousand, even more. If only a man kept digging he would strike it rich and never work another day.

After four days in camp, drinking *pinga* and enjoying the girls, the *garimpeiro* had no more gold left to exchange with Jim for reals, not even enough for a seat on the plane to Manaus. He needed to tramp back to his deep hole in the forest and begin shoveling more mud and gravel, slowly accumulating gold until he could return to the city and his family. Then the same thing happened again unless his difficult work was interrupted by an anaconda in the river or he succumbed to malaria.

The life in this place is an illusion, Setimbrano said. All the men knew it. And yet they savored it. They dreamed of striking it rich until they could no longer manage the backbreaking work. When elderly *garimpeiros* lived out their days in Manaus they reminisced about the perils they'd braved, the cantina nights and fervent dreams while sleeping deeply in a hammock between the trees.

One morning Phyllis was awakened by the chauffeur's wife. There were fifteen men standing outside the gate to Jim's estate, one of them with a warrant. Soon the attack force of cops and IRS agents was combing the main residence and Jim's game house for hidden wall safes. They found three. They looked for cash, securities, jewelry, and any records that might help their case, but all they discovered were a few porno tapes and two small bags of marijuana. One of the men snickered. The agents catalogued Jim's boats, cars, furniture, everything of any value. They pretended Phyllis wasn't there, watching. They went through her underwear. They took Jim's paintings off the walls. She worried they'd be damaged and raised her voice. The agents were dismantling her world, piece by piece. Everything Phyllis owned was handled. They took her engagement ring. She should have sold it. Jim was right.

Many months earlier, before he'd left for Brazil, Jim said to her, If the police come hide your passport. When she had the chance, she took the passport from her makeup drawer and slipped it into her pocketbook. She believed in Jim. She was listening for his voice for guidance. The passport would save her. She could fly to him in Manaus. The police gave her and the boy two hours to leave the house.

Michael shivered violently while he clutched Ava's ratty little dog. What he must have thought while Phyllis rushed up the stairs to pack some of their clothes. The chauffeur and his wife were right after all. Hell and madness and cruelty had descended upon them. The boy's mother was gone. The house was gone, almost gone. Soon they would take his dog.

One of the men drove off with Phyllis's car. In a minute, she had been dealt a whole new reality. She had this crazy teenager, no money, and no home. There wasn't any way to reach Jim. He was still living his life in the jungle as though he had millions up north to back up his play.

She made a quick call to her sister. By nightfall, Phyllis, the boy and dog were staying with her sister in a small one-bedroom apartment in downtown Toronto. The chauffeur and cook were gone. The dream house was gone. The only things of value Phyllis had been able to save were two signed Monet prints Jim had given to her before he'd left for Brazil. They had been sitting in a framing shop in Toronto.

Phyllis tried to befriend the boy, but he was fierce and very strange. He was repelled by tenderness. Michael simmered and you didn't want to touch him. He would burn you. Phyllis wondered if he could accept love from anyone, his mother? He fixated on the idea of dyeing his hair green as though it were crucial to his welfare. Phyllis gently tried to talk him out of it but ended up helping him do it in the bathroom. They made a mess and laughed at the green dye on the tiles. It didn't matter to Michael that people on the street looked at him. But he let Phyllis in, just a little, maybe because she was harmless, just barely managing, and she was trying to understand things that were beyond her horizon. Michael had this cutting off-the-wall humor that made her laugh and cringe until tears were rolling down her cheeks. Then, in a heartbeat, he'd close down. She could not imagine Jim tolerating such a person.

Every eight or nine days, occasionally he could stall it off for two weeks, Jim, Luis, and three gunmen flew back to Manaus with gold Jim had collected from his *garimpeiros*. Seeing the girl was the best part of these trips. Jim was eager to tell her what was happening at the camp. Soon they would build an enormous sluice box, a hundred and fifty feet long. Everything would change for the better with the sluice box in place. The gold would flow into their hands. The real life would begin.

She nodded, tried to imagine what he was talking about. She felt his urgency. Jim no longer had patience for the view outside his picture window of fruit trees and lethargic caimans. His whole manner had changed. His body had grown harder.

Jim could not afford impediments. He was running out of cash. He tried to pick up the pace. He urged his men to work harder, the small construction crew and the gunmen who resented doing manual labor. He needed Luis to make phone calls, find a more trustworthy gold buyer, locate a shop to fabricate aluminum cross members for the sluice box that would make his fortune. The sluice box became everything. There was a long list of things to do. He needed Luis to get moving. But there was a distracted look in Luis's eyes that Jim didn't like. Jim pushed them all. Although Luis he had to coddle along.

Jim pulled out the scroll of old promises. He was well practiced, having recited them, with variations, for more than thirty years. The gold was for all of them, he pledged. Soon, very soon, Jim's gunmen would never again need to risk their skins for ten bucks a day. Jim became emotional. He cared for all of his guys. It was true.

He lured them ahead. That was also true. He offered them attractive packages. He'd pay them a little less now, five or six dollars a day instead of ten, and give them much more later. Jim could negotiate deals, even in the steaming jungle. Soon they would all be driving around Manaus in big, powerful sedans. He spoke beneficently of bonuses and little partnerships. He'd take them all to Rio for lavish vacations or he'd take them to Vegas, why not? He'd fly them to Las Vegas.

Jim summoned the endless future of lavish cars and boats and idyllic islands off the beaten track. Jim had always mainly sold happiness and optimism. The gold was for all of his children, not just Jim. Just work with him, put in the hours, take a little less now. Because it's coming. He talked to each man. He probed for the hot button, even in the absurdly remote camp. What do you want out of life, really want? Jim's hired guns smiled at him with their fat greasy faces and sweaty camouflage shirts; they shook their heads and grinned, even the ones who hadn't visited emotion in half a lifetime. They called him Jim in a lingering way that implied *gringo maluco,* crazy American, who will do anything to win.

Jim promised to make Luis and Ribamar wealthy men. Soon Jim's top guys would never have to work another day in their lives.

Ribamar stood outside the circle, watching and smoking a cigarette, listening to the sounds beyond the clearing. He was a sentinel among fools. Jim cast him a glance. No more time for the music, Ribamar, not now. Ribamar nodded. He drew his own conclusions.

Except for the girl, trips to Manaus felt to Jim like bloated time, dragging his heels, waiting for Luis. Too much eating and sitting around Brazilian steak restaurants, driving to stores flanked by his big men mopping their faces. He put off calling Phyllis—tried to force the dying world out of his head. He had work to do back in the camp. They were rolling, and the gathering pace of it thrilled him. He needed to be back there. He wanted to start cutting timbers for the sluice box. He needed Luis, and more often than not he couldn't find him. Luis was irreplaceable for his gift for drawing talent from a hat. But Jim also counted on Luis to translate when he sold the gold to one of the local buyers, and twenty other things. Jim wasn't getting the best prices. It was impossible to negotiate in Portuguese.

Without Luis, Jim had too much time to think and he felt dragged down by his own deficiencies. He wasn't sure if they were making a profit or even breaking even. He had never learned to read spreadsheets. He didn't know how to do research. Jim didn't have patience for such things. He wasn't Marvin Gesler.

Luis went off to his women friends. He needed time for himself. He tried to tell Jim that something was wrong. Luis had become afflicted by dread. For no reason his heart would begin racing. He had premonitions. It was something more cataclysmic than worry about disease or animals. An expression would pass across his face, terror and loathing for the work they were doing in the jungle, as though he were casting a warning.

Luis, what's wrong, man? Why are you looking at me that way? Don't you see what we're doing here! Luis covered his face with his hand, a delicate, girly gesture, trying to erase his expression. He tried to change himself for Jim, but Luis was losing his grip. He ran off to his girls for solace and to search for himself apart from the camp and Jim's unwavering convictions. Luis dreamed of corpses crowding him in his own bed. One day, out of the blue, he grasped Jim's arm and said, I know you are leaving me, going back to America. Please, Jim, don't go. Luis's face was awash and he looked a little green and teary. Jim shook his head, no. I'm not going anywhere.

Jim needed the gold. He had to have it. It never occurred to him that he might lose the house on Lake Ontario. He was jarred by this news much more than by the reappearance of Ava. He'd always believed that she would show up one day. Even after learning that the government had seized his factories, he never thought that they could take his house. With that place sitting on the lake he could thumb his nose at Marvin Gesler. He could succeed in the gold business or fail because he had the house behind him; it was worth millions; he had been esteemed for owning such a place. Now he was playing without a safety net. He only had the girl whom he didn't understand (but he loved her more and more) and the gold, which only came in trickles. Jim could make it work in his favor. He'd done that as a boy, come back from zero. He'd saved his family when they were starving. These were the stakes he liked best, all or nothing. He could do it, rev up the energy and conviction and win.

Jim showered all the men with promises and hope. He inspired them, even Luis, though he came ahead half-crazed.

Luis wrested the idea out of his tortured being. It was so obvious. Why not bring Iliana into their operation? She had studied geology at the university. She was available, waiting for the chance to launch her career. What would be the risk? Jim needed a real expert who knew where to look for gold. They had five hundred people out on the land, guessing where to dig. At least talk to her. Maybe she would make some suggestions about where to construct the sluice box. She could save them months of trial and error.

What a smile she had, broad and captivating and self-assured. She spread her geologic maps and aerial photographs on Jim's rough-planked dining room table. Iliana was wearing rayon pants, an off-white silk shirt, and sandals with three-inch stiletto heels, everything classy and expensive. Iliana put the stakes right out there with maps, charts, the insider lingo of meandering rivers, black shale, granite, earth fissures. She was here for considerable money. She would deliver. He should take a long look. She sold herself like a Mercedes.

That Hollywood smile and great legs made him a little breathless. She laid out her ideas. There were things to look for, drainage patterns, other clues about the evolution of the landscape. She was very firm and sure-handed. She would cost a lot. A lot. Iliana was high maintenance. And Jim felt the danger, right then, in the first minutes. She was Ramon's girl. They would be in the jungle together. That tension was a part of her proposal. She liked risks and money. Iliana was very smart. She could deliver the gold.

The smells of Angela's dinner seemed to seal the deal. Jim always relished her stew with meat and potatoes. He remarked on the smells from the kitchen, but there was an expression on Iliana's face, some mild distaste.

Listen, for all her fancy geology talk, Jim didn't know if Iliana was a real scientist. He knew she'd cost plenty. She appealed to him and that's how Jim did business. He went with his gut. In minutes, maybe in the first minute, she'd become his hired expert. His mind was racing. She could take over the Manaus end. She could sell the gold for him in town, get better prices than Luis. Jim wouldn't have to worry if Luis was off with his girlfriends. Luis didn't know the ins and outs of selling gold. She did. Maybe she was feeding Jim a line, but he didn't think so. He didn't comparison shop. When he liked a car he bought it right off the showroom floor while he felt first love. Iliana was a beauty.

Angela served the food and Jim kept his eyes on one of the maps. All of a sudden he felt ashamed about Angela. He didn't want Iliana to know that his girl was a peasant with no education, no good clothes; she was dirty every night from planting in the field.

Angela was clearly pleased with herself. She had prepared his favorite meal, and he nodded, pretending to be focused on big business. Then she was back in the kitchen. It was an awkward situation, but he started to enjoy it. Jim got away with things his whole life. He always believed that he could slide through and win.

He and Iliana were drinking red wine. She was beautiful all right, long legs, lustrous black hair. She liked to run her hands through her hair. He wanted to touch her hand and then he did, let it linger for a moment, making his point. She smiled at him. All of this was happening very fast.

He'd eaten half his plate before he noticed she wasn't touching her food.

What's wrong? he asked.

I'm not very hungry.

Come on. You don't like meat or something? It's delicious.

Do you know what she's cooked for you?

It's a stew.

She wrinkled her nose. Jim, the name of it is *nutria*. It means "rat." A big rat.

Iliana spoke perfect English with barely a trace of an accent. She had spent three years in Chicago going to high school while living with an aunt.

When I was a kid, I'd smell them roasting behind the house, she continued, the dinner for our servants. In my country, poor people will eat anything. She's feeding you rat.

Iliana shook her head, to brush aside the subject. He smelled the light fragrance of rose and lavender. Then he breathed her again; he couldn't restrain himself. She nudged him ahead with hints and dares. What arrangement do you have in mind, Jim? She smiled. It was a large question. She had a very big ambition. He needed a lot of help. He needed to find the gold and sell it at the best price. Jim knew where this was leading, but maybe it was okay. If she could find the gold.

She backed off a little, tucked her feet up underneath her. She told him a little about her background. Her father had owned an anthracite mine a hundred miles north of Manaus. After returning from the States she had studied geology and mining at the university so she could help her dad with his operation. She adored her father. During her last year in school, he got sick and soon after he lost the business. He died one year later. It happened so quickly.

Iliana was biting her lip. Everything was lost. She'd trusted her father. Her dreams were linked to his. Each month she sent money back to her mother, who was looking after Iliana's three younger sisters. All this tragedy had made her angry and very directed. There were many sides to Iliana. She wanted Jim to see this. But she always kept her eye on the mark. She could come at you from many angles. She was faster than he was, and probably smarter. She was hard to locate. No one possessed her.

Jim nodded.

Look, Jim, I'm not looking for a salary, not even a good salary.

Jim nodded and pushed his plate away.

She waited until it was almost awkward. Jim, I think this could work out. For both of us, I do. She took a breath and then the softness was all gone. You're finding gold on your property every day. Not so much, but every day your men take some from the ground. That's important. Many areas in the Amazonas region have no gold. There is a chance to be wealthy, exceedingly wealthy. You need to find a dense concentration or you're wasting time. There are clues. I can help you with this part. There are signs to look for. Maybe you are sleeping on top of it. I'll find the gold and I'll sell it for you. I can do this, but I don't want to be cut out. I'm not coming into this for a few dollars. I'm not looking for a salary. I want a deal based upon what I produce.

Iliana wanted a piece of the action. She would deliver a lot. His choice.

For a few minutes now, Angela had been standing in the doorway and she could feel the room alive with bold plans. Soon there would be a course change in her life. But where would it lead? She came to Jim and leaned against him with her arm draped softly on his shoulder. She had no idea of the scope of Jim's conversations with this stranger or how they might come to affect her. Most of her life with Jim was based on guessing. Whenever Angela listened to his business dreams her wonder took the shape of a slightly be-mused smile that he loved, even now, when he had been revealed.

Each morning Iliana and four men headed out from the camp, hack-ing their way through heavy underbrush and tough, tangled vines. They inched north toward the Rio Novo, clearing away swatches of vegetation so she could measure rises and dips in the land and in some areas digging down until they found gravel; then they moved a little to the east and worked back to camp; it was exhausting work, back and forth, steadily edging east toward the far end of the landing strip. Even in the baking heat and humidity, Iliana dressed in tailored khakis like a model on a shoot. But she kept pushing into the forest, nearly oblivious to the hordes of gnats and sand flies and the danger of the cats, and she was methodical and forceful with the men. She brought a few instruments to make basic tests, but mainly she was looking around. There were certain key tells: the color of the topsoil, the placement of rocks. Again and again, she ordered them to clear patches of earth so she could examine the shape of the exposed land. She worked long hours. Once she got to the end of the landing strip, she planned to widen the search to the east and, if necessary, she would study the land closer to the river, but for logistical reasons it would be much better if the sluice box could be constructed close to the camp.

At dark she slumped down on a rough bench in front of the can-tina and drank a beer. She was exhausted from the heat and swat-ting bugs. She pulled off her socks and massaged her feet. She had pretty little feet. The gunmen looked her over. A few of them knew that she was Ramon Vega's girl, or had been, and the news spread through the camp and spawned rumors and racy conjectures about the future. In a little while, she asked Luis or Ribamar to watch the door while she washed herself in the communal shower area, just off the dining hall.

The finished camp consisted of three rectangular thatch-roofed buildings, held up by rough-hewn wooden poles that had been the skinny trunks of young *açaí* trees. The buildings were strung along the western end of the landing strip. The dormitory, farthest to the west, had twenty-five cots and was where Iliana slept, curtained off from Jim's gunmen and Luis. Jim's small sleeping and office space was on the east end of this building. Next came the cantina, a plain room large enough for seven tables and a small bar where late at night a short raven-haired Indian girl named Maria danced for the men. Each night of the week men fell in love in this unadorned place with uneven planks resting on the dirt and a leaky roof. The six tiny cubicles where the girls worked and slept were a separate structure just east of the cantina.

Iliana sized up the cantina, did some math in her head. She was very good with numbers. She considered the irony of these uneducated girls lying on their backs and making more in a month than she could in seven or eight years. She thought about what it would be like working for one year in the jungle and then living rich for the rest of her days. She thought of the gold coming into her hands each day and it made her peevish and then slightly forlorn. If the arrangement with Jim didn't pan out, and finding a rich vein of gold was a long shot, Iliana would be back in Manaus working as a shopgirl. She was only twenty-six, but in this part of the world that was old. Any of these whores could have bought her. It was maddening and she had to remind herself each day to smile and be lovely.

At night Ribamar set up his chair in front of the door to Jim's little room on the east end of the dorm. In a side holster Ribamar carried a pearl-handled .38-caliber revolver that was a gift from Jim. Leaning against the wall was the single-shot bolt-action rifle that Ribamar had carried into the forest for thirty years. He smoked a cigarette and listened closely to the jungle and the occasional barking of the dogs. The camp was falling asleep. Sometimes he closed his eyes, but he was listening. He was no longer protecting

Jim so much from animals. Ribamar's concern had passed to Jim's own gunmen, or maybe there was something else. He was listening deeply. There were too many deals in the air. Too many promises. Too many delays and disappointments. Some of Jim's men would have killed him for a better deal, for money instead of promises. Jim never took this seriously. He believed too much in what he was selling.

Ribamar was a force of nature. The men thought of him as a spirit, perhaps impossible to kill, and that helped to keep Jim alive. There were favorite stories and speculations about Ribamar's unusual powers that the older *garimpeiros* passed along. It was said that he had developed immunity to malaria and even to some snakebites, and that he could find food in the jungle when *garimpeiros* would have starved, that he could will himself to heal from diseases and even grave wounds. No one knew exactly what was true or exaggerated because he wouldn't speak of his gifts. Ribamar had become a fable even while he watched Jim's back and tried to distinguish the friends from the enemies. It was said that when he was a young man Ribamar had once wrestled with a large black jaguar. According to Setimbrano's narration, Ribamar had been surprised by the jaguar and was badly mauled. Then he rolled free and in one split second there was an opening and he threw himself onto the jaguar's back. He cinched his left arm around the animal's head and coiled his legs tight against the cat's belly. The jaguar went wild, smashed the two of them into trees, clawing, but couldn't shake this phantom fighter. While he held tight on to the neck Ribamar reached with his other hand for his knife and slit the animal's throat. The cat began spinning, with blood flying everywhere. That's the last Ribamar remembered until he came to, pressed against a tree trunk with the bloody cat on top of him. To survive, Ribamar had become a jaguar himself, Setimbrano said with reverence. Jim had seen the scars on Ribamar's neck and back, but the old man only shrugged when Jim asked about the story.

Then one day Iliana observed a pattern of declivities in the land three hundred yards east of the airstrip. Close beneath the leaves and shallow topsoil they found suspended sediment, silt, and sand. Five feet deeper there was black gravel. She could barely contain herself but didn't say a word for two more days. The men kept cutting back the bush and vines as she mapped the course of the sloping basin that snaked northwest toward the Rio Novo. It was what she'd been looking for all along, an old dried-out riverbed. Almost surely, this one had been an offshoot of the Rio Novo. Iliana knew some basics about geology, but also she'd been very lucky. The gravel was rich with gold, in some places five times the concentration of the best areas discovered thus far by *garimpeiros* prospecting Jim's territory.

In the following weeks, Jim worked alongside his men for sixteen-hour days. He had more energy than any of them, and he was game for the dirtiest jobs. Jim and his crew burned down the trees and hauled away charred limbs and mountains of green bramble and young vines that wouldn't burn. The tractor shoved the mess into the dense jungle, terrifying spider monkeys, *jaguatiricas,* birds, and snakes. A few of the little cats became disoriented and sprinted across the newly scorched ground. Jim was beating back the jungle. His surly gunmen worked without complaint alongside fifty *garimpeiros.* The time for promises was past. Everyone could see the gold flecked in the gravel.

Before breakfast Ramon Vega's brightly painted orange helicopter whooshed over the tree line; beneath its belly hung a heavy load of aluminum cross sections, called riffles, for Jim's sluice box. From the air Ramon could see a swath newly cut into the jungle as though a meteor had burned out the trees and left a large crater. In a few days, Jim would divert a stream to fill the huge hole with water. Just east of the landing strip a vast superstructure rose from the jungle floor like a flattened-down ski jump. No one had ever built anything like this before in the Amazon. Men were climbing all over it, hammering and sawing. Soon the riffles would be bolted in place, perpendicular to the long sluice, and Jim's water cannon would bust loose tons of gravel. It would rush down the chute carried by a flood of water from the dam and the riffles would make small eddies in the sluice water to give the heavier material, black sand and gold, a chance to drop to the bottom behind the aluminum riffles. Gold would gather behind a hundred riffles, buckets and buckets of gold each day—that's what Jim was counting on.

The morning air was fresh smelling and dewy, newly born. Jim's girls were lovely at the start of day washing their clothes like innocents. Ramon took in the sights of the camp. Already there was bustling, building, a hundred great plans spooling out. Martha was hard at work preparing the evening feast. Even before sunset, the music and dancing would begin, hand-holding, caressing; Jim's girls would incite dreams and yearning. Ah, there was so much good fortune here. Ramon watched his friend, rushing here and there, directing a dozen projects; there wasn't any time for small talk. They shouted to each other, promised to meet up in the city. Ramon Vega smiled and shook his head. Jim was into his long sprint. Jim was winning. Jim. Ramon had this way of saying the name, Jim, so that it rang with irony and lament.

One night she came to visit Jim in his little room. Ribamar was in his chair leaning against the door frame. He didn't want her to pass. He hadn't liked her from the first day. She could feel his rebuke and great strength, though he wasn't a large man. With Ribamar you were either in or out. You couldn't buy his love. She had to slide past him to get inside. Iliana smiled back at him. She liked dares and crossing lines.

The gold had opened her up. She felt flamboyant and newly minted. It was such a big relief to find it—no more sullen shopgirl afternoons. All the money was playing out in front of her like a gaudy movie. They were both watching it, the gold flooding her ancient dried riverbed. Life would rush ahead from this point. It was almost funny. She was free and didn't have to pretend. She and Jim had had sex twice before this in Manaus, and she had been tentative, like a sweet girl trying her hardest. This night, however, they started to laugh while they fucked. They were watching the same movie. They were both coming home from disaster waving a banner. She became excited almost immediately and started to come, but then she shook her head, no, made him back off. In a minute, they had started again. She took his hands and put them on her throat. Jim didn't get it. She ground her hips into him. She then took her hands and put them on top of his hands and began to squeeze his hands with hers. She arched her head back, extending her neck. Harder, she said. Jim had never even heard of such a thing. Iliana started to gasp and he took the pressure off of her throat. She nodded to him, yes. After a minute or two she looked at him and nodded again. He put his hands on her throat. Jim was a very strong man. He could have easily broken her neck. That occurred to him. Surely it occurred to her as well. She began to gasp, change color, and two veins in her forehead engorged. He loosened his grip. Her eyes were bulging and she began to kiss him passionately. Then she wanted more. It went on like this for an hour, with Iliana nearly passing out, cutting the edge closer, until she was drenched and exhausted.

29.

In February 1984, about a half year after I had first met Jim in
the Bahamas, he and Phyllis were newly ensconced in their posh
condominium on the Intracoastal Waterway in Miami and were
already holding parties four and five nights a week, recruiting
salespeople for his new business. I came to a half dozen of their
network-marketing bonding sessions. I couldn't take my eyes off
my new friend while he worked the room, describing how easily a
man can make a residual income for the rest of his life. Jim was
charming and convincing, at least for this sad group. Even shy
types opened themselves to him. Men and women became emotional and surprised themselves telling him their secrets. Jim honed
in on disappointment and avarice as he probed for the hot button.
What do you really want? he asked confidentially, enigmatically, or
impishly depending on his customer.

Sometimes, it was adventure. Many of his recruits were so flattened down by long expanses of mundane lives, or in some cases
poverty, that they didn't know life held the capacity for real adventure. The faces of men and women glowed when he told his sto-

ries while Phyllis walked around in a low-cut gown serving her delectable hors d'oeuvres. She was a wonderful and inventive cook.

More times than I care to remember, I watched him go to his custom Plexiglas gun locker with a few starstruck network-marketing recruits in tow. He would push the magic buttons with a grin, and the Plexiglas door glided open with a rush of air and Jim would reach inside and pull out his stainless-steel .232-caliber miniature M16. It was the gun he'd hunted with in the rain forest, the very same semiautomatic he used to fire rounds at the Colombian speedboat while I was crouched down on the deck of his yacht cowering in fear. He said a few words about the gun and then let each of the men handle it, and feel the thrill, because that gun had a lethal, deadly look with its vicious little cooling slits like nostrils. It seemed to have a conviction, a living presence.

Then Jim told a few of his yarns. He was a little drunk, and the stories weren't interesting to me. But he knew his audience. Jim wasn't entertaining me at these parties. He crafted his adventures to impress recruits and sell product; at first it was a health line of powders and vitamins, but a couple of years later he was using the gun and Amazon stories to hawk magnetic back braces and mattresses. He knew just what to tell and what to leave out. He had perfect pitch for selling: Yes, I lived in the jungle for a while. No, right in the middle of the Amazon jungle. He told a few hunting stories to close deals for $79.95. The men looked at him as though he had traveled inside a black hole and survived. They were right about that much. Sure, we'll take a trip to the Amazon, Jim would say. As soon as you're up to speed in the new business we'll fly into Manaus. He made this promise a hundred times, maybe more. He promised them the Amazon.

I would leave the room when he began talking about Brazil to this needy group. I was trying to keep the fragments of the story I knew straight in my mind. I didn't want them getting mixed up with therapeutic magnets or some mundane or carefully crafted sense of right and wrong; night after night he watered down the jungle for his audience, leaving out the real things.

Jim's Brazil life just wasn't something you could tell at a PTA meeting or a bonding session for network marketing, or later on he couldn't tell it to Mara's little kids. They would never understand how this new father in their lives could have done such things. He couldn't even tell large parts of it to Phyllis, who adored him.

As the years passed, Jim told his Brazil stories ever more cleanly. He wanted to be a saint in the Amazon. He just wanted to use the jungle to sell products and meet new people. I tried not to listen.

And meanwhile the real story grew darker and more astonishing as I learned more. My friend had fashioned a reality that mirrored his ambition and avarice and the aspirations of his father. Jim had written an original and then had fallen into his own illusion along with his men. He'd made up rules and enforced them. He'd done this at fifty-five, when many men are beginning to focus on early retirement. Every afternoon, he'd run into the jungle with Ribamar without fear of dying. He'd constructed a machine that pulled buckets of gold from the earth. He'd captured the imaginations of jaded, vicious men who would do anything for a few dollars. Even Ribamar had fallen under Jim's spell. He had loved a young Indian girl from the jungle. I think he would have married her if he'd had the chance. That would have changed the story greatly.

I hated when Jim showed off the gun and then described the time he shot some animal off a tree limb. But Jim knew better than me. He knew just what to say and leave out. He had the recruits nodding and fawning. He told his stories and he signed up hundreds of men. The distance between freewheeling desire and deafening banality is a flicker.

———

In the late afternoon Jim walked with one of his men from the cantina toward the edge of the forest. He was a gunman named Rolf whom Jim had put in charge of scheduling flights to Manaus. There were few seats available for *garimpeiros* to travel on Jim's planes and it was common knowledge that Rolf demanded payoffs to get out. Jim had brought up this matter several times, but Rolf heeded no one. Over time he had carved out his own small but profitable power base within Jim's operation. Except for booking flights, miners and other gunmen stayed clear of Rolf, who was a flagrantly cruel and violent man even by the standards of this lawless world.

That morning there had been two mortally sick workers with dengue fever scheduled to fly home. By chance, Jim had noticed that the men hadn't boarded the plane. Later in the day one of the miners came for Jim and brought him to the bodies of the sick men who had been dragged into the forest, not two hundred yards from the clearing. Their throats had been slit and they hadn't been buried or even covered over with foliage, as if they had been served up for the cats.

Rolf shrugged. It didn't matter, he explained, because the men would have died within a day or two. They were finished and didn't need to go back to Manaus. He'd put them out of their misery and then sold their space to two others, doubling his profit.

It was the amused expression on the gunman's face, a kind of dare, that cut through Jim's distraction. On another day, in a better mood, Jim might have allowed Rolf's explanation, which was significantly true, if lacking any trace of remorse: the men would have suffered terribly and died. Jim could accept Rolf's business shenanigans, and even his brutality, because he was a very efficient worker, highly unusual among Jim's hired guns, who mainly sat around smoking and drinking beer while waiting for war.

Jim was exhausted and irritated. He had been working around the clock on his enormous machine. In its tentative first hours of operation, tons of raw gravel and water had come shooting out the front of the sluice box, without filtering out any gold; time had been lost. Jim was trying to determine the optimum mix of gravel and water pressure so as to not overrun the riffles. Jim and Rolf walked past the east end of the runway. Ahead of them, Jim's apparatus was daunting in the austere evening light.

Over time the machine would give Jim everything, but first he needed to master its beastly appetites and messes. Just turning the thing on created hills of waste gravel called *cascalho*. Mountains of the stuff rapidly built up on the ground along both sides of the long trough and especially on the open front end where the men did the final sifting for gold. After one sixteen-hour shift the mounds had become unmanageable and it was necessary to bring in the Cat and push away the gravel, which left a four-foot gully. Jim usually drove the Cat himself.

The sluice box had taken over his imagination. Each morning Jim could hardly wait to race from bed and get his hands on it again, to learn something new, and to pull out the gold from behind the riffles, which was pure lust.

Jim walked east with Rolf, explaining the rules of the camp and what he was trying to accomplish with the sluice box while Rolf nodded as if the machine were key to his welfare and prosperity as well as Jim's. He told Rolf that he was trying to improve things for all his men and that rules were rules, no exceptions. Finally they were past the sluice box and up against a seeming impenetrable wall of darkening forest. Jim pointed the stainless-steel rifle at Rolf and told him to get moving. Everyone in the camp knew what it meant to walk in there alone, and particularly at dusk. Had Rolf even turned around to plead his case, Jim would have shot him.

Luis had found Maria in the slums of Manaus and she soon became the feature act in the cantina. The men called her Maria Full of

Grace. She was short, less than five feet, with small breasts and a petite ass, and she had a dark mark on the end of her little nose. Maria was a kind of sexual child. She had jet-black hair that she kept short, like a boy. She could be adorable and flirtatious, but other times she had an inner smile that was spiritual and entirely captivating.

Many evenings, when it was late and the music was no longer playing, Maria was lifted onto the bar by the men and she would begin to dance while leaning back against a rough wooden pole that rose into the thatched ceiling. Her lips glowed soft pink. When she lifted her skirt her womanly legs came as a shock because the rest of her was childlike. Maria closed her eyes and thrust her hips ahead and swayed to the rhythm of the droning and screaming insects and birds outside that came in waves, in this odd cadence of shrieks and soft eerie silences. She fell deeply into herself while she slowly took off her clothes until she was completely naked. The men were riveted by her dance. Each of them tried to catch her eye, wanted her to dance for him alone. She wore only a distant smile. Who are you smiling for, Maria?

By this late hour the girls were no longer innocents. The tenderness of earlier encounters had passed. The girls were undressed or mostly undressed. It was the last of the night and they sat on the laps of their suitors, fondling their genitals and putting their breasts into the faces of the men, some of them still smeared with dried mud from the day's labor. The faces of the women were swollen with desire. No one was pretending. The men reached for their pouches of gold to check what was left.

On the little bar Maria made love to herself. Her shaved mound was pure as a baby's ass. She was into her own world, untouchable for all the pleasure she promised and allowed on special nights, when she was in the mood. A hundred men yearned for her. Many would have married Maria and believed in the sanctity of their lives together. Though Maria aroused the cantina with her dancing, many nights she would not go with a man. She could have made much more than any other girl in Jim's cantina, but she made less. After her dance she would come off the bar and sit in a corner by herself lost in thought. The men knew they must leave her alone. If you talked to her or touched her arm she became incensed and then the night fell apart, and the men left the cantina feeling forlorn.

30.

Iliana continued to keep her room in a small residential hotel near center city but now she was using Jim's estate as her home base. She set up her office in one of the bedrooms and more often than not she stayed the night. Each week the gold was delivered to the estate. It was guarded here by Jim's men until Iliana made her weekly sale and then she called him on the radio with the news. She was now a 10 percent partner in the operation, but she acted like the boss. Iliana drove to town in Jim's old Mercedes surrounded by his gunmen. She directed them to do personal chores. She was an independent operator, virtually unchecked and unchallenged. Jim couldn't be everywhere at once and he preferred spending his time in the camp, particularly now with the precious metal literally flowing down the chute; also, he didn't have patience for negotiating with vendors in Portuguese and he disliked keeping the books.

Iliana stole from the first week. She negotiated for the highest selling price and then she reported to Jim a different amount, 5 percent less or 7 percent less, always less. How could he know for certain what she was getting? He didn't speak the language and the gold numbers were always fluctuating; scales were calibrated differently; there were many explanations. And she was always reporting large sums of money, which gladdened him. In the first month, even with the sluice box at half speed, Jim's gold sale had soared from $30,000 to nearly $150,000. The weekly report from Iliana was a high point for Jim in the camp.

Iliana pushed the envelope. In addition to her conventional chipping, she coerced gold buyers to pay her commissions under the table. If they refused she took away her business. She threatened and bargained relentlessly or she used her appealing smile or she suggested even more was possible if the money was right. She didn't care. Her primary convictions were about money. She was appeasing herself after a run of heartbreaking losses. She was very smart and she had tools. Men were easy to break down. They were weak and foolish and easily blinded by an attractive woman. She believed that she could navigate herself out of any mess. She held Jim's face between her two hands and extolled their growing success. Their enormous machine would feed them gold for years, she assured him. They would keep moving the sluice box north to the Rio Novo. They were just beginning.

Iliana had traveled fast from having nothing to needing everything. She didn't love Jim, but she had to possess him and deceive him.

Her impediment was Angela, a Caboclo without style or education. Iliana ordered the girl around crudely or ignored Angela altogether. Whenever Jim was away, Iliana wanted to drive the girl from the house, but she didn't dare. She was bursting to say to Jim, Why do you need this whore? She's so crude. I'll give you everything.

For Angela, the new woman was hardly more than a nuisance. Angela was very hearty, but also, she operated on a different wavelength. She didn't share Iliana's ambitions, so there really wasn't any fight except in Iliana's head. Angela didn't think about a future with Jim—the idea was inconceivable. She was from the jungle and yearned to go back. She was tuned to the wind and night sounds, the screeches, yelps, and growls from over the green security wall that gladdened her and made her think of home.

Angela wasn't resentful about Jim's long periods away in the camp. But when he came back she was happy to see him and live with him inside their guessing game. When he fell asleep she gently closed the door behind her and returned to her little room. The future, or any pledges he might make about the future, meant little to her. Repeatedly, this struck him as fresh and appealing and also it made him yearn for her all the more.

Angela's charm and beauty were irresistible. Iliana couldn't top it, but she tried. She pulled Jim into her room. She always left the sheets for the girl to wash.

Iliana tried everything to win him. She tried to please him with great runs of passion. She offered him cocaine, but Jim didn't like the feeling. She acted like a little girl. She discovered that the best way to convince him was to please herself, to put his hands on her throat. He found it astounding that this driven woman would allow such vulnerability; it was this contradiction that kept him believing they were on the same side, more or less. She trusted Jim to give her back her breath. But if he'd lost himself and squeezed the side of her neck for an additional few seconds their partnership would have ended on the spot. More than once, with his hands squeezing her throat and her face turned crimson, he considered allowing this mistake. It was such a powerful fantasy that she seemed to engender.

The situation in the house persisted, with quiet changes, for almost three months. Iliana angled for every loose dollar. When Jim was in town she dressed in smart outfits from New York or Paris and continued to act like they were a couple, yet she slowly came to accept that the girl was a facet of her life.

The Manaus house was an unusual cocktail of muted passions. Angela remained in her own space. He would watch her from his window, moving across the field or planting. Sometimes she would notice him and they'd wave. She didn't seem to mind if Jim visited the other woman. This confused him, but he was grateful. In the afternoon, even if Jim was visiting for a day or two, Angela was glued to her favorite soap opera. He waited patiently as she watched the tube; afterwards, she smiled at him and when he took her in his arms she gave him kisses and gently bit his lips.

Jim had changed a lot. He rarely thought about the great house on the lake, and if he did it seemed gloomy and shrouded like an unhappy past. When he was away from the camp, he soon missed it. He wanted to get back with Ribamar, working out details, burning back the trees and underbrush so there would be more room to store mounds of gravel. Jim had become very directed and what remained of his softness was focused on the girl whom he couldn't manage to possess.

Jim had been waiting for Angela's birthday. He wanted to make it up to her for his preoccupations, for Iliana and his long absences in the jungle. Most of all he wanted to win Angela completely, bowl the girl over with a gesture and eliminate all doubts. The day before her nineteenth birthday he told her about the gift. He slowly described it and repeated himself until he was sure, at least fairly sure, that she understood him. He didn't want any guessing. By now Jim had lost all patience for the game that had defined their relationship.

The following afternoon, after he had finished his banking, Jim would send the car back for her and she would meet him in the lobby of the Tropicana, which was the finest hotel in Manaus. Together, she and Jim would roam the free-trade shops where tourists from all over the world came to buy fine clothing, the best luggage, expensive jewelry, perfumes from France, watches, electronics. Anything a girl could dream of owning was available in the gift shops at the Tropicana. Jim asked Angela to think about what she would like to have so she wouldn't be stagestruck while surrounded by rich tourists. She could have anything at all. She could spend a thousand dollars or three thousand dollars. He wanted her to let herself go. He tried to explain what this meant. Whatever you want. Take anything at all. He gestured large things with his arms. Take them. They're for you.

Angela laughed at his foolish pantomime, but then her smile grew distant. He decided that she didn't understand the meaning of so much money. A girl from the jungle wouldn't earn three thousand dollars in ten years, unless she was one of Jim's whores in the cantina. Angela understood what it meant to spend one dollar or perhaps three dollars. She couldn't wrap her mind around three thousand dollars. This hesitation made Jim think even larger. They'd spend five thousand dollars on her birthday gift. What did he care? He was finally making money again after nearly four years. She could buy enough in the hotel shops to sink her tiny village. He wouldn't say no. He'd take her from one shop to the next and help her select.

He watched her while she tried to absorb his largess. His idea was beyond her horizons; at least that's what he conjectured. She was from another culture. He was charmed anew by her naïveté. He could barely sleep thinking about Angela's birthday shopping spree in the Tropicana Hotel the following afternoon.

The next morning Jim left with his gunmen around ten. He called the estate three hours later to tell Angela that the car was on its way back for her. One of the gunmen told him that she wasn't in the house. She had left an hour earlier on the bus.

Angela must have come into town on her own. It was her little surprise, Jim decided. He went to the Tropicana and waited. He read the newspaper and waited. But he had a feeling in his stomach she wasn't coming. Something was wrong. Something about the birthday present. There had been a misunderstanding. After two hours he called home and she wasn't there. No one knew where she had gone. She must have misunderstood his intention, or she would have run to meet him. Any woman would have.

Angela didn't come back to the house that night, or the next night.

She didn't come back. He decided that she must have returned home to the village to visit her parents and little sisters. There was nowhere else she could have gone. Surely she would come back in a week or two. Or if she didn't he'd go to the village and bring her back. He settled on this idea and calmed himself down. Jim returned to the camp and went back to work. The camp was the solution to all his problems. It quickly absorbed him.

After six months operating the machine, and nearly four years since losing his factories in Canada, Jim was back in the money. He had more than eight hundred thousand stashed in his wall safe in Manaus, and each week there were more thousands coming to him from the gold sale. Only he didn't know what to do with the money. His whole adult life, he needed wealth as a test of character—for Jim, simply the act of making money was the hot button—but after buying the basics he wasn't sure what came next. Having a glut of wealth was the backwash of having none, and each generated pools of anxiety.

Marvin Gesler had always made the large-money decisions beyond houses, cars, and boats. Jim couldn't keep stuffing money into the safe. One of his men could have pried it out of the wall. Jim was afraid to use the local banks. He called Phyllis because he didn't know where to stash his money. He instructed her to fly to

Miami and take a room for a week in the old Eden Roc hotel on the beach. He prepped Ribamar about the trip, warning that the sluice box mustn't be operated unless he was standing there himself, monitoring the final sifting of rich gravel. If he turned his back for a minute, the gold would walk. Jim reminded Ribamar to keep logs across the runway, although he understood the implications better than Jim. While Jim was in Florida, Luis would also remain in the camp. Luis was broken with anxiety, but Jim couldn't bear to let him go and kept up the pretense that Luis was his key guy. He was a dear man and Jim believed he'd snap out of it. Before Jim left he gave Iliana his room number at the Eden Roc, where Phyllis had already checked in. Iliana offered to fly into the camp, to make sure things were running smoothly, and he reminded her to call Ribamar on the radio first and ask what supplies or spare parts he might need.

Jim flew to Miami feeling an unfamiliar gloom. The good life, all of his dreams, was back in the jungle clearing. It was like a premonition, he reflected to Mara and me. He felt impatience and dread at the prospect of sharing a room with his young wife. Jim was safe in the rain forest, but she could maim him.

I should never have married Phyllis, Jim said to us, and Mara nodded solemnly, as if they were back again on the same team. And he believed her, believed all her junk like the biggest sucker in town. But it was easy for me to say he should never have married Mara. Another man couldn't have found respite in the jungle.

In the vast but worn lobby of the hotel, Phyllis greeted Jim standing beneath a giant discolored chandelier. She wore a puzzled smile and her body was all soft, particularly her shoulders and arms. It was the first glimpse of his wife in two and a half years.

She was the same age as Iliana, but Phyllis couldn't have survived two days in the jungle.

She took his hand and guided him to a restaurant near the pool, ordered a bottle of red wine. The place smelled of chlorine and laundered towels. Phyllis was looking at him for clues, for a way inside. She was shaking her head, amazed. Jim had grown so taut, all sinew and brambles. He'd lost thirty pounds. What? he asked her impatiently.

I'm just so happy to see you, she said.

She jumped into the narrative to fill the void. Marvin had run off to Europe without ever making a court appearance. No one knew where he was.

You know, Jim, you and Marvin have become big mystery celebrities in Toronto. Both of you on the lam like bank robbers. You've been in all the papers.

Now her big daffy smile.

His eyes kept slipping away from hers. He asked her a few questions about Marvin. After so much mileage Jim still had a taste for his partner. But she didn't know much. Marvin also had lost his house, and soon after his secretary left him for a salesman. The government had built a massive case against Jim and Marvin for just under $20 million in back taxes and penalties. In the indictment Jim's crime had been described as a tax evasion scheme as financially sophisticated as it was venal. He smiled at that. Jim could barely balance a checkbook. She smiled back.

But he had nothing else to say. He'd become so skinny she couldn't find him, and he had so much disdain. In her desperation, she talked a jag. Facts, goodwill, stories burbling out. Michael had left for California to join Ava. He'd done things before he left Phyllis hadn't wanted to tell Jim on the phone. Michael had run around with a group of boys who took drugs. One night they stole a car. Jim nodded. That was it, next subject. He didn't want to think of the boy or anything in her world. Phyllis's singsong voice was wrenching.

After three days in the hotel he said he needed to get back to Manaus. There was no discussion. Jim, she said, shaking her head. She'd just wanted him to feel her caring heart; she'd kept it for him. But he couldn't. Despite the savings accounts they had just opened together in ten Miami banks, she never expected to see him again. She could never have guessed that from this point in the story they had another twenty years of marriage ahead, many of them rich with travel and friends and Jim's contagious optimism.

31.

On a clear Sunday morning, Iliana flew from Manaus to the camp with Ramon Vega and his youngest brother, Herman. When they were ten miles out, she called the radio operator to say she was arriving in Ramon's helicopter and there was no need to remove the logs from the airstrip; they'd set down in front of the cantina. She added to tell Ribamar, if he was around, that she'd managed to find a replacement water pump for the spare generator and that Ramon had brought gifts for the men. That was code for Cuban cigars and fine Kentucky bourbon. Jim's men all liked Ramon. He was one of them.

Ramon banked the orange helicopter over the tall trees on the east end of the clearing, passing over Jim's gold sluice, and then at twenty feet he came racing down the center of the landing strip. He took a swing over the dormitory and cantina, and he hovered there, creating a tornado above the buildings. A few of the girls ran outside and waved. What a cowboy!

As he brought her down in front of the cantina he could see Jim's gunmen appreciating their lazy Sunday morning. Most of them

were relaxing on benches and chairs along the two westerly buildings, about twenty men, Ramon guessed. Some were talking to the
girls, who looked angelic with their sleepy faces. He knew the men
would be hungover from Saturday night.

The day was gorgeous, not so hot as usual, and yet the morning
sun cloaked the jungle in a honeyed glow. Ramon stretched and
smiled at his kid brother, who nodded once, sharply. If Jim had been
here to see the helicopter bank down over the trees on this lazy day
of rest, he might have recalled Ramon's warning.

While the rotors idled to a stop Ramon waved to the men from
his window. Ribamar was standing a few yards away at the corner
of the barracks, leaning against his old carbine. Iliana, seated behind Ramon, took in the morning camp and gestured hi to Luis,
who smiled back meekly. Then one of the girls waved and Iliana
turned away.

Jim had always liked Ramon's brother, who was a strong kid
of about twenty-four. Herman was fearless and he understood the
jungle. He could track game and despite a thick-muscled body,
he could pull himself up a tree like a cat. And he was true, like
Ribamar. Herman would gladly take a bullet for Ramon, whom he
adored. Jim would have hired Herman, made him a top guy, but that
wasn't possible. Herman always wanted to be with his older brother.

Ramon was smiling as if he were off to a picnic with his wife
and kids. Herman was wired, but he was also pleased about the
morning's adventure, nodding to some *musica* inside his head. On
their laps, beneath the line of the Plexiglas window, the brothers
were holding short-stocked Uzi automatics with long clips that rode
up into their bellies. Herman kept finding the trigger with his finger.

Don't shoot your legs off, Brother, said Ramon. The brothers
grinned broadly, and then on the beat Herman pushed open the door
on his side and stepped out, blocked from Jim's men by the cockpit.
There was no one on the outboard side of the helicopter and Ramon

took his time climbing down like an old creaky guy, he was such a player, and he liked tweaking his little brother, who was very high-strung. Herman shook his head, oh man.

Then the brothers took four long steps in tandem, clearing the front of the fuselage, and they leveled the guns and started firing. They fired and fired with the guns pulled tight against their shoulders, fired at everyone in sight. The men dropped like deadwood and the air was filled with burning metal and smoke. In the cockpit, Iliana was shouting, No, no! and shaking her head.

Most of the men and women were already down and the brothers stood shoulder to shoulder, glued to their guns, crisscrossing their fire, showering everything with lead.

Ribamar managed to get off one shot before he was hit. He struggled to get around the corner of the building.

Then Herman seemed to stumble over his own legs and he flopped onto his back. He reached up with his hand, grinning toward his brother.

Ramon slapped one more clip into the gun and began firing at bodies, though most of them were still. Herman couldn't get off the ground, though he tried to get his powerful legs moving. He was holding his belly. Iliana was staring out the window with a dead expression.

In less than half a minute the brothers had shot off four hundred rounds into twenty-odd men and five women. The air smelled like it was burning up.

Ribamar had made it behind the barracks. He had been shot through a leg. Ramon thought about chasing him down. Ramon could have caught him in a minute, but Herman was bleeding through his fingers and Ribamar was as good as dead. He'd try to make it into the jungle before Ramon's men arrived. The men would kill Ribamar before the day was out or the jungle animals would do it, unless he first bled to death. Everyone else in the camp was dead except for the radioman and one of the girls. They both came outside with their hands up. Ramon shrugged. Now they worked for him. He hauled his brother into the helicopter, started the engine, and pulled out of the clearing.

The following afternoon, when Jim arrived at his estate in Manaus, he found the front gate open and the place nearly deserted. Everyone had left except for a maid and two of his gunmen who were packed to go and clearly unnerved by Jim's unexpected appearance. They told him of the massacre in measured words. Now it was Ramon's camp. Jim could feel loyalties shifting even while they spoke. He asked about Luis and Ribamar, and one of the men shrugged. They'd heard that many had been killed, even some girls. Jim needed to get out of the house fast. Any minute, Ramon could drive through the gate with his men. He would kill Jim on the spot unless Ramon restrained himself to first enjoy a beer and a few laughs. Jim went to his bedroom, took the remaining cash from his wall safe, a few pieces of clothing, and the stainless rifle, and shoved them into a large duffel bag. He left in the waiting taxi.

He recalled something Ribamar had once said to him. All problems are small problems. He wondered if this was a small problem. He got out of the cab in the downtown area of the city, across from the opera house, and walked a few blocks down a side street until he found a nondescript hotel. He checked in and went up the elevator to his room. Jim, when you are afraid, don't move; think about the situation. It was Ribamar's steadying voice.

But in fact, Jim didn't feel afraid. He needed to decide what he wanted to do. The logical alternative was to go back to the States. But the Manaus airport would be very dangerous. Ramon Vega ran a charter service and his men were usually sitting around. If they saw Jim, they would kill him and the police would be paid off. Jim was a fugitive. If he went to the Canadian embassy for help, he'd be arrested and sent back to Canada.

The life in Brazil had led him to a set of alternatives that would have been unthinkable three years earlier. But Jim was no longer that person. Phyllis had recognized this immediately in Miami when she saw him and touched his arm. This moment was an expression of who he had become.

Jim could try to escape or fight. His education in the jungle had prepared him to do either of these things with considerable skill. If he had the opportunity he would kill Ramon Vega. Killing was no longer a line that stopped Jim or even caused great turmoil. It was one of his options. This pleased him, although he knew it was much more likely that he'd be seen by Ramon's men and killed himself. Either way, it didn't seem earth-shattering.

Jim had a lot of cash. He could hire a car and drive to Barba or Ayrao or perhaps take a slow riverboat to Tabatinga. From these places maybe he could rent a small plane and get to Rio. He had to decide.

He kept imagining Ribamar, wounded and hiding out in the trees, waiting for him. He tried to shake it off as a bothersome fantasy. Ribamar was dead. But sneaking out of the country felt wrong.

Jim had long been guided by appetites, needs, and urges, like his own father half a century before. In this one respect Brazil had not changed Jim. He had never been moved greatly by formal religion or social conventions except insofar as precepts that might facilitate his selling. His fidelity toward family and friends flowed naturally from his affection and caring, which was intense and deeply felt. Loved ones were a sublime pleasure and yet over the years their faces changed like the seasons. Old favorites were cast out for misunderstandings or financial treasons or because Jim grew bored and needed to change venues, but for that finite and acute period of inclusion those closest to Jim were held very dear, and for them he'd walk the line.

In Brazil, he had been greatly affected by certain people. He loved the girl, and increasingly so. In the passion of traveling from the city to the jungle and back again, while he built his own world with his own hands, Angela had made it possible for him to slow down a little and savor the ride. He would have missed most of the best except for her. Ribamar had become Jim's soul, perhaps his true father. Certainly his good father. Jim was haunted by Luis, pathetic and loveable, brilliant, possessed.

Jim was still engaged with his jungle theater. Florida was dead to him. He didn't want to go back. He was fascinated by the clearing and he yearned to see it again. He felt that it was his, even though Ramon had taken it away. Jim didn't feel outraged so much as perplexed and stopped in place.

Jim had left twenty gunmen in the camp. They knew exactly how to defend the camp. Ribamar was there directing things. Something had gone wrong. Jim had an inkling, but he really didn't know. It wasn't classical revenge that drove him ahead. Even now, Jim could imagine sitting down with Ramon Vega and reflecting about what had happened at the camp. If they did that, Ramon could almost surely make Jim smile, even now. He felt like they were still playing their game, conning each other, posturing, testing.

Jim wanted everything as it was before. He couldn't turn off the switch. He was hearing the voice of Ribamar as though they were walking in the forest together hunting for tapir and monkey for Martha's barbecue pit. He wanted to do that again. Lust was making this key decision for him, as it always had. He couldn't stop thinking about the sluice box. It was a beautiful thing, the way he'd built the dam and directed the flood to strain tons of gravel in a day; buckets of gold fell into the riffles. He couldn't give it up.

The following morning he walked to the tiny shop of the white-haired gun vendor he and Luis had often visited. It was a big chance going in there. The old man could easily have heard about the massacre. Such news from the jungle travels fast. But the gun seller acted normal, not a twitch or tightness on his face. Jim said that he needed two good men for the camp, and the old man nodded and dialed a number. Jim had no idea who he was calling; it might have been Ramon. After a half hour, two men came to the shop wearing fatigues and uncaring faces that Jim knew so well. He left with his new friends.

Even at this late hour, he didn't have a plan so much as a direction. He decided that he needed to go north to get south. If Ramon Vega had learned that Jim was back in Manaus, his men would be checking the traffic on the two-lane road leading south from the city in the direction of the camp; they wouldn't care about the few cars leaving the city on the dirt road north. Jim and the men bumped along in a taxi seventy kilometers to the town of Ayrao, where there was a landing strip. He paid triple the normal price to charter an old four seater for the four-hundred-kilometer flight south to Angela's tiny village on the Igapo-Acu River. The pilot knew of the river but hadn't heard of Angela's village. He wasn't confident there would be any place to land. Jim listened and nodded, but these weren't his concerns.

He fell asleep with the engine roaring close to his head. An hour south of Manaus, the old plane entered a broad, dark storm and was thrown all over and pelted by rain. They were flying in a black pit. For twenty minutes the pilot struggled to hold her, and the gunmen feared they would be thrown from the sky.

Finally, they were into the clear, and the pilot tried to get his bearings. Below there was a vast expanse of burly green jungle, lakes and blue ribbons of rivers and streams. All the green terrain was indistinguishable. It went on like this for an hour, many, many winding rivers, none with defining features, and Jim wondered if the pilot was just conning him, trying to make a show of finding the village before turning the plane back to the north. Jim understood that he couldn't allow the man to land his plane at the Manaus airport even if it meant forcing him to put it down in a field. Then the pilot turned toward a river that was perhaps broader than the others. The little plane headed east, a few hundred feet above the muddy water, for about ten minutes and then Jim began pointing, There, he said, there!

Jim could count five, no, six hovels on the riverbank. Not much. There were a few grazing cattle. Kids were waving up at the plane. Just to the south of the village, if you would call it that, there was a wide dirt swath, a rudimentary landing area just as she had said. The whole place could have been pushed aside with a shovel and a rake.

Jim was suddenly aglow, waving stupidly and trying to catch a glimpse of Angela running out to see the plane. His heart was beating all over his chest and stomach. She'd described the village perfectly. The children were playing by the river, beautiful kids with black curly hair. He'd come just as he'd promised. She'd be amazed.

For a few delirious minutes he forgot about Ribamar, Luis, and the others. He said Angela's name to six or seven kids who now surrounded the plane, and they all pointed to her house only a hundred feet away. Everyone knew Angela. There was her toothless father, Juici, sitting on the porch working on his fishing nets. There were a dozen gray squirrel monkeys watching him or fidgeting or climbing off and on the simple raised porch. Also, there was a beautiful little girl with lustrous black hair and a slightly flattened nose. She was resting her head on a sleeping monkey. She was Angela at three years old. It was her baby niece.

Angela's father was a very nice man, simple and pleasant, happy to meet his daughter's good friend from far away. He clearly knew about Jim and didn't seem to mind that his daughter had an older boyfriend. She had been home visiting for weeks, but a few days before she had left the village with three *garimpeiros* who were passing through. She's gone back to her work, her father said with pride. It was highly unusual for a girl from this tiny place to work in the city.

This news only made Jim happier. Angela had left the village to come back to him. He'd been worried that she wouldn't want to leave her family. Jim was on a roll of good luck. He'd have to find her in the city, but he could do this, easily. Right now he needed to put Angela out of his mind.

The four men slept the night sitting up in the plane. At dawn Jim instructed the pilot to meet them at the village in five days and to wait an extra day if they weren't back. Then, Jim and the two gunmen ate an early fish breakfast with Angela's father and mom and Jim accepted a gift of some dried fish for their trip. The three of them caught a lift across the river with one of the village fishermen.

32.

The early morning coolness of the rain forest is precious and a traveler wants to breathe it deeply. The leaves have a fresh, fragrant wetness and the ancient place seems newly spawned. Even while walking fast, a man feels like a lighter person. Seamen have a similar experience when the distant shoreline drifts below the horizon. The heaviness of one's being stays behind.

On the south bank of the Igapo-Acu River, fallen trees from past rainy seasons had miraculous shapes, some of them curled around one another like petrified cobras. Now pushing into the virgin jungle, Jim looked at tall trees, *sumaumeira,* with very thick trunks and huge buttress roots that stood higher than a man. Above the buttress roots, twelve or fifteen feet from the ground, he could see the watermark from past rainy seasons. In a few months the rains would come again and four-hundred-pound fish would swim right here where the three men were walking.

Jim had no map. He navigated through the jungle using a little hand compass. Some months before, when Angela visited his camp, they'd looked together at a map and she pointed to where her village was located on the river, although the map didn't show any village.

Jim knew the distance from her community across two rivers to his camp was sixty kilometers and the heading was, more or less, southeast. He hoped Angela had been accurate when she'd pointed to the map. Jim had explored stretches of the Rio Novo and figured that if they crossed the river anywhere within five or six miles east or west of his camp he would be able to find his way.

When they had first started taking walks and hunting together, Jim couldn't keep up with Ribamar. Jim had struggled not to fall on his face or break an ankle, and he couldn't keep air in his lungs. When the brush was nearly impenetrable, the older man seemed to swim through it while Jim's face was whipped by branches and coarse vines. Ribamar had teased and pushed Jim to move faster, trained him to run across logs until he didn't worry about falling and to feel his way through the trees and vines at night because one day that might be important.

Ribamar had prepared Jim for this jungle passage. He knew that to be safe from cats, or fairly safe, he must sleep in a natural clearing, never in dense jungle. He knew where to look for hearts of palm and Brazil nuts to eat on the run. He had learned the habits of many animals from Ribamar. Jim knew to steer clear of coatimundis, fierce thirty-pound creatures that looked like little bears with long snouts. Coatimundis are brilliant animals who kill cobras but understand that they must not take on the deadly snake unless there is a tree root with an anti-venom nearby. When wounded by a hunter, these uncanny creatures play dead and are known to rip a man apart when he approaches incautiously.

Jim could see it like a photograph, Ribamar waiting for him high in the foliage of a tree, maybe sixty feet above the jungle floor. There he'd be safe from the cats and covered over by vegetation where Ramon's men couldn't find him. Ribamar could survive for a month like this and the idea of it made Jim giddy. Ribamar wouldn't try to escape. He wouldn't try to walk out of the jungle. He would survive eating honey from beehives, hearts of palm, and the sticky sap from milk trees that actually tastes like cow's milk. He could heal his wounds with plants and barks. Jim felt sure that Ribamar was alive. He could last for a long time and they'd never find him. Jim would find him.

Ribamar had said that in a twelve-hour day a man could cover forty kilometers in the forest if he kept moving and eating some dried meat or fish every two hours. But in order to keep going at such a pace a man needed to have a goal. Jim was traveling to save Ribamar, that's what he told himself, but sometimes the girl came into his head. He was running to Angela, though she was in Manaus, looking for him. It was a strange thing.

By the middle of the second day, the walk was no longer pleasant. The heat had become oppressive and Jim's light clothing felt leaden. The temperature and humidity wiped out thoughts and daydreams. Jim focused on his breathing and placing one foot in front of the next. There was no excitement or fear about what lay ahead. He just kept walking with his eyes fixed on the ground. Jim's men were twenty years younger, but they couldn't go at his pace. Every half hour he'd sit on a log and wait impatiently, and when they'd caught up and given him a sullen nod he pushed back into the dense forest with branches and fronds and biting insects in his face. He listened to the men's muttering and heavy breathing falling behind. Jim avoided shallow streams and more open stretches where Ramon Vega might have patrols moving about.

They arrived at the north bank of the Rio Novo at about 3:00 P.M. on the second day. They had to make it across, about eighty feet, without soaking their rifles. This was a very nervous moment. The only way, Jim figured, was to rest the guns on logs and push them across. Once the men were floating in the river, they'd be sitting ducks for Ramon's men. Worse yet, to get the logs across, the men had to kick with all their strength. It was the dry season and the river was teeming with red-bellied piranhas. Any commotion in the water was a dinner call: come feast on flesh. One of the gunmen became sick with fear and was certain piranhas were attacking his legs. But it was all nerves. The men got across to the other side and scampered up the bank with their packs and guns.

Jim figured it was about one mile to the camp from the river's edge. He could do this last part blindfolded. Now he had a plan. Approaching the clearing from the northwest, the men would come to a small bluff at the west end of the landing strip that looked down on the buildings. From this hill they would be about eighty or a hundred yards from the barracks. Jim would take a look and decide. He had no idea how many men Ramon had left guarding the camp. If it was twenty men, the situation was hopeless. Jim would have to crawl back down the hill and hike back to Angela's village. Also, he was concerned about the camp dogs. Were his two dogs still alive? Or had Ramon Vega killed them and brought new dogs that would begin barking the moment Jim and his men approached the ridge or maybe before?

After resting for a while, the men neared the clearing about a half hour before dark, as Jim had planned. Early in Jim's jungle education, Ribamar had reflected that as the forest cools down at the end of day the jaguar come out to hunt, when it is practically invisible approaching through the foliage. It was an appealing idea. Jim hoped that Ramon's men would be relaxed and perhaps hungry after a long, hot day.

Jim poked his head above the ridge. It was perfect, almost too perfect. There were two men cooking meat on Martha's outdoor grill between the cantina and the small building where the girls entertained. Jim's dogs were sitting beside them waiting for food. Suddenly the dogs started wheeling around and wagging their tails, but they weren't barking. The two men must have thought, Such foolish animals. There were three other men drinking beer outside the cantina. Jim couldn't see any more, only five.

Now was the moment, before someone went inside. Jim signaled the other two men to come onto the ridge alongside him. He would kill the two who were cooking. His gunmen would shoot the others who were twenty yards closer. Jim's shot was about a hundred yards, long for a rifle with an open sight, but he felt certain he could hit them. One of the men by the grill was facing Jim and gesturing with his arms as if narrating a story.

They would all shoot on the count of three. Jim aimed for the center of the storyteller's chest. One. Two. Jim squeezed it off and the man crumpled and went down on his side. Jim tried to shut out the gunfire of his men. His other target was confused, like a turkey trying to decide where to run. Jim shot him in the neck.

Jim's men had dropped two of three beside the cantina. The other one ran into the forest.

Okay. It was the best they could have hoped for. Jim wasn't concerned about the one who had run off. There was no telling if there were more men inside the buildings or if Ramon had patrols coming back in. They'd wait and watch.

In the jungle, it always seemed miraculous, the way night fell like a black curtain. Jim and his men stayed on the hill, listening, dozing. It felt like a reprieve.

At dawn, he walked back into his camp. The air was still and chilly and perfectly lucid. The four men lay where they had fallen. The buildings were all empty. Everything hung in the balance. It could have gone either way. He might still have left the clearing with his dreams.

That was the moment. But Jim sat on the dirt for a while across

from the cantina and shook his head. He felt this powerful emptiness close over his arms and chest like a net. There was no answer
to it. No moves to make. Nothing. It was too late now.

One of the men was calling to him from the direction of the
sluice box. Jim came ahead sullenly like a big kid. He didn't want
to open that door. He had never smelled anything like it before.
Maybe his father long ago.

Jim and the men started pulling bodies from the gully beside
the sluice box, but mostly it was Jim. He pulled and lifted with
wrath. He wrenched them out of the gravel, hoping, but no, he saw
the two of them very quickly, Luis and Martha, who was wearing
her white apron. Oh, their legs and arms were tangled; he couldn't
get them out of the gully. He pulled them, but they were stuck in
the gravel.

He was fierce or he couldn't have done it, one body after the
next covered with flies and maggots. He was soaked from the effort. Some of them he couldn't recognize at all. Many faces were
gone altogether. It was too horrible to look and Jim rolled them
onto their bellies. Luis hadn't wanted to stay behind. Twenty bodies Jim counted, but Ribamar wasn't here. Jim wanted to run away,
because he was scared that he hadn't looked closely enough and
that Ribamar might be lying on his belly beside the others. Jim
couldn't bear to turn them all over again.

One of the men was calling him and he tried to tune him out.
No, Ribamar wasn't here. None of the men had scars on their
backs. He wasn't here. Enough of this.

There were more bodies in the little creek that fed the dam. It
was a lottery and Jim was expected to make each selection. If he
could just will it his way, please, just once.

Four more bodies. Two girls. One of them was wearing red sandals and a skirt. She had no face at all. It took him a moment to
understand. He'd bought her the imported sandals in Manaus, but
she hardly ever wore them. No, impossible. This wasn't her. He took

a breath. She wouldn't be here. It was one of the other girls. Why had they killed the girls? He tried to keep moving down this path. They were innocents.

She'd gone back to him in the city. It was settled. Her father had said so. He loved her. He'd had a plan. The sandals stuck in his mind. Angela didn't like heels, even little ones. She loved to walk in her bare feet. He'd wanted to take her back to Florida. She was trying to be beautiful for him. She was just a poor girl.

It wasn't his fault. She didn't need to dress up for him. He would have taken care of her. He would have kept her safe in the big house. He loved it when she walked in the field in her bare feet. She'd hiked here for two days from her village to surprise him and fly back with him to Manaus.

There was so much he wanted to give to her. The flies began to settle on her legs, and he brushed them away. He would give the money to her father and mother and beg them. Her parents would love him. He'd convince them. He'd go to them and weep. Forgive me.

Ribamar wasn't in the creek. Jim needed to find Ribamar. That was the only answer. Maybe the bodies could then disappear and Jim would be able to move on. Luis had dreamed of bodies crowding his bed. Luis had pleaded; it was embarrassing. Ribamar must be alive. Nothing could kill him. Ribamar moved through the bush like a spirit. Jim couldn't push the red shoes out of his head.

Jim headed into the jungle behind the barracks. One of the gunmen tried to follow and Jim waved him off. He plowed right into branches and vines, let them beat against his face. He wanted to feel it. He was hoping the little cats came to him in the light when he could see. He craved them with their whining baby sounds and yellow eyes. He'd kill them. He'd fling them against the trees and laugh. Let them rip his chest and neck. He'd kill them all.

Jim fell asleep curled beneath a tree and when he woke up it was night. Maybe he'd be eaten before the morning. The idea made him happy and he closed his eyes and waited.

In the morning he was walking again. He and Ribamar always headed this way, working south along a dried creek. They could always find something to shoot for Martha. Every fifteen or twenty minutes Jim pounded on the base of a *sumaumeira* tree and the sound echoed deep into the forest. He'd been swimming way off-shore. He'd wanted to get out so far he couldn't make it back to land. But as the morning grew hotter he wasn't so sure which way to go. He was feeling hungry and light-headed, losing his clearest intentions in the heat. He wanted to do the right thing, but Jim was walking back to who he was. He began thinking of breakfast and a good bed. He walked on and on, beating the tree trunks to locate his conviction, but he couldn't capture it back; he was hungry. He couldn't keep going like this, deeper into the jungle. But he kept walking while making little bargains like a salesman. Only an-other half hour and he'd turn back. Maybe he would return to Florida. He had money there. He would need to get back to the river before dark. Ramon's men would be out searching for him. But once he had decided to turn around, it felt pleasant to keep moving ahead a little farther. It felt like he was being pulled ahead, gliding. The heat and thirst were playing with his head and Jim was moving much more slowly when he heard the distant sound. Two beats, just the way he and Ribamar had practiced. Jim beat his stick against a tree and there it was coming back to him. Ribamar was alive and sending back the signal. He had stayed alive for Jim, liv-ing in the trees for nearly two weeks, waiting to tell him.

After another half hour Jim pushed through a dense tangle of vines and limbs and there in a tiny clearing was the old man sitting on some leaves and leaning against a thick tree that had been his drum. Ribamar was exhausted and weak, but he wasn't surprised. He had a serene expression. He had envisioned this moment for days; he willed it. Not one word, but he reached out his arms to Jim like a man who had been waiting patiently for his family to come for him.

One last stop.

He knocked on her door.

It's Jim, he said.

There was a pause. He knew she would quickly reinvent herself. When she threw open the door she embraced him. Oh, I'm so relieved, Iliana gushed. I thought he'd killed you. I tried to reach you in Florida. Jim could feel the emotion rippling through her body. She was a marvel.

He had never visited her little hotel room that was dark and dreary with all of her failures and disappointments. He slowly took it in. She had money now and the prospect of much more, but Iliana kept this lonely place, maybe as a reminder to keep herself sharp.

Let me see you, he said, but she held on to him tight. She knew.

He pushed her away and looked at her face. Her expression was wounded and needy, as though she wanted to touch his cheek but couldn't quite manage it.

No foreplay. He grabbed her by the neck, the thumb and fingers of his right hand digging into her windpipe as if he'd wrench it out of her throat.

How many points did he give you? Jim asked, Twenty points? She shook her head.

Thirty points? Thirty points to kill them all? Even the girls? Tell me.

She tapped his leg, an old habit. He let her breathe.

She gasped. Don't, she managed, before he throttled her again.

Tell me. He squeezed until she turned bright red and her eyes bulged.

She gasped, Fifty percent.

Equal partners, he said, very good. But you know he would have killed you in a few days. It would never have held up.

She looked at Jim with terrified little-girl eyes.

When Jim had imagined killing her, it was very satisfying. In the jungle he played it over many times in his head, and each time she fought like a devil. She coiled around him like a python, scratched him with her nails, or she reached for some hidden weapon and then he broke her neck. But at the moment, the real moment, she didn't do anything of the sort. She yielded. She hung limp like a rag. She gave herself to him.

He let her breathe. Jim couldn't do it. They were both breathing very hard. She began to cry. He shook his head no as if to say, Okay, okay. It's finished. He gave her a last embrace.

She sobbed. I didn't know he would kill them. Believe me. She cried.

I do, he answered. She probably didn't know. Ramon wouldn't have told her.

I never thought he'd kill everyone. There was no reason. They would have all given up and gone to work for him. He didn't need to shoot the girls.

Jim nodded, but she'd made a mistake. Don't keep selling when a deal is already agreed upon. She'd woken Jim and his mind was racing again. "Everyone" stuck in his mind. Did she know that Angela was in the camp, had been shot and thrown into the ditch? She must have seen Angela from the window of the plane? Did it gladden her? Of course it did.

I'm going now, he said to her slowly. I'm leaving Brazil. She looked at him with pleading eyes. I don't want you to go, Jim. He smiled, because she was so quick and nimble, but she had misjudged him. He was watching her eyes. She was still whimpering but already thinking about the money and how to handle Ramon. Maybe kill him. She'd have to kill him to ever see the gold. You had to admire her. But Jim had played these games his whole life and no one was a better reader of intention.

After a pause, he said, There's a whole part of the story you don't know about yet. It's the one good part, the only good part.

Jim opened her front door and Ribamar walked in, still dressed in torn, stained shorts, his wound seeping through a clean bandage, and he smelled from the jungle. Ribamar said something to her in a quiet voice, and Jim stepped out and closed the door behind him.

33.

In the fall of 1983, while Jim was still recuperating from Brazil and beginning a new life with Phyllis in Florida, Marvin Gesler was living in a rooming house in the East End of London. For more than two years he had been spending cash he had taken from his safe in Toronto while rushing to leave the country one step ahead of the police. Whenever he left his sparsely furnished room, he dressed in a long coat and sunglasses, fearing that he would be identified by the police and extradited to Canada for tax fraud. He spent most of his waking time on park benches, riding buses, or wandering aimlessly.

Marvin was a very wealthy man with secret accounts in Geneva and the Cayman Islands, but he was afraid to travel to these places to collect his money. He believed that if he entered one of these financial institutions and identified himself he would be arrested and flown back to Toronto.

Finally, when he was down to his last three hundred dollars and there was no other alternative besides life on the street, Marvin took a train to Geneva and walked into the chilly front room of the Anker Bank in the city center. He had never been here before.

He presented his passport and driver's license while dreading that the pencil-thin bank manager would check a computerized list and make a phone call. Marvin was thinking about spending the next twenty years in prison and he wasn't listening.

The banker patiently repeated his question. Marvin gathered himself, gave his password, and then asked for $1 million in cash. The man nodded and Marvin tried to control his nerves. In fifteen minutes the banker had returned with Marvin's briefcase filled with large bills. Marvin didn't bother to count the money. He said thank you, and then, as an afterthought, he asked for the wire transfer protocols for future transactions.

Marvin walked to a travel agency while trying to decide where he should go. He might have chosen any destination on the planet. He was a fugitive. He suspected that no one, save his elderly parents, cared if he lived or died.

With cash, he paid for a one-way ticket to Nassau. The Bahamas came to mind because Marvin had traveled there a few times with Jim.

Marvin walked through customs at the airport in Geneva without incident. He boarded the plane, got off in Nassau, showed his driver's license, and passed through Bahamian customs. It began to dawn upon him that outside of Canada, no one cared about him and his legal problems. The joke was that he had jailed himself for two years, worried, and lived on pennies for no reason. How could he have been so stupid?

Marvin Gesler had nearly $60 million in his bank accounts, but this wealth, and the knowledge that he could access it, didn't make him happy. He could no longer remember what it felt like to work on a project that excited him or to have an inspiring idea or to enjoy reading a novel. This exceptionally smart man had lost the capacity to think. He had become idle and useless. What good were the millions?

One afternoon, while shuffling along the beach in Nassau, he had a thought that was both obvious and very powerful. He missed Jim. The good times had shut down when Jim left their business. Marvin had made terrible mistakes; indeed, he had destroyed himself and everything he had built over many years. Really, Marvin had ceased to exist.

As this idea sunk in, he experienced an emotion that was wrenching with both grief and intense pleasure, a longing that went beyond any nostalgia he'd ever known. Marvin was worried that this feeling would go away and he wanted to horde it as he once tried to embrace all of his many dollars and business ideas. For a moment, at least, he was feeling alive.

That night, Marvin dined in a renowned island restaurant, Lord Rum Bottom's. Over the years he had eaten here with Jim six or seven times. It was a gorgeous place with tables arranged on a raised veranda surrounded by tropical gardens. There were orchids on every linen tablecloth and elegant ceiling fans sumptuously pushing the evening air scented with jasmine. Marvin began watching the front door half-expecting Jim to walk through. He indulged this fantasy for a time but then realized that he was unprepared for such a meeting. What would he say to his partner who had left without a trace and probably still despised him? Marvin didn't want to blow this last chance.

Then it came to him: he would make Jim a proposition that he couldn't refuse. Marvin would offer Jim a fortune in cash if he would go back into business, some new enterprise they would devise together.

Later, in his room, Marvin counted out five hundred thousand dollars and put the cash in a black satchel. For the next three months, each night, Marvin came to the restaurant waiting for Jim so that he could make his offer, outrageous though it was. Some nights Marvin brought the satchel and laid it beside his feet, as though it would have the power to draw Jim through the door. This immodest proposal seemed like the answer to Marvin's life. Every night he sat at a table with a view of the heavy front door bejeweled with shells and sea glass, drinking alone with his sunken jowls, tapping his foot. He felt confident that if he waited long enough, Jim would eventually walk through with his big smile and verve, his winner's way. Then Marvin would give Jim the satchel and Marvin's life would begin anew.

Marvin relocated to Cincinnati, Ohio. Really, he might have moved anywhere, but he had a distant cousin living in Cincinnati and, following an uneventful but pleasant visit, Marvin decided to stay longer. He eventually married a stately, independent woman, invested his money conservatively in commercial real estate. Marvin enjoyed holidays in New York, going to museums and the theater. He read copiously.

He opened a small construction business mainly as a hobby. He designed prefab fiberglass modules that could be configured variously to form a line of low-cost houses. It was a clever and promising idea, but he never felt motivated to aggressively market the houses. He didn't need the money.

Marvin was no longer afflicted by churning business notions and runaway lust. As a seventy-year-old, he was no longer excited by financial scams, and his crudeness had mostly burned away. But Marvin wasn't a moralist and he didn't feel bad about past indiscretions, business, sexual, and otherwise. Indeed, he believed that the smartest people often explore unusual and dark paths.

From time to time he thought about the black satchel with the half million for Jim and it made Marvin's heart skip. It was an ecstatic and outrageous notion and he'd preserved it in his heart while he'd lived a fairly humdrum life. The idea of a last chance can be even more delicious than the illicit affair itself. The black satchel gave Marvin a little edge, until the very day Jim called him on the phone.

Even though he had daydreamed about this call for many years, Marvin Gesler was dumbfounded. On the end of the line, Jim's voice was filled with temptation and chances for victory of legendary proportions. Marvin didn't know Jim's circumstances. He didn't know that Jim was broke and half-dead with high blood pressure and gout. Marvin was holding his own fantasy in his hands. He had been waiting twenty-one years for this chance.

It was hard for Jim to dial his former partner. But Jim was at the very end of his game. He had no more stories to tell Mara and she was packing her things. She didn't want the past. She wanted a big house for her children with a backyard. She wanted to create her own past.

And there was one punishing moment when she stared at him on the ratty couch and she shook her head as if he were a stranger, someone's doddering grandfather. What had she been doing in this wretched house?

He could see it clearly. In a day or two she would be another of his stories. He would try to recall her needy little sounds, her fine neck and white arms that helped him fend off demise. Soon he'd be dying alone in some hospital or nursing home. That's why he made the phone call.

In the first half minute, Jim could feel Marvin's vulnerability. Jim heard a thumping, needy heart and it made him very keen. He slipped right back into the hunt. He was tingling. He might have been tracking game by the dry riverbed with Ribamar. Jim backed off, became a little distant. He had deals, he told Marvin, yeah, he was considering this and that. Maybe he was going into the diamond business. He had just been wondering how Marvin was doing. He deflected the talk away from any business deal they might do together. How was Marvin feeling? Did he still watch the ball games? Did he still make his pro football bets? Yeah, Jim was still betting the games himself, doing pretty well.

Jim didn't have a dollar, but he felt himself racing back into form. He knew how to win. It was built into him, like desire.

They worked it out on the phone in less than an hour. Marvin would put Jim in charge of sales. Jim would build a sales force as he'd done many times in the past. Marvin offered three hundred thousand to start along with a new Lexus and the down payment on a home in the best section of Cincinnati. Marvin gave Jim the black satchel and Jim grabbed it. It had taken Jim twenty-one years to walk through the door at Lord Rum Bottom's.

FINAL RECKONING

For nearly three years I moved between two worlds. Writing and researching the book, I became like one of my characters, taking what I needed without remorse, like Jim or my dad before him. Closing the deal justified almost anything. One night I took Phyllis to a fancy restaurant in Miami. She had been living on the street for a half year and she had livid sores on her face and hands, although she had tried to cover them with thick makeup. I asked her questions about the past while she drank Merlot and wept. She still loved Jim, she managed to say while blowing her nose. Even now she believed he would save her, and recalling his promises elicited a brief smile. While she spoke I took notes and envisioned where I would add these details to my pages. I even considered including a chapter on her woeful street life. Incredible. But I felt like their story was owed to me and I felt righteous taking it. When I was outside the book, this seemed absurd and wrong to me, unclean. And yet I moved back inside the pages easily.

———

I came to Cincinnati to visit Jim in the late summer of 2005, a few weeks past my sixtieth birthday. There were a few more things I needed to know and then I could finish.

My friend lived in a lovely house on a shady hill with a view of Cincinnati in the distance. The place was filled with the rueful, haunting sights and sounds of growing up in the suburbs, kids nervously getting their books ready for school, a rambunctious Lab puppy racing around the basement, the smell of cut grass in the evening, chicken baking in the oven, cookies on the kitchen table eaten by the fistful while Mom and Dad move around upstairs for all of eternity.

I felt an aching nostalgia. For a moment, I could be the child here. It was very confusing. All of time was mixed up in this house. Only Jim could do it.

Adorable young moms came by after school for a cup of coffee and gossipy conversation with Mara. When he was back from work, he flirted with these children who had their own children and they flirted back.

There was no heartbreak anywhere that I could tell. He and Mara cared for each other. Mara was composed and happy and her trashy side was no longer apparent. This was really all she'd ever wanted. A beautiful house for her kids, a lovely car. She might have killed him—one way or another killed him—or loved him for the rest of his life. It turned on a phone call to Marvin.

All of the many schemes and scams and poor Phyllis and even Brazil were swallowed up by this lush suburban plenty that promised more and more, always Jim's favorite tune. More money, more victory trips to Israel to visit Mara's family, more time for red wine with big spreads of food. One by one she was bringing her family to the States from Israel. Already two of her brothers were settled in Cincinnati. Her brothers and their children would grow up alongside Mara and Jim and their children.

Jim was nearly eighty.

Including his bonus check, he'd made four hundred thousand dollars the first year selling the fiberglass houses. This year he would make a million. In three years he would be a full partner.

Jim and Mara had saved the special news to tell me. They giggled at each other. Her face glowed. She was going to have a baby. She couldn't stop giggling. I told you, she said, shaking her head at me. Jim looked goofy with love.

I just hadn't understood, and Mara forgave me graciously in her new home.

Jim and I were standing on the front lawn. Every house on the block was a minor masterpiece, one successful family after the next. The mayor of Cincinnati lived two houses down. In the morning, he and Jim chatted over their wrapped newspapers at the end of the driveway. There were no impediments that I could see; somehow he had made it through without a wound. Everyone in the neighborhood loved him. The adorable young mothers waved as they drove their children to school.

Mara was going to take me to the airport in her little white BMW. He was training the dog when I left him. Jim had time enough for everything. Time to cut the lawn with his fire engine red Toro mower and to fix the bikes for the kids. Time to go with her to Kabala class. Time to make a million dollars. Time to train the puppy who so badly wanted to run into the street, to break free, and Jim yelled at him, No, Lucky. NO, Lucky! And then Lucky bolted off and ran into a jolt of electricity from one of those invisible fences for training dogs. The puppy was all rippled up with current. Worse yet, its world was rocked. The street looked so exciting and yet it couldn't go there. Jim grinned. It's hilarious what we do. In that instant he seemed to glimpse the big picture. We mustn't underestimate him. That is the moment I like to remember. He'd won again, made it all the way back and beyond. He'd cast off the devastation of growing old.

Jim was kneeling, consoling the dog, when Mara pulled up. He looked over to me and said, Take care of yourself, Bub.

ACKNOWLEDGMENTS

Inspiration for *The Dream Merchant* came from many people, dreams, secret urges, and places that I love. But significantly it came from my father, who was a great lighting-fixture salesman, and a half dozen other exceptional and unforgettable salesmen I have known over the years.

My wife, Bonnie, has edited all my published writing. But beyond making graceful changes to my paragraphs, she is the navigator in my writing life (as she is on our fishing boat), often providing the direction when I get lost, not to mention her loving and at times fierce encouragement over the years. People know Josh Waitzkin as a many-time national chess champion and martial arts world champion. And yet, I've learned so much from my son about deep lessons drawn from defeats, and about humility and perseverance. Also, Josh is the very best reader I have ever known. I could not have written this book without Bonnie and Josh.

I am enormously indebted to Don Fehr, my friend, agent, and editor. Don loved the novel from the start, and during hard times in the business, he has been a relentless, eloquent, and passionate advocate. Thanks so much, man.

I want to especially acknowledge Maya Brenner and Hannah Beth King for their contributions, some of them ineffable. Each of these deeply insightful women could make a fortune offering their services as "professional muse."

Katya Waitzkin, my brilliant, beautiful daughter, helped so much with her savvy readings of my early drafts.

Much appreciation to Thomas Dunne and Katie Gilligan at St. Martin's Press.

My friends in Brazil introduced me to the beauty, mystery, and dangers of the rain forest.

For friendship, readings, advice, and inspiration, I want to thank Amelia Atlas, Mike Bryan, Cal Barksdale, Lou Cassotta, Desiree Cifre, Paulette Chernoff, Tom Chernoff, Paul Chevigny, John Clemans, Don Friedman, Nancy Gabriner, Susie Goodman, Jesse Kates, Antonia Meltzoff, Jake Morrissey, Jeff Newman, Megan Obymachow, Bruce Pandolfini, Paul Pines, Elta Smith, and Binky Urban.